YESTERDAY'S ISLAND

D0532759

Just at the right moment in her life, Caroline had been left a half-share in a house on picturesque Nantucket island, off the east coast of America—and she decided to leave England and go there to live. But the other half-share belonged to someone called Hawkesworth Cabot Lowell the Third! What difference would *he* make to her plans?

YESTERDAY'S ISLAND

BY

ANNE WEALE

MILLS & BOON LIMITED
15–16 BROOK'S MEWS
LONDON W1A 1DR

First published 1983
Australian copyright 1983
Philippine copyright 1983
This edition 1983

© Anne Weale 1983

ISBN 0 263 74285 4

Set in Monophoto Times 9 on 9½ pt.
01-0783 – 70861

Made and printed in Great Britain by
Richard Clay (The Chaucer Press) Ltd,
Bungay, Suffolk

CHAPTER ONE

CAROLINE was still reeling from the shock of losing her job, when another blow fell.

Watching the television news, she was startled and saddened to learn that Kiki Lawrence, once a great star of stage and screen, had died at the age of eighty-four in her luxurious house at Palm Beach, Florida.

Kiki had been godmother to Caroline's mother. One of Caroline's earliest memories was of the unexpected arrival of a glamorous woman wearing a black fur coat with beads to match (the famous black pearls) and bringing all kinds of exciting presents for everyone, including a brilliant green malachite egg for Caroline, a French knitting dool and a beautiful, very old box, all of which she still treasured.

Kiki must have been sixty-six then, but she hadn't seemed like an old person. Nor had she seemed old last summer when Caroline had spent a week with her at the lovely house at Antibes on the Riviera; a house left to Kiki by her second husband, a French marquis. There had been three husbands and many lovers in her life; but, after falling in love when very young, and being persuaded by her parents that the man was hopelessly ineligible, she had never been able to give her heart to anyone else.

Within ten days of Kiki's death, there was a third surprise. It arrived by mail from New York; a letter from a firm of lawyers informing her that the late Mrs Katharine Lawrence had bequeathed her a house. Not the Addison Mizner-designed house on North Ocean Boulevard, Palm Beach, or the spacious white villa at Antibes. A house on the American island of Nantucket.

Caroline was at first incredulous and then, almost immediately, overjoyed. For years she had longed to return there—her birthplace and her father's favourite weekend place. However, because of the tragic accident in which he had lost his life when her mother was eight months pregnant, the island had been somewhere which was never mentioned.

Even though, for more than twenty-two years, her mother had been happily married to an English landowner, by whom she had had three more children, Caroline had grown up feeling that Nantucket was a taboo subject.

Only to Kiki had she confided her interest in the island. Which she wouldn't have, had she realised that for Kiki also the place held unhappy memories. But it hadn't been until their last meeting that Kiki had mentioned that Nantucket had been the scene of the youthful love affair which had left her heart permanently scarred.

Before Caroline had finished reading the lawyers' letter—the mail came late and as she had been out all day, job-hunting, it was now early evening—someone pressed the bell-push outside the door of her flat. In spite of her American parentage, she had grown up in England and never re-crossed the Atlantic, so she thought of the place where she lived as her flat rather than her apartment.

She opened the door to find a young man with sun-bleached hair and a tanned complexion standing outside. He was wearing a French fisherman's jersey of navy blue oiled wool with buttons on one shoulder, and an old but clean pair of jeans. A bulging nylon backpack on a light alloy frame was propped against the wall beside the doorway.

'Rob!' Her grey eyes lit up at the sight of the elder of her two half-brothers.

He stepped forward to give her a hug. 'Hello, Caro. How are you?'

'Fine. I needn't ask how you are—you look as fit as a fiddle. You must have had much better weather than we've had while you've been away.'

'Yes, marvellous—only two wet days. I'm hoping you'll let me sleep on your sofa tonight. I've one or two things to do here before I go home.' As he spoke, he lifted the backpack and dumped it inside the doorway.

'Of course. It'll be lovely to have you,' she said warmly.

Although, at twenty-one, he was three years her junior, they had always been very close. From the beginning she had found a baby brother much more fun than inanimate dolls. When he could toddle, she had kept so close a watch on him that he had been in danger of over-protection. But later, when he was nine and she twelve, it had been Rob who had sensed that she was the one member of the family who wasn't happy on horseback, and who had helped her to overcome her secret mistrust of the animals which most of her school friends adored.

Because, physically, they both took after their fair-skinned, blonde mother, many people didn't realise that Robert and Caroline were the children of different fathers. Occasionally, with her polo-playing stepfather and horse-mad young brother and sister, she was conscious of being, if not exactly an interloper, an alien who did not really belong in their environment.

With Rob she never felt that. Although he was an excellent horseman, horses were not an obsession with him. He had a gift for languages and was currently at a university. This being the Easter vacation, for the past three weeks he had been on a walking tour in France.

While they were drinking coffee in her small but comfortable living-room, Rob suddenly broke off his account of the tour to say, 'You're thinner, Caro, and you've got what Nannie used to call your "peaky" look. Is something the matter?'

Reluctant to mention the disaster which had befallen her within days of his departure, she said lightly, 'I only look pale because you're so brown.'

'Your cheekbones are sticking out,' he said, with brotherly candour. 'In fact, on closer inspection, you look like hell. What's the trouble?'

Caroline had always been slim. Since losing her job, and with it her appetite, perhaps she had lost a few pounds. She had been vaguely aware that her waistbands were looser than usual, but had not seen any marked change in the face reflected by her mirror when she put on and took off her make-up.

She had always had prominent cheekbones and a noticeably square, stubborn chin with a dent in the centre. Her father's chin, and her father's cheekbones, presumably.

Her mother's face was the classic oval. Still lovely at forty-four, at Caroline's age Barbara Halland must have been stunning. Caroline missed being a beauty because, although she had Barbara's large dark-lashed eyes and pretty nose, below it their features were different, not only in the resolute firmness of the daughter's chin compared with the mother's rounded one, but in the shape of their mouths. Barbara's lips had the symmetry of a lipstick advertisement. Caroline's mouth was too wide for perfection, the lower lip fuller than the upper.

'The worst thing is that Kiki has died,' she told him reluctantly. 'I thought you might have heard that in France.'

He shook his head, looking distressed. 'No, not a word. Where did it happen? In Florida?'

'Yes. During her afternoon nap. Her maid went to wake her up because she had guests coming to tea, but Kiki had died in her sleep. We ought to be glad for her—no illness, no real old age. But oh dear, we are going to miss her.'

Rob murmured agreement. After a pause, he said, 'Do you remember the last line of Nancy Mitford's biography of Madame de Pompadour?'

She shook her head.

'It was *After this*—referring to Madame de Pompadour's death—*a very great dullness fell upon the Château of Versailles*. That's how we shall feel without Kiki. You said that was the worst thing. What else has happened in my absence?'

'My job has gone down the drain. I'm out of work. Not for long, I hope, but it has been rather traumatic to find myself unemployed. Everyone knew a merger was imminent, and that some people would be redundant, but I never dreamt that my boss would be axed. Naturally, my job went with his.'

'I can hardly believe it,' said her brother. 'You seemed set for life—or at least until you got married.'

His sister had been personal assistant to a senior executive with a large company which, until recently, had seemed to be one of the most stable businesses in the country.

'It's not the end of the world—at least not for me, with a family to fall back on. But I'd rather not ask Mummy and Daddy for help if I can avoid it. If I can't find a job which appeals to me, I shall just have to take one which doesn't.'

Rob nodded. Although he would eventually inherit a seventeenth-century manor house in the beautiful county of Gloucestershire which the Prince and Princess of Wales had chosen for their country home, neither he nor his brother and sisters had been over-indulged by their parents. From childhood, he and Caroline and the younger two had supplemented their modest pocket-money by doing various chores in the house and grounds.

Both by nature and training, Caroline was a person who would tackle any difficulty unaided unless there was absolutely no option but to turn to someone else for help. He could remember how doggedly she had endured falling off her pony. His mother had had no idea that, after a lesson in jumping, her elder daughter had been in the habit of retiring to a hiding place in the garden, there to cry in secret. It had been he who had guessed that every jump had been an ordeal which, for a reason he hadn't understood at the time, she had not dared to baulk.

'Oh, I almost forgot,' said Caroline. 'When you arrived I was reading a letter from Kiki's lawyers. She's left me a house, would you believe? A house in America which I didn't even know she possessed. If I can't find a suitable job here, I might try my luck over there.'

'What a strange thing to leave you. I should think you'd have much rather have had a few of her jewels, wouldn't you?'

'She'll have left those to Mummy, I expect—or some of them. She had a lot of other godchildren, remember; not to mention all the godchildren's offspring. For someone without any direct descendants, she had an enormous "family" of people she loved, and who loved her.'

While she was speaking, she had walked through to her tiny kitchen to fetch the letter she had left there. As she came back, her eyes skimmed the paragraphs already read and continued further down the page. Then she gave a muffled exclamation, causing Rob to ask, 'What's the matter?'

Without looking up, she answered, 'I hadn't read this bit before. I seems that the house isn't mine—at least not completely. I only have a half share in it. My co-owner is someone called Hawkesworth Cabot Lowell the Third. What a mouthful of a name! I wonder who he is—and why Kiki left the house to both of us? They say here that neither of us can dispose of the property without the other's consent. Wait a bit while I read the whole thing—this American legal jargon is as complicated as the English version.'

The letter covered two pages. It took her a minute or two to digest it. When she looked up her eyes were very bright, and her voice was husky as she said, 'She *has* left me one of her jewels—an antique diamond and emerald brooch in the form of a lovers' knot. Oh, Rob, what a darling she was! You wouldn't remember, but she wore that brooch once, years ago, when she came on one of her flying visits and Mummy was giving a dinner party. Everyone else was in long skirts, but Kiki wore black silk trousers—she called them pants— and a black silk shirt with this fabulous brooch pinned on the collar. It was the most beautiful thing I'd ever seen, and she let me try it on. I was about thirteen or fourteen. Fancy her remembering how I drooled over it! I'd completely forgotten until now.'

'She was—to use one of her own expressions—a very caring person,' said Rob. 'You're a lot like her. Caro. Look at the trouble you take to find just the right birthday presents for all of us—and to give people unbirthday presents if you see something you know will please them. When you come home for a weekend, you spend half the time listening to Nannie wittering on about Daddy's teething troubles, or reading books about the Royal Family to her.'

He was speaking of Miss Edith Pell, a children's nurse originally engaged by his grandparents, who now, after caring for two generations of Hallands, was comfortably ensconced in a cottage on Sir John Halland's estate.

'Not all her conversation is about babies,' said Caroline. 'And think of the hours and hours she spent reading to us when we were tots. I like sitting with Nannie.'

'I'm damned if I do,' he said frankly. 'She's a crashing old bore, and you know it. You sit with her because you've a much nicer nature than the rest of us. Look how you put up with all the incessant horse-talk which goes on at home. Nobody ever talks about the things which interest you.'

'One person does—*toi, mon frère*,' she said, with an affectionate smile. 'Would you like to have a bath while I rustle up something for supper?'

They spent a companionable evening, mostly reminiscing about their teenage visits to Kiki's house in France, and discussing the unusual terms of Caroline's inheritance and the identity of her co-owner.

'Maybe Kiki had it in mind to do a spot of posthumous matchmaking,' Rob suggested, as they had a late snack of what was left of the Camembert and crusty bread he had bought in France that morning. 'She seems to have had connections with lots of America's first families. Hawkesworth Cabot Lowell the Third sounds no end of a grandee—maybe a millionaire to boot. Nobble him and you won't need to find another job!'

Caroline laughed. 'I think if Kiki had wanted to organise a "good" marriage for me, she would have tried it before now. Actually she shared Mummy's views about marrying young—but for different reasons. Mummy is against it because she thinks people aren't mature until they're at least twenty-five. Kiki's view was that girls should do what men have always done—have two or three lovers before committing themselves to one person for the rest of their lives.'

Her brother gave her a thoughtful glance. She guessed he was wondering if she had followed Kiki's precept. She had certainly had the opportunity, living on her own in the small flat, answerable only to herself.

But if he was curious about her love life, or lack of it, Rob did not ask. Presently they went to bed; he in his sleeping bag on the sofa, and she in the double brass bedstead—brought to London from her stepfather's attics—which several young men would have liked to share with her, but in which, up to now, she had always slept alone.

At the crack of dawn, or so it seemed, the telephone rang. Usually, Caroline left the door between bedroom and sitting-room open. Now it was closed, muffling the sound of the bell. The telephone was on one of the end tables by the sofa, and she didn't have an extension on her night table.

Also the bottle of wine which she and Rob had shared during the evening had made her sleep more heavily than usual. By the time she reached the other room, the ringing had ceased and Rob was answering the call for her.

Evidently it was not—as she had half expected—someone misdialling a number.

She arrived to hear Rob saying, rather irritably, 'This is Robert Halland. Yes, you have the right night, but Caroline is asleep—as most people are at this hour.'

He saw that she was now awake and ready to take over the

call. 'It's for you. A call from Barbados.' He handed her the receiver.

At work, alert and efficient, she would have answered an overseas call with a brisk, 'Caroline Murray here. Who's speaking, please?' But, still groggy from being wakened out of a deep sleep, and bewildered by a call from Barbados, she reacted with a puzzled 'Hello?'

The voice which answered was male, American, and as incisively businesslike as hers would have been in other circumstances.

It said, 'Good morning, Miss Murray. I'm sorry if I've broken into your beauty sleep, but where I am it's four o'clock in the morning and I'm up this early in order to catch you at home. I don't have your number at work. Maybe you don't work?'

Caroline was about to retort that of course she worked, when she remembered that, at present, she didn't. A glance at the clock showed that in fact it was not unreasonably early to receive a telephone call. It was eight o'clock. What with going to bed later than usual, and not having set the alarm which normally roused her at seven, she had overslept.

Before she could explain that she happened to be between jobs, the voice continued, 'My name is Hawk Lowell. It seems that you and I are joint heirs to a house which belonged to Kiki Lawrence. Have you received details of the bequest from her lawyers?'

For a few seconds after he had given his name, she hadn't connected it with the Hawkesworth Cabot Lowell the Third who was also Kiki's legatee. But now she was beginning to pull herself together, and to respond with her usual quickness.

'Yes, I received them yesterday, Mr Lowell, but I didn't expect to hear from you as soon as this. Kiki has never spoken of you, and her will doesn't explain why she left the house to both of us. Perhaps you can throw some light on that?'

'None at all. I've never heard of you either, and I'm equally baffled,' was his answer.

'Do you know the house? Have you ever been to Nantucket?'

'Yes, I know the house—I once lived in it. I have no desire to repeat the experience.'

The question *Why not?* trembled on the tip of her tongue,

but remained unuttered. Her English upbringing made her hesitate to put a personal question to a stranger.

What did he look like, this fellow countryman who was speaking to her from an island in the Caribbean? Perhaps he wasn't an American. For all she knew, his accent might be Canadian. She could recognise the drawl of the Deep South, but the other regional variations of the unimaginably vast continent of North America were as unfamiliar to her as the many variations in British voices were to people from across the Atlantic.

What she knew of her homeland had been gleaned from the cinema and television, and from reading American novels. It didn't enable her to 'place' Hawk Lowell either geographically or socially, in the way she could have placed an Englishman merely by listening to him on the telephone.

'Do I gather that you haven't seen it? was his next remark.

'No, I haven't, but——'

'Then take my word for it, Miss Murray, neither the house nor the island would appeal to you. The house, even when I lived there, was in a bad state of neglect; by this time it's probably falling apart. As for Nantucket, it has its enthusiasts, but it also has many disadvantages. For a start, it's thirty miles off Cape Cod, which, as you may or may not know, is the narrow peninsula which sticks out into the Atlantic from the south-east corner of Massachusetts.'

There was a crackle on the line, but the connection was still good as he went on, 'Nantucket isn't as accessible as Martha's Vineyard, the larger and better-known island in the same area. In winter it's not unknown for the harbour to be frozen solid. In summer the town and the waterfront are infested with day-visitors who come over from Hyannis on the Cape. The place is only livable in spring and fall, and even then it's basically a small, isolated New England town where everyone knows everyone else, and where, unless you were born there, you'll always be "someone from off".'

Caroline almost said *I was born there*. But again something made her keep silent. Was it merely that he didn't like Nantucket, or had he some devious reason for trying to put her off the island? The fact that Kiki had liked him enough to include him in her will was some guarantee of his integrity, but it was such a strange bequest, and——

Her train of thought was interrupted by the crisp, authoritative voice saying, 'My advice is that we should sell it.'

'Your advice may be sound, Mr Lowell, but I should at least like to see it before deciding to dispose of it.'

'By all means. Why don't we meet there? Could you make if four weeks from now? I have no free time before then.'

Caroline had often organised short-notice trips overseas for her boss. The arrangements, as such, were no problem. But he had been travelling at the company's expense. If she made the journey to America, she would have to pay for it herself, and she wasn't sure she could afford it. She had always tried to manage her salary sensibly, but, with prices rocketing all the time, there was never much left in her account at the end of the month.

Recklessly, because although she knew her current credit balance she had no idea how much it would cost to reach Nantucket, or how long she would need to stay there, she said, 'Yes . . . yes, I can manage that. Four weeks from today—that will be the twenty-fourth of May. I'll look forward to meeting you, Mr Lowell.'

He did not return the courtesy, but said, 'My apologies to your . . . friend for disturbing him. Goodbye'—and rang off.

The sardonic tone of this parting shot was not lost on her. But it wasn't until she had slowly replaced the receiver that she understood what he had thought when Rob had answered the telephone and told him that she was asleep. Because their surnames were different, he had taken Rob for her boy-friend and thought they were in bed together.

A flush of annoyance and chagrin tinged her clear but winter-pale skin. Her life-style was none of his business. Why should she mind what he thought? And yet, for some reason, she did mind; and would have given a good deal to be able to ring him back and clear up the misunderstanding.

That afternoon she went home to Gloucestershire with her brother. They had telephoned their mother to expect them, and Lady Halland was at the bus station to welcome them, driving her large estate car with two of her six dogs in the back.

During her twenty-two years in England, Barbara Halland had embraced the English way of life with the fervour of a religious convert, and by now had scarcely a trace of her American accent.

As a much younger man, Sir John Halland had been a frequent visitor to Kentucky where he had friends among the horse-breeding fraternity. It was there that he had met his wife, at that time a twenty-one-year-old widow with an infant daughter. She had been living with her parents, and was only gradually recovering from the shock of her first husband's death followed, within a few hours, by a difficult premature birth.

The child had been in the care of a nurse. To the concern of her parents, Barbara had shown no interest in her baby. Although assured by their family physician that this was a temporary reaction to what she had been through, they had felt very worried about her.

However, the advent of John Halland had marked the beginning of her recovery. Ten years older and of a different temperament from the husband she had lost, he had quickly won her parents' approval. Within a year they were married and, with the birth of her son, Barbara had become more maternal towards her first child.

The conversation on the drive to Thornbridge Manor was mainly about Kiki Lawrence. As Caroline had predicted, she had left her black pearls to Barbara, and a Fabergé box to Sir John, to add to the collection of Fabergé objects he had already inherited from his grandmother. To the two younger children, Jack and Rebecca, with whom she had had less to do, Kiki had left funds to be invested on their behalf.

'There's a letter from New York waiting for you, Rob. Have you heard from the lawyers yet, Caro?' her mother enquired.

From his place in the back of the car, Rob leaned forward. 'Enough of this talk of legacies! Don't you want to hear about my tour?'

He began to describe his experiences. Caroline flashed him a grateful glance. She did not want to broach the subject of her legacy until later. Perhaps her mother would not be as anti as she imagined. But the one and only time in Caroline's life when her mother had talked about Nantucket at length—

and beseeched her not to marry young and thereby repeat her own mistake—she had ended by bursting into most uncharacteristic tears at the memories the subject had evoked.

That had happened five years ago, when Caroline was nineteen and involved in what Lady Halland had seen as a budding romance. In fact, like all her relationships with the opposite sex, a promising beginning had eventually come to a standstill because, on Caroline's side, there had always been something lacking; whatever it was which gave friendship the wings to fly to the higher plane of love.

The opportunity to test the subject on someone who knew her mother's history but had not been involved in that tragic period of her life came when Caroline and her stepfather were the first to assemble for drinks before dinner.

With evening had come light spring rain and a chilliness which had made Sir John put a match to the drawing-room fire. The logs were beginning to burn in the blaze from the kindling, and her stepfather was standing with his back to the wide brick-lined hearth, and sipping a glass of pale dry sherry, when she joined him in the large, slightly shabby room with its English country house smell; a combination of beeswax furniture polish, old books in worn leather bindings, and the pot-pourri, in porcelain bowls, which Lady Halland gently stirred with her fingers whenever she passed them.

As soon as he had given her a glass of sherry, Caroline told him about the loss of her job—which she had kept to herself in the hope of quickly finding another one—and about her legacy and how, unprepared for and somewhat flustered by Hawk Lowell's telephone call, she had committed herself to going to Nantucket in May.

'But I don't want Mummy to be upset,' she concluded. 'Do you think my going back to Nantucket *will* distress her very much?'

Her stepfather was a man of medium height, well-built, with thick, steel-grey hair. He was fifty-five, eleven years older than her mother.

His light blue eyes studied Caroline's anxious face for a moment or two before he said, 'How very odd of Kiki to leave you a place there. Still, she always was an eccentric, unpredictable woman. Yes, I think your mother is bound to be upset by this news. She dislikes any mention of that time. Perhaps it would be a good idea for me to have a word with her in private ... give her a chance to take it in before we discuss it at dinner.'

'Oh, yes, if you would,' she said thankfully. 'I've been trying to get her alone ever since we arrived, but with Rebecca around and people telephoning, there hasn't been a chance.'

On his way from the room, he gave her a pat on the shoulder and Caroline felt a responsive upsurge of affection— as if he were truly her father. But although he had always been kind to her, there was something missing between them, a lack of the deep-rooted affinity she felt sure would have existed between herself and her natural father.

Rob came into the room, looking buoyant.

'Kiki's left me the library at Antibes! Not the room, but all those fabulous books from her second husband's *château*. Lord knows what I'm going to do with them—unless whoever has inherited the villa is willing to house them for me. Of course, they may not be too pleased that the books aren't included with the villa, but presumably she thought I was more likely to appreciate them.'

He went to the side table where bottles, decanters and glasses were arranged on a large silver tray.

'Think of it! Two thousand vols of French antiquarian treasures! It will take me a lifetime to read them all. Kiki, wherever you are, I drink to you'—raising his glass in the dirction of the ceiling.

His mother, when she heard, was not delighted.

'I'm beginning to think Kiki must have gone slightly gaga in her last months,' she said, frowning. 'If whoever has inherited the villa won't continue to house the books—and, if we don't know them, why should they?—they will have to come here, and where can we put them? Your bedroom is already like a second-hand bookshop, Robert.'

'We'll find somewhere, m'dear,' her husband said soothingly. 'Perhaps we can weed out some of the stuff in our library.'

'Certainly not. Robert will have to fix up one of the attics for his French books,' was her answer, expressed in a much more curt tone than she usually used to her husband.

Caroline sensed that it was her legacy, not Robert's, which

was the cause of her mother's sharpness. An old wound had been reopened. Like anyone in pain, Lady Halland was easily annoyed.

'What did you get, Caro?' Jack asked her.

Dark-haired like his father and Rebecca, he was eighteen, soon to leave school and go to an agricultural college to learn farming and estate management.

'A diamond brooch,' Caroline answered. Her uncertain glance at her stepfather being acknowledged by a slight nod of the head, she added, 'And a house in America.'

'Then you may have room for Rob's books,' suggested her sixteen-year-old sister. 'Where in America?'

'In Nantucket, which is an island off the Atlantic coast,' Caroline explained, knowing that Rebecca's geographical knowledge was confined to places famous for horses.

Although the two youngest members of the family knew that she was their half-sister, with a green American passport instead of a navy blue British one, neither of them had ever been inquisitive about their mother's first marriage. Nantucket was a place of no special interest or significance to them.

She turned to her mother. 'Does the name Hawkesworth Cabot Lowell the Third mean anything to you, Mummy?'

Lady Halland shook her head. 'Nothing. But I think that to leave you a half share in a house there proves that Kiki was not *compos mentis* when she took that idea into her head. I'm surprised that her lawyers weren't able to dissuade her from making such a ridiculous bequest. Your father says this man Lowell wants to sell the place. I shouldn't think it can be worth much, a tumbledown house which Kiki herself never bothered with. I should write to the lawyers, tell them you agree to sell, and leave them to handle the whole thing. There's no necessity to go over there yourself.'

'No, there's no necessity. Except that I've said I will . . . and I want to,' Caroline replied quietly. 'It's the place where I was born. I can't help being curious about it.'

Her long-lashed grey eyes held a silent appeal to Lady Halland not to oppose her in this, the first important decision she had ever taken without consulting her mother beforehand.

She had been quite a small child when someone had said something to Nannie about Caroline being a living reminder of tragedy to her poor mother. Whoever it was had been swiftly hushed by Miss Pell. But that unguarded remark had made the child grow up feeling that, if she didn't take care, she might lose her mother's affection for her.

Consequently all her life, and particularly during her teens, she had stifled the impulse to do anything which might incur Barbara Halland's disapproval.

They had been regarded as having one of the few harmonious mother-and-daughter relationships in their circle. Only Caroline knew how much that harmony had depended on her forcing herself to submit to her mother's choice of clothes and activities.

On leaving school, she and a close friend had wanted to spend a year working their way round Europe. Her friend's parents had been agreeable, but her mother had vetoed the plan, and Caroline had spent the year at a secretarial college, laying the foundation of the career at present interrupted by the aftermath of the merger.

'If I had still been working, I shouldn't have been able to go—or not until my holiday in August,' she went on, when her mother said nothing. 'But as I'm not working at present, and may have to forgo a summer holiday when I find a new job, I might as well take a break now.'

'Your father told me this man was unable to meet you before the twenty-fourth of May. Surely, with your excellent qualifications, you will have found another post long before then?' said her mother.

'Perhaps . . . I'm not sure. There are a lot of well-qualified people out of work at the moment. Anyway, talking it over with Rob on the train, I thought I might go straight away and have a look at New York and New England before making the meeting with Mr Lowell the grand finale, as it were.'

She waited for her mother's comment. When none was forthcoming, Caroline's square chin lifted slightly.

She said, 'This morning I went to see my bank manager and showed him the letter from Kiki's lawyers. In spite of my being unemployed, he agreed to let me have an overdraft to cover my expenses. If I fly there and back by standby, and travel around by bus, the trip shouldn't cost a fortune.'

'There was no need to ask for an overdraft, Caro,' said her stepfather. 'You know you mother and I will always help you with any finanical problems.'

She smiled at him. 'Yes, I know—but I'd rather stand on my own feet. Twenty-four is too old to be anyone's dependant.'

Much later that night, Rob came to her bedroom.

'Good for you! I didn't think you'd stand your ground when Mummy withheld her blessing on your expedition. Don't lie awake changing your mind, Caro.'

'I shall probably lie awake, but I'll concentrate on what to pack,' she assured him. 'All the same, I hate not having her approval. Perhaps it's too much to expect when you think of what she went through there—in Nantucket, I mean.'

'But it was twenty-four years ago, and she's had a happy life ever since.'

He sat down on the end of her bed and looked thoughtfully at her as she leaned against the headrest, her Victorian-style nightgown and shoulder-length mane of fair hair making her look much younger than she did in her neat office suits, with her hair confined in a coil at the back of her head.

'It will do you good to get away and do your own thing for a change. Even though you've been living in London for several years, you've never really cut the apron-strings. You don't need Mummy's approval any more. You shouldn't need anyone's approval. As you said yourself at dinner tonight, twenty-four is grown-up. Being grown-up means doing what *you* think is right even if *everyone* else is against it.' He grinned. 'Sez I, with the wisdom of twenty-one!'

'But you are wise, Rob,' she said seriously. 'Much wiser about life than I am.' She leaned forward, clasping her knees. 'Losing my job was a terrible shock at first. Now I've had time to think about it, I'm not sure I want to go on being a P.A. But what else can I do?'

'Perhaps you'll find the answer to that in America.'

Nine days later, Caroline sat in a crowded bus station in midtown Manhattan, using the time before her bus left for Boston to scribble a letter to her brother.

N.Y. is completely different from the way I visualised it, she wrote. *The streets are* not *like narrow canyons between the skyscrapers. All the long straight north-to-south avenues are very wide, and plenty of sunshine reaches the sidewalks. The*

*layout of Manhattan Island is so simple that, in two days, I felt
at home here. I've walked miles, and am sad to be leaving. A
week isn't nearly long enough to explore this fabulous city.*

The departure of the woman sitting next to her left the seat
vacant for a few minutes before it was taken by a man who, to
her relief, was not one of the many drop-outs who seemed to
frequent the station. So far, the only thing about New York
which she hadn't liked was the subway. She was beginning to
think that the bus station, where many seats were occupied by
unwashed men and women who looked like alcoholics or
worse, was not a very nice place either.

However the man who had seated himself beside her was
visibly clean and well-groomed. He was wearing a grey chalk-
stripe suit and a pink cotton Oxford cloth shirt with a button-
down collar. She recognised the source of the shirt because
she had been into Brooks Brothers, the élite store on Madison
Avenue and had bought an identical shirt as a present for
Rob.

He caught her glance, smiled and said, 'Hi.'

'Hi,' said Caroline politely.

He looked nice, and would probably chat if she gave him
encouragement. In general she liked chatting to people, but at
the moment she wanted to finish her letter before the bus
journey in order to concentrate on the scenery.

It wasn't until she had written *Another bulletin soon.
Meanwhile, best love—Caroline* that she noticed her neighbour
was also busy with pad and pen.

But he wasn't writing a letter. He was drawing an unkempt
youth who was sleeping on a seat a few yards away. From
what she could see of the sketch, her neighbour was no
amateur artist but a professional.

His absorption in his task enabled her to study him more
closely than she had at first. Probably in his late twenties, he
had thick but fine mid-brown hair with a lock which slipped
across his forehead when his head was bent over his sketch
pad. His eyes, she had seen, were hazel; and his features were
good but not handsome. He had a pleasant, reliable face, and
an air of good standing which made it a little surprising that
he should be travelling by bus rather than in his own car.
Unless he was only at the bus station to make drawings of
winos and their kind.

'What do you think?' he asked suddenly, showing her the sketch of the youth.

Startled, she murmured, 'It's very good.'

In fact she thought it was brilliant. Every detail from the youth's long bedraggled hair to the down-trodden heels of his sneakers and his dirty fingernails had been captured by the quick, sure strokes of the artist's pen.

He gave her a long smiling look which brought a faint flush to her cheeks. She couldn't be sure whether his scrutiny was that of the artist or the man. Either way, it was disconcerting to be studied so intently, even though she herself had been guilty of staring at him a few moments earlier.

'You sound British,' he said.

'I know I sound it, but actually I'm not. I'm an American, although I've never lived over here.'

'There can't be many Americans who can say "actually" like that!'

She laughed. 'Probably not. I must try to stop saying it.'

'No, no—don't change a thing. You're perfect just the way you are. You also smell great—which is more than can be said for some of the people around here,' he added dryly. 'What's the perfume you're wearing?'

This was flirtation at a faster pace than she was accustomed to, especially in a public place.

She said, 'Excuse me, I have to go now or I may miss my bus. Goodbye.'

Picking up her small soft-topped suitcase, she walked briskly away.

She had already discovered that the long-distance buses took on their passengers from a lower level of the concourse. As she made her way there, a glimpse of her reflection in a mirror made her wonder if her former colleagues would recognise her.

At the office she had always been shod in well-polished leather shoes with fairly high heels. Throughout her week in New York, except in the evening, she had gone everywhere in the comfortable black and white running shoes which had made it possible to walk all over Manhattan without becoming footsore.

In place of the coil, she was wearing her hair in a plait

which started almost at her crown and ended between her shoulder-blades. It looked casual and young, but was tidier than completely loose hair in a city where the high buildings created strong gusts of wind.

As for her clothes, instead of suits and silk shirts, she was living in grey flannel pants—more adaptable than jeans in a wardrobe pared to a minimum—with a couple of Liberty print shirts and a grey cashmere sweater. If it rained, she had a black showerproof blouson which, rolled up, went in her shoulder bag.

About a dozen people were already standing in line for the bus to Boston. Caroline joined the queue and unzipped the compartment of her bag which contained a guide to sightseeing in New England on a tight budget.

When the line began to move, she put the book away and picked up her case. However, after several people had boarded the bus there was some kind of commotion inside it and boarding stopped.

This delay—apparently caused by the loss of someone's contact lens—didn't bother her. She resumed her study of her guide book until, presently, boarding continued.

The search for the missing lens was still going on as she made her way towards the rear of the bus. As she was hoisting her suitcase on to the rack, a man said, 'Let me help you with that.'

To her surprise, she discovered the traveller immediately behind her was the artist.

'Thank you.'

Having taken a seat next to the window, she was not surprised when, after stowing the case, he said, 'Do you mind if I sit here?'—indicating the seat beside hers.

She shook her head. Where was his baggage? she wondered. Perhaps his suitcase was too large for the overhead rack and had gone in the main baggage locker underneath the bus. His only hand baggage was a leather satchel which presumably contained his sketching equipment. She didn't think he had had a case with him in the waiting area, but he might have checked it in somewhere before coming to sit by her there.

'If we're going to be travelling companions for four hours, maybe we should introduce ourselves. I'm Todd Blackwell.' he offered his hand.

'I'm Caroline Murray. How d'you do?'

'Now you can tell me what that perfume is,' he said, as they shook hands.

'It's English ... something I get from a shop called L'Artisan Parfumeur in London.'

'Is that where you live, Caroline? In London?' When she nodded, he said, 'I'm a New Yorker. I live in a loft in SoHo. Have you been here long enough to find where that is?'

Again she nodded. 'It's the area south of Houston Street where a lot of artists live and work. I explored it the day I went to look at Greenwich Village. But what is a loft? Is it the same as an attic?'·

'No, a loft is larger than an attic. In the nineteenth century SoHo used to be a commercial district with warehouses and factories which artists have converted into apartments and studios. I don't need a lot of space for my work, the way a sculptor does, but I like to have it anyway. I have twenty-four hundred square feet, most of which is my living-room, with a kitchen and bathroom in one corner.'

Caroline said, 'I don't know the floor area of my apartment, but I should think it would fit into your loft a dozen times over. I'm at the top of an old house, in what used to be the roof space before the owners put in partitions and windows. I have to hang some of my pictures on the doors because there isn't enough room on the walls. You would think it terribly cramped, but I like small rooms and clutter— provided it's orderly clutter.'

'We may have different ideas about living space, but I'm sure we can find something in common.'

His eyes held hers for some seconds until, disturbed by the intimacy of his glance, she turned to gaze out of the window.

She liked the look of him, and was even rather pleased that his destination was the same as hers. But she didn't want to flirt with him. It wasn't her style.

'Goodness! I shouldn't have thought the loss of a contact lens would have called for four policemen!' she exclaimed, seeing the drama going on outside the door of the bus.

In fact only one of the officers was actively engaged in the incident. He was taking notes while his three colleagues, and the bus driver, stood by, listening to an agitated outburst from the owner of the lens, an elderly man, and his even more agitated wife.

To see what was going on, Todd Murray had to lean closer to her, his shoulder pressing against hers, his cheek inches from her temple. She thought he protracted his inspection of the scene a good deal longer than was necessary.

'You mentioned your pictures,' he said, as he sat back. 'Don't tell me you're also an artist? No'—as she shook her head—'that would have been too good to be true.'

What did he mean by that remark?

Aloud, she said, 'My pictures are paintings I've picked up in junk shops, or prints cut from magazines—anything which I like enough to justify the expense of having it framed. One of my favourites is *The Magic Apple Tree* by Samuel Palmer. Do you know it?'

It was Todd's turn to shake his head.

'It's the painting I'd most like to own,' she went on. 'But even if I were a millionaire, I couldn't. It's in the Fitzwilliam Museum at Cambridge.'

He said, 'You mean Cambridge in England? There are ten or eleven places called Cambridge in the United States, including Cambridge, Massachusetts, right next to Boston.'

'Yes, I meant England's Cambridge. A couple of years ago I made a pilgrimage there to see the original of the painting. It's not very large. Just this size'—demonstrating with her slim, capable hands. 'But to me it's the most beautiful watercolour in the world.'

'If I every get to that Cambridge, I'll make a point of going to see it. Have you looked round any of our art galleries here in New York?'

'Only two. There wasn't time for them all. I chose the Metropolitan, and the Frick which I thought was stunning. More like a private house, which of course it was originally, than a museum.'

'How long are you here for? Or have you come back to stay now?' he asked.

'I'm not sure yet. It depends. I must say that if I like where I'm going as much as I've liked New York, I shall be very tempted to stay on.'

'Where are you heading? To Boston itself, or somewhere nearby?'

'I'm spending a few days in Boston, but I'm really on my way to Nantucket. Do you know the island?'

It seemed to her that a strange expression flickered across his face when she mentioned her final destination.

But his tone was normal as he said, 'Yes, I know it. It's a delightful place. About as different from New York as your little apartment from my large loft. Do you have any special reason for going to Nantucket?'

'Yes—it's my birthplace. I guess'—already she was beginning to use I guess in place of I suppose—'people are always curious about the place where they were born if they left it too early in life to have any memory of it.'

He smiled. 'If they were raised there, they mostly can't wait to get away. I was born in a small town in Iowa. If it weren't for visiting my parents, I doubt I'd ever go back there. It's not my scene.'

Caroline surprised herself by saying, 'I don't know what my scene is yet.' Quickly she brought the conversation back to an impersonal plane by saying, 'One of the things which has impressed me is the New York Post Office. Not only does it look like a Greek temple, but it has that marvellous inscription on the façade. *Neither snow nor rain nor heat nor gloom of night stays these couriers from the swift completion of their appointed rounds.* Who wrote that, I wonder?'

'I don't know, but I can find out. Where will you be staying in Nantucket? If you'll give me your number, I'll call you.'

Inwardly amused by his quickness, she said blandly, 'Oh, I shouldn't dream of putting you to that trouble.'

'It will be a pleasure.' he produced his sketch pad and pen, and looked expectantly at her.

She said, 'I can't give you my number because I don't know where I'm staying.'

'You've no relations or friends in Nantucket?'

'No, none. I'll stay at an hotel or guesthouse. Perhaps, if you've been there, you can recommend one?'

'Sure I can.'

Instead of using a leaf from his pad, Todd produced a wallet from which he took a business card. As he wrote on the back of it, he said, 'The couple who own this guesthouse are nice people. You'll be comfortable there, and it's inexpensive if you're watching your pennies. It may be mentioned in that guide book you were studying a while back.'

'Thank you. Yes, I am watching my pennies very carefully,' she admitted.

Having read the address he had written, she turned the card over and discovered that Todd was Design Director for a magazine she had seen on all the news-stands. No doubt that accounted for his style of dress being more like that of a business man than an artist.

At this point the bus started moving and, tucking the card in the outside pocket of her bag, she prepared to take leave of the city which had given her such a favourable first impression of her native land.

Todd proved an agreeable companion. He seemed to sense that she wanted to spend part of the journey not talking, but quietly admiring the low, rolling, wooded hills and the large stretches of water which in England would be called lakes and in New England were usually known as ponds.

Here and there she caught glimpses of villages and country towns, but the bus was travelling by the Interstate highway and didn't pass through any places, not even Hartford, the state capital of Connecticut, of which she saw only its rooftops and a golden dome.

'You should go there some time,' Todd advised her. 'You must see the Mark Twain memorial. It has to be one of the most extraordinary houses in America. A lot of the original décor, including some amazing silver stencils, was designed by Louis Comfort Tiffany. After a period of neglect, the house has been very beautifully restored to the way it was when Twain and his family lived there. Are you familiar with Tiffany's work?'

'Oh, yes. I saw some of his stained glass windows in the Metropolitan Museum, and so-called Tiffany lamps are becoming a decorator's cliché in England. I think most of them are rather bad copies, nothing like his original designs.'

'That's also true here,' he agreed. 'I've seen some atrocious objects masquerading as Tiffany designs. If you want to see some of his best work, go to the Episcopal Church on Fair Street in Nantucket Town. Behind the altar there are five little Tiffany windows called the Nantucket wild flower windows. And the three west windows were also made at his studios in 1902. Are you interested in needlepoint?'

'Very much.'

Kiki who, during her screen career, had whiled away the time between takes by stitching pillows and rugs, had been needlepointing a stool cover the last time she had seen her. Caroline's mother did needlepoint and had instructed her daughter in the simpler stitches when she was quite small. Unlike learning to ride, needlepoint had been something which Caroline had enjoyed from the outset, and still did.

'The Episcopal Church has some excellent kneelers and seat covers. They were designed by Erica Wilson. Maybe you've heard of her?'

'Yes; she's a big name in embroidery circles. I passed her shop on Madison Avenue. I couldn't afford to buy one of her canvasses, but I had a long gloat at the designs.'

'You can gloat again in Nantucket. Her first shop is right on Main Street. In the summer she lives on the island and holds a needlework seminar. She's British, you know, not American.'

'Really? I didn't know that. I'd love to go to the seminar.'

'Go in the shop and talk to her,' he advised. 'I went in once with a girl-friend. Mrs Wilson's a charming person—tall, good-looking and very friendly. She's lived in America for years, but she still has her British accent.'

'Tell me more about Nantucket,' invited Caroline.

'No, I don't think I will,' Todd replied. 'If you have two good friends who haven't met, and you want them to like each other, it's usually a mistake to praise one to the other beforehand. What I like about Nantucket may not be what you like. It's better you find out for yourself if it's your kind of place or not.'

Thinking about the man she was going to meet there, she was tempted to ask Todd if he had heard of Hawkesworth Cabot Lowell the Third. Even if he hadn't, working on a leading news magazine he must have access to files on or directories including almost every person of note in the United States. Even if H.C.L. the Third had no personal claim to fame, he sounded as if he must be the scion of a distinguished family.

However, upon reflection, she decided not to mention his name. Todd would naturally be curious to know why she was interested in the man, and her English upbringing made her reluctant to confide in a stranger, however nice he seemed.

Before setting out that morning she had fixed herself a snack for the journey consisting of wholemeal pita bread stuffed with shredded Iceberg lettuce and salami. Every day since her arrival she had eaten similar picnics wherever she happened to be when her appetite told her it was lunchtime.

Sharing the picnic with Todd—luckily she had filled two pita pockets and insisted on his having one of them—she told him the places where she had lunched while she was sightseeing.

'I think the two best were the observation roof on the seventh floor of the R.C.A. building in Rockefeller Center, and a tiny public garden which I discovered at the end of Riverview Terrace. Do you know it? It's a cul-de-sac of small, old-looking houses off Sutton Place. There was rather a lot of noise from the traffic on the Queensborough Bridge, but the view of the East River was lovely.'

'Yes, I know the spot. I've drawn those houses. But as often as not in secluded places like that you'll find a wino or a junkie asleep on one of the benches. You could have been mugged down there, Caroline.'

'There were a couple of other tourists there. I wasn't at risk,' she assured him. 'I know New York has a high crime rate and parts of it are better avoided, but I must say I always felt as safe as I do in London. Everyone was polite and helpful. I thought New Yorkers had excellent manners.'

'Maybe you brought out the best in them.'

Once more he gave her the warm look which made her feel suddenly shy of him. To avoid holding his glance, she rummaged in her bag for the apples she had brought to complete her meal.

They were nearing the end of their journey when she asked him, 'What takes you to Boston? Something to do with your work?'

Todd slanted an amused glance at her. 'No, as a matter of fact my secretary was quite startled when I called her and told her to cancel all my appointments. As I've already mentioned, I'm making this series of drawings of society's misfits which is a project of my own, nothing to do with the magazine. Mine isn't a nine-to-five job. I often take work home, but also I may take an hour during the day to do my own thing. That's how I came to be at the bus station this morning. There are always some interesting studies there.'

He paused, his hazel eyes quizzical. 'However, today, the person who caught my attention was a very nice-looking blonde girl. I managed to strike up a conversation with her, but then she had to go catch her bus. I wanted to go on talking to her, so I caught the bus too.'

Caroline stared at him blankly. 'Y-you can't be serious!'

'Why not? if I hadn't got on the bus, I might never have seen you again. I didn't know then that you would be going to Nantucket, where I happen to have a weekend place.'

She still found it hard to believe that a man in a responsible position would impulsively shelve all his commitments to pursue a chance encounter with a girl—at least when the girl in question was someone like herself with no claim to be stunningly beautiful.

'You're frowning, Caroline. Are you angry?'

'I . . . I'm incredulous,' she said helplessly.

'There's no reason why I shouldn't have followed you, is there? You're not already taken? I saw you weren't wearing a ring and I assumed you were free. But maybe you have an unofficial relationship—I should have considered that possibility. You're too special not to have some kind of involvement, I guess. I've probably made a fool of myself.'

He sounded so genuinely downcast that she found herself saying, 'No, you haven't—I am free. But what a crazy thing to do! How will you get back?'

'That's no problem. I'll take the bus back—no, I won't. I'll rent a car so that I can take you to dinner and drive myself back to New York. I have a small car in Nantucket for going to the beaches, but I fly back and forth to New York and there I don't need one. If it's further than walking distance, I take a cab or use the buses. I can take you to dinner, can't I?'

How could she say no when he had ditched his appointments and made an unnecessary journey in order to get to know her? She was flattered and touched. But also a little uneasy about encouraging him, because when she had left him in the waiting area she had had no instinctive feeling that she was walking away from a man who might have been important to her.

'Yes . . . yes, if you wish,' she agreed. 'But first I must find myself somewhere to stay. I've made a list of telephone numbers, but my guide book says that accommodation can sometimes be a problem in Boston.'

However, the bus station at Boston had a Travellers' Aid desk where the man on duty recommended an inexpensive guesthouse, and telephoned to make sure they had room for her. It was not far away. Todd carried her case to the door, then left her to unpack and change while he went to organise a car.

While she took a shower, Caroline debated what to wear for the evening. If she was going to see him again, when she got to Nantucket, it would be time enough then to dress up a little. For the present she felt it was wiser to keep things as casual as possible, which included an obvious effort to look more glamorous. She changed her shirt for a clean one, brushed and re-braided her hair, put on slightly more make-up and left it at that.

It was still only mid-afternoon when Todd took her to the Quincy Market in an area which had once been a waterfront slum, and was now one of the city's most attractive places, with granite block pavements and benches between the old market buildings housing dress shops and craft shops, restaurants, food stalls and bars.

Later, after strolling along part of the city's famous Freedom Trail—red lines painted on the sidewalks to lead tourists past historic buildings—they dined on chicken verdicchio in a small Italian family restaurant.

It was not late when they said goodnight.

'I'll be using my place in Nantucket every weekend from now until late fall,' Todd told her. 'I'll look forward to seeing you there. Goodbye for the moment, Caroline. Take care of yourself.'

Giving her a gentle pat on the cheek, he climbed into the car and drove away.

After a day looking round Boston on her own, the next day she went to Concord, mainly to see the house where Louisa May Alcott, author of *Little Women*, had lived.

The small town, not far from Boston, was a beautiful place of fine old houses, green lawns and tall trees. It was the site of the first battle of the Revolutionary War and, as well as seeing Orchard House, the home of the Alcotts, she walked to the

North Bridge spanning the Concord River, the place where 'once the embattled farmers stood, and fired the shot heard round the world.'

These lines by Ralph Waldo Emerson, another of the town's famous inhabitants and one of her favourite poets, were inscribed at the base of the statue of the Minuteman, a broad-shouldered young colonist representing those who had fought against some of the eight hundred British troops sent to seize the war supplies stored in the town.

As Caroline stood on a replica of the wooden bridge which had separated the colonists from the redcoats, she wondered if that spring morning in 1775 had been as perfect as today. Everyone knew about the glories of New England's maple trees in the fall, but she had been unprepared for the beauty of the flowering dogwoods. Their white or pink blossoms were everywhere; both in the open countryside and in the well-kept gardens of the gracious town.

Her enjoyment of the slow-flowing river and the wooded meadows which surrounded it lacked only one thing—someone to share her pleasure.

Thinking of Todd—still amazed at his impulsive action—she wondered if she would like him more or less when they met again. First impressions weren't 'always reliable. And he, when he knew her better, might find that, far from being special, she was really quite ordinary. But the fact that, if only for a day, he had thought her worth following to Boston was something she would always remember, whatever the eventual outcome of their encounter might be.

His hire of a car to get back to New York made her wonder if the cost might be lower in America than in England. Next morning she made enquiries and found that it was—much lower. She also discovered that, for an additional charge, she could pick up a car in Boston and drop it off somewhere else.

The drop-off place had to be fixed in advance. Caroline studied her map and debated which way to go, and when and where to hand the car in. In the time before May the twenty-fourth, she couldn't possibly visit all the six states in New England, or even explore one of them thoroughly.

In the end she decided to rent a car for one week, in which time she could go to Plymouth to see where the Mayflower

had landed, explore Cape Cod and hand in the vehicle at
Hyannis, there to take the ferry to Nantucket. She would then
have ten days on the island before her co-owner arrived; time
to get her bearings and reach her own judgment about
whether the house should be sold as he had suggested.

*Ladies and gentlemen, if you look to starboard—to the right—
you will see a school of dolphins.*

Caroline was already leaning on the starboard rail when the
voice on the public address system directed the passengers'
attention to the half dozen sleek dark shapes leaping from the
calm, sun-lit ocean a few hundred feet away from the Hy-Line
ferry *Brant Point*.

The boat was named after the lighthouse, a small wooden
structure, which was already in view. For almost two hours
the ferry had been cruising south across Nantucket Sound.
Now the island which, on the map, was shaped something like
a lamb chop, was only minutes away.

Its outline, which she had been watching emerge from the
sea for the past half an hour, was a low one. The island, a
product of the Ice Age, was the terminal moraine of a great
glacier. It had no tall cliffs or high hills. What she saw was a
shingle-grey town built on ground rising gently from the
harbour, its roofs interspersed with trees, its skyline marked
by two steeples, one a pointed white spire, the other topped
with a dome.

From the dock where the ferry berthed it was only a two-
minute walk to a cobbled square, surrounded by shops, which
seemed to be the heart of the town. The sidewalks were
shaded by elms, with many comfortable benches for shoppers
to rest on. Cars moved slowly over the cobblestones which,
where there were side-streets, gave place to flat-surfaced
crossing stones.

Caroline asked a woman to direct her to the guesthouse
recommended by Todd. Less than ten minutes later she
was being shown into a pleasant bedroom with ruffled
white curtains at the windows and a patchwork quilt on the
bed.

While she was unpacking, she noticed a map on the
dressing-table. It was a street map of Nantucket Town, and it
showed that the house Kiki had left her was not far from

where she was staying. As soon as she had emptied her suitcase, she set out to see her inheritance.

She had already learned from her guide book that the town was a unique example of the style in which a maritime community, made prosperous by whaling, had lived in the eighteenth and nineteenth centuries. But what she had read had not prepared her for street after street of the beautiful architecture of the past, with little or no modern building to mar the sense of stepping back in time.

The house, when she came to it, was much larger than she had expected. Its sides were clad with cedar shingles, but the front was once-white clapboard, the paint now flaking away from the wood beneath it.

When she had collected a set of keys from Kiki's lawyers in New York, they had told her that the place had come into Mrs Lawrence's possession about three years earlier. At the time, they had suggested to her that it should be repaired and kept clean, but she had chosen to disregard this advice.

Wondering what state the interior would be in after three years' disuse, Caroline climbed one side of the double flight of steps leading to the front door and selected the largest of the keys for her first attempt to open it.

Although the drawn blinds at all the windows gave the house a mysterious air, she felt no misgivings at entering it by herself. Even her co-owner's somewhat ominous statement that he had once lived there and did not wish to repeat the experience did not worry her. She felt only a strange sense of expectancy.

The hall had the musty smell of a place long closed up. Shutting the door behind her—a fanlight enabled her to see—she advanced a few steps to open the first of several internal doors. As she had anticipated, this was the entrance to the living-room or parlour, or whatever the principal room was called in Nantucket.

Here it was both musty and gloomy until she pulled up the blinds at the two tall, many-paned windows. As she turned to inspect her surroundings, she drew in her breath.

Hanging above the empty hearth was a large, gilt-framed oil painting. It was a head and shoulders portrait of a man—a man with almost-black hair and extraordinarily piercing blue eyes.

He seemed to be fixing Caroline with a stern and critical stare. As she stared back at him, her heart gave a queer little lurch. She had never set eyes on him before, yet she felt she knew him—had always known him. It was the strangest sensation; this instant feeling of recognition. Particularly when she realised that the clothes he was wearing were those of the distant past, a black silk neckcloth, a dark coat with many brass buttons.

Meeting those fierce, vivid eyes, she was conscious of disapppointment because she would never meet him. He had lived and died long ago, perhaps at sea—she felt sure he had been one of Nantucket's many master-mariners—or perhaps in a room in this house.

She had forced her gaze away from his face, and was striving to re-focus her attention on the room and its furnishings when there was a sound which, after a moment, she identified as someone knocking on the front door.

When she opened it, she found a small, grey-haired woman standing at the top of the steps. She looked Caroline up and down before she said 'I'm Mary Batson from across the street. I saw the blinds go up and thought I should see who was in here. Sometimes, in the season, young people break into the empty houses—but I can see you're not that kind,' she added with a smile.

Caroline guessed that Mrs Batson had seen her unlock the door, and was curious to know who she was.

She said, 'No, I'm legally entitled to be here—but it was neighbourly of you to check me out, Mrs Batson. My name is Caroline Murray. How do you do?' She offered her hand.

Taking it, Mrs Batson said, 'You're British, aren't you?'

Foreseeing that this was an explanation she was going to have to repeat many times, Caroline answered, 'No, I'm an American, but I've never lived in America.'

The woman's glance slid inquisitively past her to peer into the hall. Caroline did not feel disposed to invite her inside, but she was prepared to satisfy her curiosity to a certain extent.

She said, 'This house has been left to me.'

'Oh? Is that so? We wondered what would happen to it. At one time we thought the old man would have left it to Hawk. Whatever their differences, the boy was the only kin he had.

But, as my husband says, Hawk may have died before the old
man did—he was too wild and reckless to live long. What did
happen to him?'

'He's alive, but that's all I know about him. You knew him
when he lived here?'

'I wouldn't say we knew him well. We saw him coming and
going, and we'd speak to him sometimes. He was always very
well-mannered, and so he should have been. He went to
Deerfield Academy, which is one of the best schools in
Massachusetts. Later, he went to Harvard. He was very
clever, by all accounts. Then he and the old man had a fight—
not for the first time!—and Hawk left and never came back.
We never heard what became of him. There was more than
one girl in Nantucket who lost her heart to him, poor thing.
He was a devil for the women; not only girls of his own age,
but older women, summer people from New York and
Boston.' She clicked her tongue disapprovingly. 'Are you and
your husband planning to live here?'

'I'm not married, Mrs Batson, and, as for living here, I
doubt it. It's a much larger house than I imagined. But I shall
be here for at least two weeks, so we'll see each other again, I
expect. Goodbye for the present.'

With a friendly smile, Caroline retreated and closed the
front door.

Three days later, when the house had been aired and no
longer smelled musty, she spent her first night there, after
warning the Batsons not to be alarmed by seeing lamplight
shining through the blinds. The house had no electricity.

She had to admit that it was a little eerie going upstairs by
the flickering light from a candlestick because the oil lamps
were heavy to carry. All the bedroom doors had old-fashioned
thumb-latches without locks or bolts. Not that there was any
need to lock her door when she was alone in the house and
the front and back doors were locked. But it would have
made her feel more secure as she lay in the antique bed,
listening to the unfamiliar night-sounds of a very old, timber-
framed house.

By the time she had discovered that it had been built in
1829 by Captain James Starbuck, one of the many
descendants of Edward Starbuck who had been among the ten

partners taken by the nine First Purchasers. It was Captain Starbuck's portrait which hung in the room below her bedroom.

She had been correct in guessing him to be a master-mariner. Since then she had learned that he had been among the most renowned of the whaling captains, winning his command at an early age and several times returning to Nantucket with more than two thousand barrels of sperm oil on board his ship, *Damaris*.

Of his personal life she had yet to discover any details. But the house was full of his presence, not only because there were many mementoes of his voyages, but because every time she went into the parlour she was sharply aware of his harsh, rawboned face looking down at her.

Not only was the portrait far superior, technically, to most of those she had seen in the Whaling Museum, but the man who had sat for it had been unusually striking—not handsome, not even good-looking. But somehow extraordinarily compelling. A man born to command other men; to give orders rather than to take them; and, by the proud set of his head and the disciplined firmness of his mouth, to inspire a wary respect in everyone with whom he had dealings.

What of his effect upon women? Caroline only knew that she couldn't stop thinking about him ... wishing she had known him.

The other man who occupied her thoughts was Hawk Lowell. But thinking about him was like working on a jigsaw puzzle with most of the important pieces missing. She didn't even know how old he was because she hadn't thought to ask Mrs Batson when he had lived here. It might have been ten years ago, or it might have been twenty. None of the bedrooms showed signs of having been a boy's room. Perhaps, after the quarrel, the old man—his father? his grandfather?—had deliberately disposed of every reminder of him.

A devil for the women, her neighbour across the street had called him. Was he still? Was that what he was doing in Barbados? Chasing the golden girls to be found in all those winter-sun places? Or—and this was a more disturbing theory—pursuing some rich, bored older woman because he enjoyed the flesh-pots but couldn't afford that lifestyle out of his own pocket? The fact that he was a philanderer wouldn't have put Kiki off him. She had always had a soft spot for a rake.

If he's that kind of man, she should have left him the Palm Beach house, or the villa in France, thought Caroline. She began to wonder if 'the old man' had been the one whom Kiki's parents had dissuaded her from marrying, and if he had left her his house as a sign that he had always loved her.

If so, she would have left Hawk his share because he was the logical heir to the property. But she might have known he would want to sell it and had included Caroline in the bequest simply as a means of breaking the taboo on Nantucket and forcing her to return to her country of origin.

For several days she divided her time between exploring the town and putting the house in order. This was a task calling for a lot of elbow-grease. Clearly it was years since the fine old furniture had been properly polished, the wooden floors thoroughly swept and the hooked rugs taken out and shaken.

One night, tired by her exertions, she went to bed early, intending to read for a while. During the day she had come across one piece of evidence that her co-owner had lived in the house. It was a copy of the great American classic *Moby Dick*. On the flyleaf, in a bold, clear hand, was written the name *Hawk Lowell*.

After reading only two or three pages of Herman Melville's masterpiece, she must have fallen asleep. She was woken by a sound which was not made by a mouse scuttling beneath the floorboards, or by the roof trusses expanding or contracting. For some seconds the sound had her puzzled. Then, with a gasp of dismay, she realised that someone was moving about on what she was learning to call the first floor instead of, as in England, the ground floor.

Sometimes, in the season, young people break into the empty houses.

As she sat up, listening with alarm to the slow-moving footsteps downstairs, she remembered Mrs Batson's excuse for knocking on the door. But the season wasn't in swing yet; and, as her lamp was still burning, it could be seen by anyone in the street that this house was not one of the empty ones.

Whoever had broken in appeared to be looking round the

first floor, presumably with the aid of a flashlight. It seemed to Caroline that any man who forced an entry into a house which he knew to be occupied must have some motive other than theft. Could it be that some unpleasant character had noticed she was living here alone and, knowing there was no telephone, meant to . . .

Her heart thumping, she scrambled out of bed, snatched up her dressing gown and thrust her arms into the sleeves. As she pulled the garment around her, her eyes searched the room for something with which to arm herself.

At first there seemed to be nothing she could use as a defensive weapon. Then she remembered the window sticks.

Although they looked as if they would operate by sash cords, none of the windows in the house opened and closed by this means. The upper sashes were fixed. The lower ones had to be propped open with a long notched piece of wood which, when not in use, lay on the window-ledge.

A window stick was not as sturdy a weapon as she would have liked, but it was better than nothing. Wondering if the Batsons would hear her if she screamed for help, she trod into her slippers and braced herself to confront the intruder. She had never been more frightened in her life.

When she opened the door, the glow from her bedside oil lamp illumined part of the landing, but not the dark depths of the hall at the foot of the staircase.

At that moment the intruder was emerging from what she had mentally dubbed Captain Starbuck's room. His flashlight was beamed on a fine antique barometer which hung near the front door. All she could see of him was the outline of a very tall man with shoulders in proportion to his height. A big, powerful man against whom if he once got his hands on her, she wouldn't stand a chance.

It was then—too late!—that she knew what she ought to have done. On the roof of this house and many others there was what was known as a walk. It was a look-out platform built over the ridge and surrounded by a wooden rail.

If she had turned out her lamp and felt her way up to the third floor, she could then have used her own flashlight to climb to the walk where she would have been safe. One loud yell from up there would rouse not only the Batsons but the neighbourhood.

She was wondering if it was still possible to get up there when the light swung away from the barometer and up to where she was standing near the head of the stairs.

Momentarily hypnotised by the narrow beam of brilliance now focussed on her frightened eyes, she said sharply, 'There's two hundred dollars at the back of the centre drawer in the kitchen dresser. Take it and get out.'

It wasn't true. Her money, all in dollar travellers' cheques, was in her bag in the bedroom. But it was a desperate attempt to give herself time to reach the comparative safety of the roof walk.

The beam fell away from her face. A voice she had heard once before said, 'Miss Caroline Murray, I presume? Don't be frightened. I'm not a burglar.' As relief flooded through her, he began to come up the stairs.

It wasn't until he reached the top that she was able to see him clearly. Only when he stepped into the area lit by the oil lamp in the bedroom were his features revealed—and recognised.

For it was no stranger from whom, instinctively, she recoiled. Since her first day at the house, those penetrating blue eyes and the aquiline nose and lean cheeks had become as familar to her as the features of her brother or stepfather.

'Captain Starbuck!' she whispered hoarsely.

At that moment, in the aftermath of terror, she felt that no living man could be the image of a dead one; and that somehow, by thinking about him and feeling that, if she had known him, she would have loved him, she had conjured up James Starbuck's spirit.

She swayed, feeling suddenly dizzy. She had never fainted before, but she knew that she was going to now.

Before her legs sagged beneath her, the spectre of Starbuck stepped forward and, with warm strong, flesh and blood hands, made her sit on a chair and pushed her head towards her knees.

CHAPTER TWO

'DON'T move. I'll get you a glass of water,' he said, a minute or two later, after helping her to sit up.

Caroline had no wish to move. The giddiness had passed off, but she felt it might yet return if she attempted to stand.

'There's a glass by my bed,' she murmured. 'It's had milk in it.'

She watched him go into the bedroom and return with not only the glass but also the oil lamp which he carried with ease in one hand. He placed it on top of the tallboy where its light spread over the landing, and, when he opened the door, into the bathroom.

She heard him running water, rinsing the glass and filling it. By the time he reappeared she was beginning to feel annoyed with herself for entertaining, even momentarily, the idea that he might not be real. She was not a superstitious person, certainly not to the extent of believing in ghosts. Her only excuse for so foolish an aberration was that she had had a bad fright. Also it was pretty incredible that, after so many generations, a descendant of Captain Starbuck should bear this uncanny resemblance to him.

However, when he brought her the water, and then seated himself on the blanket chest opposite where she was sitting, she saw that in fact he was not as exact a replica of his ancestor as she had thought.

Their hair was the same, and most of their strong, rawboned features. But whereas the Captain's heavy black brows almost formed a single thick bar across the breadth of his forehead, Mr Lowell's eyebrows had a space between them. There were other subtle differences, but she could not define them without studying him; and, as he was scrutinising her, she preferred to keep her gaze on her glass.

'God knows why my grandfather didn't have the house wired at the same time as he had the bathroom installed. Oil lamps might have their uses when the power's cut, but having

41

nothing but oil lamps is ridiculous,' he said crisply. 'What made you move in here, rather than staying at a hotel? When I came by and saw the lights on, I thought we had an unofficial tenant—one of the barefoot brigade who make a nuisance of themselves in most resorts in the summer.'

'For one thing, it seemed a waste of money to stay in a hotel when there were eight perfectly good bedrooms here.'

'But no comfort to speak of,' he said dryly. 'Are you short of money, Caroline?'

'No, but I haven't any to waste. I admit I do miss a hot bath. But that could be remedied if I knew how the boiler in the basement worked. Meanwhile I manage with kettles.'

'Talking of kettles, would you like me to make you some coffee? Or tea, of you have any with you. Tea is what the British calm their shattered nerves with, isn't it?'

She said, for the umpteenth time, 'In spite of my accent, I'm not British. I'm as American as you are, except that I haven't lived in America since I was fifteen months old. I was born right here in Nantucket.'

'I see. That makes Kiki's will a little less incomprehensible. Why don't you go back to bed, and I'll make us both a cup of coffee. Then I'll go pick up my bag from the White Elephant and tell them I've changed my plans. I'm staying here.'

'But you can't do that!' she expostulated. 'I'm here. We can't *both* stay here.'

'Why not? It's my house, too. After the fright you've just had, I don't think you'd sleep very soundly if I left you here on your own for the rest of the night.'

'I've slept very well, until tonight. If you thought there was someone up here illegally, why didn't you call the police?' she asked. 'And why were you looking downstairs before coming up to the room with the light on?'

'If I'd had any reason to think that the person in here might be dangerous, maybe I would have called the police. But I felt I could probably handle the situation,' was his answer.

Glancing at him, she had to concede that there wouldn't be too many situations someone of his size and physique couldn't handle.

He had probably dined at his hotel, a modern resort complex on the edge of the harbour away from the historic part of the town. Even if there wasn't a strict dress code in force there, most people would dress for dinner more formally than at the guesthouses. He was wearing a navy blue blazer with a button-down Oxford-cloth shirt and classic grey flannels. The well-tailored, conventionally Prep clothes played down but didn't conceal that he was very fit, with long muscular thighs under the flannels and strong, sinewy wrists showing under the half inch of shirt cuff which extended below the edge of his coat sleeves.

'I was looking round to see if anything had been stolen or vandalised,' he went on, in answer to her second question. 'I realise that must have made it more frightening for you, and I'm sorry about that. But you know what you should have done, when you heard someone downstairs, is to have pushed something heavy across the doorway, and then yelled for help from the window. A window stick'—he bent to pick it up from the floor where she must have dropped it when her head started to swim—'isn't any protection against a burglar.'

'I know. But it was the only thing to hand. Perhaps I didn't act sensibly, but most people's wits aren't at their sharpest when they've just woken up. I'd been reading, and had fallen asleep with the light on. Anyway, this isn't New York where break-ins seem to be commonplace. From what I gather, there's very little local crime on Nantucket. What there is is mostly committed by the summer transients. It's quite unnecessary for you to leave your comfortable hotel on my account. Besides which, the bed I'm sleeping in is the only one which has been aired. All the others are probably damp.'

As she rose to her feet, she added, 'I'm feeling fine again now. I'll come down and make us some coffee. What time did you arrive, Mr Lowell, and how did you get here?'

He picked up the lamp to light their way down the stairs. Before moving ahead of her, he said, 'Don't you think that, as friends of Kiki, we can count that our introduction and call each other by our first names? I intend to call you Caroline.'

'Very well . . . Hawk,' she amended.

'That's better. You sound almost friendly.' His smile held a hint of mockery before he turned to lead the way.

Flushing slightly, she followed him down the staircase, noticing the way his thick, crisp, almost-black hair showed an inclination to curl into ducks' tails at the back of his deeply bronzed neck.

'I flew in from New York,' he told her. 'I'd been to see Kiki's lawyers. They were holding various other keepsakes which she had left me—a very fine piece of scrimshaw which I had admired, and an antique sextant. They told me you'd called in about two weeks ago and were planning to look round New England. I didn't expect to find you here yet. When did you arrive?'

She told him. 'I found this was the place I most wanted to see, so I cut short my tour on the mainland. I did drive the length of Cape Cod. I didn't like Provincetown much—although it has a marvellous museum—but Sandwich and Chatham were delightful. You know the Cape well, I expect?'

'Not really. I know Rhode Island better. I spent a lot of vacations there while I was at college.'

'You were at Harvard, I believe?'

They had reached the hall and were on their way to the kitchen, and her remark made him check and turn.

'Who told you that?' he asked.

'Mrs Batson from across the street. She came over the day I arrived. She was curious to know who I was, and what I was doing here.'

'She would be,' he said sardonically. 'The woman's a professional busybody. What else did she tell you about me?'

'Not much—where you'd been to school, that you had quarrelled with your grandfather and never come back to Nantucket.' She hesitated before adding, 'She seemed to think you might have predeceased him. She described you as very well-mannered but too wild and reckless to live long.'

He gave a short, harsh-sounding laugh. In the kitchen he set the lamp on the table and set about lighting another lamp which belonged there.

He said, 'Anyone who doesn't have a streak of wildness in them when they're young is going to be a dull person later.'

What does that make me? Caroline wondered, remembering her unrebellious teens.

'I wasn't that wild,' he went on. 'I got smashed once or twice. But as I only had a bike, not an automobile, I wasn't a danger to anyone but myself. I had a few midnight dips in other people's pools. That might seem wild to Mrs Batson who's never had kids of her own, and whose nephew was the studious type who preferred ice-cream to beer and never looked at girls. As for smoking tobacco or pot, I never did either. They were too expensive. Every dollar I earned in the vacations went into my Independence Fund.'

He finished trimming the lamp and replaced the glass shade. Caroline had already noticed his well-kept brown hands. They were not the huge, thick-fingered hands of some very tall men. His were lean, showing their bone structure, with long square-tipped fingers which had dealt with lighting the lamp with a deft economy of movement.

He went on, 'My education was paid for by one of my aunts. But my home—such as it was—was here with my mother's father until I could afford to support myself. Ben Chase was a tough man to live with. I was twelve when my mother died, and I promised her I would live with him. Seven years later he threw me out. Mrs Batson might say he was justified. I think otherwise—although I was happy to go. Perhaps you should defer judgment until you know me better.'

She made no comment on that, but said, 'You called your grandfather Ben Chase. I had assumed his surname was Starbuck. If he wasn't a direct descendant of Captain James Starbuck, how is it that you are so like him?—the Captain, I mean.'

'Ben was directly descended from Starbuck. The Captain's only son was lost at sea and the house came down to his daughter. She married a Macy, and her daughter married a Chase. Not so much now, but in the past there was a great deal of intermarriage in Nantucket. Husseys married Coffins and Macys married Swains until practically everyone here was cousin to everyone else.'

'I see. But your other grandfather isn't, or wasn't, a Nantucketer?'

'No. My mother married "someone from off" as they say around here. Nantucket is a pretty important place—to Nantucketers,' he added dryly.

As he had picked up the box of matches on the table to light the lamp, she had not been able to put a match to a burner on the butane gas stove.

Now, as he attended to it for her, she said, 'That's the way most people feel. Their place—be it only a dot on the map—is the hub of the universe.'

'Where's the hub of your universe, Caroline? London?'

She shook her head. 'No. Nor is it my family's village in Gloucestershire. I think the hub of my universe might be here, where I was born.'

His left eyebrow lifted. 'It was love at first sight, was it? That's as risky with a place as with a person. Sometimes picturesque places have hidden snags which the new arrival doesn't know about—or chooses to ignore.'

'If you're trying to put me off Nantucket, my mother has beaten you to it. I've already heard everything there is to hear against the island.'

'You said you were born here. Is your mother a Nantucketer?'

'No, she's from Kentucky. She grew up surrounded by horses, as she still is in England. Unfortunately, at her coming out dance, she fell in love with an equally obsessive yachtsman.'

'Why unfortunately?'

'By the time she realised they had almost nothing in common, they were married. She spent six months trying to whip up an interest in sailing—while being seasick if the water was even slightly choppy—by which time she was expecting me. My father was drowned when she was eight months pregnant. The ghastly irony was that it wasn't a sailing accident. They came here almost every weekend except in midwinter. That particular weekend she had made a fuss about being left on her own while he went off with his yacht club cronies. So he chucked his sailing arrangements and took her for a picnic at Great Point. While they were there, some bathers got into difficulties.'

She paused, remembering the day when her mother had told her the full story.

'And your father brought two of them ashore—the woman and the child—and then went back to help the man, but they were both drowned,' said Hawk.

'How did you know? Were you here when it happened?'

He looked about ten years her senior. But it was hard to be sure how old he was. Now, in the brighter light from the two oil lamps, she could see that, although there was no hint of grey in the hair at his temples, there were many fine lines fanning out from the corners of his eyes, and two more deeply engraved laughter lines running down his darkly tanned cheeks.

'No, I first came here several years later. But a tragedy of that order isn't quickly forgotten—or not in a small place like this.'

The kettle was boiling. Caroline made instant coffee, and offered him milk and sugar. The latter he refused.

Sitting down at the scrubbed pine table, she said, 'I understand my mother's detestation of the island, and perhaps yours as well. But that isn't to say I couldn't be happy here. My father adored it, and I think I'm probably very like him.'

'Do you sail?'

'No, I've never set foot in a small boat. But I know I'm not seasick like Mummy. I've crossed the English Channel several times; once when it was fairly rough.' She remembered his mention of the sextant Kiki had left him. 'Are you a sailing man, Hawk?'

It seemed to her that his blue eyes narrowed and hardened. He stared at her for a long moment before he answered, 'I'm not a weekend sailor as your father was. The sea is my livelihood.'

So he wasn't a Caribbean playboy, living either on unearned income, his wits or rich women.

'What do you do?' she enquired.

'Like James Starbuck, I'm Master of a square-rigger.'

'Really?' she exclaimed, in astonishment. 'How very extraordinary—that you should not only look like him, but also be a master-mariner. But you can't be a whaling captain, so what does your square-rigger do?'

'She's a cruise ship, with sails instead of funnels. And it's not that extraordinary for genes to jump a few generations. There's a British writer, Monica Dickens, who married an American Navy man. They used to live in North Falmouth, which is one of the nicer towns on Cape Cod. She was a great-granddaughter of Charles Dickens, one of your most famous authors. Sorry—I forgot you only sound British! But there are many other examples of a talent or a vocation reappearing in a family line. Most of my ancestors, on my mother's side, have been seafarers. Island people generally were; they didn't have many alternatives.'

'I suppose not. But if you went to Harvard you had all kinds of alternatives. What made you opt for seafaring?'

'Have you ever heard of the Sail Training movement?'

Caroline shook her head. She had once had several dates with a man who, at weekends, had been what was known as a foredeck gorilla, meaning an unpaid crew member on an ocean-racing yacht. During the week he had worked in a merchant bank in the City—London's equivalent of Wall Street. A suave young man who always wore a dark red carnation in his buttonhole and bought his shirts at Turnbull & Asser in Jermyn Street. Every Friday night, from March to October, he had rushed down to Cowes, on the south coast, to spend Saturday and Sunday in a tee-shirt and shorts, or oilskins, crewing a millionaire's yacht.

That short-lived friendship with Giles—he had never taken her to Cowes with him because the entire weekend would be spent racing to the French coast and back—had been the closest she had come to the sport which had been her father's passion and her mother's *bête noire*.

'Sail training was the brain-child of a man called Bernard Morgan,' Hawk explained. 'He thought that learning to sail was a good way to teach young people self-reliance and cooperation. If they were also able to race against crews of other nationalities, after the races they would meet and make friends. Most countries have sail training ships, and every two years since 1956 there've been international tall ship races. At least half the people on board have to be between the ages of sixteen and twenty-five.'

He paused to drink his coffee.

'When I was seventeen, I spent the summer vacation taking part in a transatlantic race from Boston to Kristiansand in Norway. By the end of the voyage I knew that sailing in tall ships was the way I wanted to live. Everyone thought I was crazy, including my grandfather. He wanted me to become a lawyer. For a while I toyed with the idea of practising marine law—it's an interesting field, and highly profitable. But long before I graduated, I knew it wasn't what I wanted. So from

Harvard I went to sea, starting as crew and gradually working my way up.'

'Where is your ship at the moment?' she asked.

'Normally she would be on her way to the Mediterranean for her summer cruises. But this year the company that owns her has entered her in a race from Newport to Portugal which starts in early July. Before that she has to have a refit at Baltimore, which is where I left her. Her first officer is also a fully qualified yachtmaster, with ten years' experience in tall ships. He takes over when I'm on leave.'

Having drunk the last of his coffee, he pushed back his chair and stood up.

'It won't take me long to collect my gear.' He turned back his cuff to check the time. 'It's a quarter after eleven. I'll be back before midnight.' Seeing her open her mouth to protest, he added firmly, 'Save your breath, Caroline. I don't know what state you found the place in, but it's reasonably habitable now, and I'm going to stay. As you said yourself, why spend money on a hotel room when there's a choice of bedrooms here?'

'But, as *you* said, no comfort to speak of. Anyway, the hotel will charge you for staying there tonight—no doubt you've already used the shower—so you may as well get your money's worth. If you want to move in here tomorrow—fine. I'll go back to the guesthouse where I was before. There's no way we can stay here together. It's not on,' she ended, her own tone equally firm.

The teasing glint she had seen earlier, after her somewhat reluctant use of his first name, reappeared in the vivid blue eyes looking down at her unmade-up face and probably untidy hair.

'Are you afraid I'll make a pass at you?' he asked.

'That has nothing to do with it,' she said stiffly. 'For all I know, you may be a married man with several children.'

His mouth quirked. 'That's no guarantee that a guy won't get out of line. If there were any statistics on the subject, I should say they'd reveal that as many passes are made by married men as by single ones—possibly more. However, at the risk of making you even more nervous, I'll admit that I'm not and never have been married. But even though I've been at sea for several weeks, and you're an attractive girl, I believe

I'll be able to restrain myself from making advances—at least until you indicate that they're acceptable.'

He was openly mocking her. Clearly he took her for the kind of girl who thought no man could resist her. She couldn't bear girls of that sort, and it annoyed her to be mistaken for one.

Striving to keep calm, she said, 'I'm sure the owners of your ship wouldn't employ a captain who was an inveterate lecher, and I'm certainly not under the impression that I'm irresistible. That isn't the point. Nantucket is not like New York or London, where more or less anything goes. As you said when you telephoned from Barbados, it's a small New England town where everyone knows everyone else, and where standards are stricter than in big cities. I'm sure Mrs Bailey wouldn't approve of our staying here together, even if we are co-owners.'

He shrugged. 'I don't care what Mrs Batson thinks. I'll return this lamp to your room and leave the other in the hall for when I come back. If I continue to use the back door, and sleep in one of the back bedrooms, Mrs Batson won't even know I'm here.'

'Oh, don't be absurd! Of course she will. She's bound to see you around town. Anyway, it's not only her reaction which bothers me.'

'You think your boy-friend wouldn't like it?'

He was mounting the stairs by this time, having placed the second lamp on the hall table.

Caroline remained at the foot of the stairs. She said indignantly, 'If by my boyfriend you mean the man who answered the telephone, he happens to be my half-brother. He was born when I was three. We're very close. He was spending a night on my sofa on his way home from France.'

Hawk paused, half way up the stairs. From that height, with his eyelids half-closed and the angle of the light accentuating his high-bridged nose, there was something about him which reminded her of the bird of prey from which his name derived.

'I see. A natural mistake on my part, in the circumstances. Would you like me to apologise?'

'No, but I think it might make you more careful about jumping to conclusions in future.'

He made no reply but continued his way up the staircase

leaving her to wonder if he really meant to check out of the White Elephant. If he did, there was nothing she could do except dress and go to the guesthouse. But why should she let him drive her out at this hour of the night?

Actually she had been surprised when he told her the time. When his footsteps had woken her up, she had thought it was one or two o'clock in the morning.

He reappeared, coming swiftly and lightly down the staircase. He said, 'Do you know about the disc in the centre of the top of the newel post?'

Caroline had one hand on the post. She moved it to glance at the disc of a paler substance embedded in the volute of the handrail. She had noticed it when cleaning the banisters of dust and cobwebs.

'Isn't it just ornamental?'

'It's a whalebone button, said to have been a sign that there was no mortgage on the house. You'll see them in many of the houses here.'

She was interested, but at the moment she was more concerned about getting rid of him.

'I'll let you out,' she said, moving towards the front door.

Her hand was inches away from the large old-fashioned key which she left in the lock overnight when his fingers closed round her wrist and drew her arm down.

'I'll go out the back way and through the garden. It's quicker. When you lock the door after me, take the key out or I shan't be able to use mine.'

Still holding her wrist, he added, 'If it's crossing your mind to leave the key in deliberately, think again. My grandfather used to lock up and go to bed at nine, and he expected me to do the same. There are several ways into this house, other than by the doors, for anyone who knows it as intimately as I do.'

He had touched her before, when he had made her sit down and, by pushing her head forward, had stopped her from losing consciousness.

But the way he was touching her now, holding her wrist loosely but inescapably in the circle of his fingers and thumb, was different. She felt her pulse start to quicken and longed to wrench it free.

'Very well, but I hope you realise that I think you're behaving abominably,' she told him stonily. 'Don't think that because you have me over a barrel in this instance, I'm going to let you ride roughshod in all our dealings. I'm not!'

He released her. 'I'll bear that in mind.'

After he had stepped through the back door, bidding her a bland goodnight as he did so, Caroline shut it and locked it. She did not think he had been bluffing in saying there were other ways he could gain admittance if she tried to lock him out.

She had noticed the absence of a bolt on the underside of the trapdoor leading to the roof walk. She felt sure that while the difficulty of climbing up there by way of the outside of the house would deter most people, it wouldn't stop him.

If he had crewed on sailing ships, he must, at one time, have been well used to swarming up and down rigging and working on the highest yard-arms. A good head for heights, and steady nerves, must be essential in that job.

Fuming, Caroline went back upstairs. Should she dress and spend the night somewhere else? Demonstrate, from the outset, that she wasn't a girl to be coerced?

Had it been Thursday or Friday, she wouldn't have hesitated. But the proprietress of the guesthouse had mentioned that, even out of the high season, they were usually full at weekends.

In the end she climbed back into bed. Knowing it was useless to attempt to sleep until he came back, she tried to calm her vexation by taking up the book she had been reading. *His* book, confound him, she thought crossly.

After a while the power of Melville's prose did distract her from her angry thoughts. He had served before the mast himself and was writing from first hand experience. When she came to the chapter headed *Nantucket*, her interest quickened.

What wonder then, that these Nantucketers, born on a beach, should take to the sea for a livelihood! she read. And, further on: *The Nantucketer, he alone resides and riots on the sea; he alone, in Bible language, goes down to it in ships; to and fro ploughing it as his own special plantation. There is his home; there lies his business which a Noah's flood would not interrupt, though it overwhelmed all the millions in China. He lives on the sea, as prairie cocks in the prairie; he hides among the waves, he climbs them as chamois hunters climb the Alps. For years he knows not the land; so that when he comes to it at last, it smells like another world, more strangely than the moon would to an Earthman. With the landless gull, that at sunset folds her wings and is rocked to sleep between billows; so at nightfall, the Nantucketer, out of sight of land, furls his sails, and lays him to his rest, while under his very pillow rush herds of walruses and whales.*

As she rushed the end of the chapter, she heard Hawk re-enter the house. Quickly she turned out her lamp, which he would not have seen, short-cutting up the lane at the end of the garden.

All the interior doors had glazed panels above them. When he mounted the stairs—moving quietly so that, had she been sleeping, she wouldn't have wakened—she could see the light of the lamp as he passed by and climbed to the top floor.

Normally her last action, after extinguishing the lamp, was to slip out of bed and raise the blinds, but if she did that the floor would creak and betray that she wasn't asleep. It was almost full moon. The night before, she had fallen asleep while watching the silvered leaves, and the dark shadows between the branches, of a large maple tree. Tonight, unable to see out, her last waking thoughts were of the man preparing to sleep in a room on the floor above.

How horrified her mother would be if she knew that her daughter was about to spend the night in an unlocked room in a house whose only other occupant was a man she had just met!

She was woken by the first of the many chimes rung every morning at seven by the Portuguese bell in the tower of the Unitarian Church on Orange Street.

They were repeated at noon, and again at nine in the evening, the curfew hour in the days when most of the islanders had been strict Quakers. For the rest of the day, the bell struck the hours normally.

It was no longer rung by hand and something seemed to have gone wrong with the mechanism which controlled it. At those special times it was supposed to chime fifty-two times; but after carefully keeping count, she had found that two extra strikes had crept in. Probably the Nantucketers were so used to the bell that they no longer noticed the pleasant, old-world sound which made it unnecessary for her to set her alarm clock.

At first even the fact that the blinds were down did not remind her of what had happened the night before. She lay in a drowsy torpor, conscious that she had slept more soundly than usual.

Then footsteps marching upstairs brought everything back with a rush. Before she had time to collect herself, there was a brisk rap at the door and Hawk walked in.

'Good morning. Breakfast will be ready at half past seven, but I thought you might like some coffee to get you going,' he said, approaching the bed and putting a cup and saucer on the night table.

'Shall I open the blinds?'

'G-good morning. Thank you. Yes . . . please do.'

Considerably disconcerted by this unforeseen invasion of her privacy, she struggled into a sitting position, pulling the bedclothes up with her, although her cotton voile nightdress was neither transparent nor revealingly décolleté.

Sometimes she had difficulty in making the blinds roll up fully. Evidently there was a knack to it. At Hawk's touch they rolled up at once, letting in a flood of sunshine. She had chosen this bedroom largely because it had a fourposter bed with a fishnet canopy, and a lovely late eighteenth century mirror hanging between the two tall windows.

'This wasn't your grandfather's room, or your room was it?' she asked.

'No, this used to be my mother's room. You keep it very shipshape. Most women have bits and pieces everywhere'—looking at the almost bare dressing-table.

'I haven't many things with me, and there's masses of storage in that tallboy,' she answered.

As if he had every right to linger in her bedroom, Hawk strolled to look at the painting of a ship which hung above a chest of drawers.

'This is Starbuck's whaler, *Darmaris*,' he told her. 'She was named after his wife. Not long after their wedding, he went away for two years. In fact she never saw much of him until he retired. Sometimes the whaling ships were away for as long as five years. In their husbands' absence, Nantucket women had to take responsibilities and make decisions which would normally have been a male prerogative. In that respect, women here were ahead of their time. Where do you stand on women's liberation, Caroline?'

She sipped the coffee he had brought her before replying.

'My stand is for everyone's liberation,' she said thoughtfully. 'I believe a lot of people, of both sexes, go through life as square pegs in round holes. Some people only ever do what they really enjoy at night classes, or weekends, or after they retire. I'm not sorry for the girl who wants to be a scientist or an engineer; if she's keen enough, that's what she will be. The people who have my support are the wives who want to stay at home, and cook and sew and give a lot of attention to their children, but who can't because rising prices make it hard to manage on one income. And I feel very sorry for the man who's discovered, too late in life, that he'd really like to be a gardener or a cabinet-maker, instead of which he's stuck in a bank or an insurance office. I——'

She stopped short, suddenly realising that she had been talking to Hawk as if he were Robert.

Nearly all her opinions had been tested and honed in discussions—sometimes spirited disputes—with her brother. It wasn't often that she aired her views with other people. Usually she listened to theirs, agreeing when she could, seldom arguing when she didn't.

'Where do you stand?' she asked.

'In general, like you, I'm in favour of both sexes doing whatever they want. I even go along with the idea of the woman being the breadwinner and the man the housekeeper if that's the logical arrangement. However on a personal level, if I ever marry my wife will have to make most of the concessions. I couldn't give up my way of life, and I shouldn't be prepared to see her as infrequently as the whalers saw their wives. She would have to live on my ship with me.'

'Did the whalers' wives never go with them?'

'A few did. There was a girl called Nancy Wyer who was only sixteen when she married Captain Charles Grant. Soon afterwards he went away for four years. When he came back, she insisted on going on his next voyage. She had her first baby on Pitcairn Island, delivered by a woman called Annie Christian who was said to be a daughter of Fletcher Christian, the leader of the *Bounty* mutineers. Later on that same voyage, Nancy was able to claim a twenty-dollar gold piece which her husband had offered to the first man to sight a whale. The story goes that she was hanging out the baby's diapers and noticed a whale before it was seen by the masthead lookout. She had two other children, one born in New Zealand and the other in Samoa. When the two eldest needed to start their schooling, she left them here with her mother while she went on travelling with her husband.'

He glanced at his watch. 'I'll go run your bath. I lit the boiler an hour ago, so there should be plenty of hot water. It may run rusty at first, but that should clear pretty soon.'

Before she could speak, he had left her.

It was twenty-five minutes to eight—*before* eight, she corrected herself—when Caroline hurried downstairs to find the kitchen table laid for a much more substantial breakfast than she usually ate.

It was difficult to remain in a state of high or even moderate dudgeon with a man who had organised hot bath water and—with a dishcloth wrapped round his lean hips to protect his clean jeans—was at the stove, scrambling eggs.

Also, although she wouldn't admit it to him, she knew that his presence in the house had been the reason she had slept without rousing at every loud creak.

'Drink your juice. These are almost ready,' he said, with a glance which took in her Liberty shirt and blue denim skirt.

She couldn't resist saying, 'Aye, aye, sir,' before she sat down at the place with a full glass of orange juice standing between the knife and fork.

Hawk had already drunk most of his fruit juice. At her saucy reply, he turned and looked at her again, a slow grin appearing. Above the rim of the glass as she raised it to her lips, her grey eyes danced in response. She put the glass back on the cloth. 'My bath was lovely. Thank you for lighting the boiler.'

He said, 'Last night, while you were glowering at me, I said you were attractive. When you smile, you're more than attractive.'

Her breath seemed to catch in her throat. She felt the same

quickening pulse-beat as when he had caught her by the wrist.

Oh, no! I mustn't—I must *not*! she thought, before he returned to his task. Her gaze on his broad-shouldered back, now clad in a white cotton shirt with the sleeves rolled up, she knew that, in spite of her anger the night before, she was in very real danger of losing her heart to a man she didn't even know.

The eggs he had cooked were fluffy, moist and delicious. As well as the hot buttered toast on which they were served, he had been out to a bakery and bought some Portuguese rolls which he had re-heated in the oven.

'For a captain, you seem a great cook,' said Caroline. 'Where did you learn to do such super scrambled eggs?'

'My mother taught me how to cook. She was confined to a wheelchair, so she couldn't spoil me the way a lot of mothers do their sons. I had to do things for her. Women do boys a disservice by waiting on them hand and foot. A man who can't sew on a button and press his own shirt is as much at a disadvantage as a woman who can't change a tyre or the washer on a faucet.'

'Why was your mother in a wheelchair?'

'She had a wasting disease which eventually killed her. My father had a drinking problem. When he was sober, he was a nice man, and I liked him very much. He was knocked down in the street a couple of years before my mother died. You know about Kiki Lawrence and my grandfather. My parents were victims of the same situation, but in reverse.'

'No, I don't know about Kiki and your grandfather. Or only that she was in love with a young man here whom her family considered unsuitable.'

Hawk split a Portuguese roll and spread it with butter and honey. 'How much do you know of the history of this island?'

'Only that two centuries ago it was the greatest whaling port in what were the Colonies, but that even before the great Fires of 1846 a depression had begun. People couldn't afford to build new houses or update old ones, and that's why the town is as it is—a lovely relic of the past with hardly any ugly Victorian intrusions.'

'That's right, and the depression lasted until the 1800s when Nantucket began to be developed as a vacation resort. Have you been over to 'Sconset yet?'

'No, I was planning to walk over there in a day or two. It's only about seven or eight miles away, isn't it?'

'Yes, it's not far, if you like walking. But the road is more or less straight and not very scenic. You'd do better to rent a bike. Maybe we should try a tandem. More coffee?'

'Yes, please.'

As he refilled her cup, he went on, 'Originally 'Sconset was no more than a group of huts used by fishermen during the seasons when the fish were running. Then it became a summer place for people from Nantucket Town, and later, in the 1890s, it began to be known as the actors' colony. Everyone who was anyone in the New York theatre spent part of the summer there, including Kiki's parents, who were both well-known stage people in their day.'

At this point someone knocked at the front door.

Caroline's eyebrows contracted. 'Who can be calling at this hour? It's not eight o'clock yet.'

Hawk put his napkin on the table. 'I'll find out.'

'No, no—you're still having breakfast. I've finished eating. I'll go.'

The elderly man she found at the top of the steps said, 'Good morning, Miss Murray. I'm John Batson. You've met my wife.'

'Oh, yes. How do you do, Mr Batson.' She shook hands. 'What can I do for you?'

'My wife insisted I come over and check that you were all right.' From his tone, and his choice of phrase, it sounded as if he had come under duress and was embarrassed by his errand.

'I'm fine, thank you, Mr Batson. Is there any reason why I shouldn't be?'

'Well . . . this is kind of a big old place for a woman to stay on her own. It's been standing empty a long while. Some young ladies would find it a mite scary . . . specially at night. But you're not the nervous type, I guess.'

Remembering her fear the night before, and how she had almost fainted when the light had revealed a face so uncannily like the portrait in the parlour, Caroline felt rather ashamed of claiming more courage than she possessed.

But in the circumstances it was simpler to say, 'No, I'm not.'

'That's good . . . that's good. If you had been—nervous, I mean—it might have upset you to tell you what my wife thinks she saw this morning. To tell you the truth, it upset *her* so bad that she had to take some of her pills and go back to bed. Normally, I would have told her she must have imagined what she claims to have seen, Miss Murray. But it so happens that, last night, I saw something strange here myself.'

'What was that, Mr Batson?'

'I went to bed later than usual. When I looked out of my window I noticed this house was in darkness. But then, just a few seconds later, while I was still standing there, a light appeared in your hallway. A short time later it reappeared on the second floor, and then again on the top floor.'

She could have told him a white lie—that she had been carrying the light he had seen. But, apart from the fact that even white lies did not come easily to her, she felt it was prudent to find out what Mrs Batson had seen before embarking on an explanation.

'What was it which upset your wife?' she asked.

'She was looking out of the window this morning, and she said to me, 'John that's unusual. The blinds are down in the room which Miss Murray is using. They've never been down at this time since she moved in. I hope she's not sick.' I said I thought that was unlikely, and then Mary gave a kind of choking sound and I saw her put her hands to her chest. I helped her to a chair. When she could speak, she told me she had seen the blinds raised, not by you but by someone who used to live over here a long time ago—the person she saw was a young man called Hawk Lowell. He was old Mr Chase's grandson. He'd be around thirty-five now—if he's still alive. You told my wife that he was; but she feels that seeing him at the window must be a sign he's passed on. Now I'm not a superstitious man, but it does seem strange that we both have seen something peculiar.'

'There's a mundane explanation for both phenomena, Mr Batson. What you saw was Captain Lowell, as he is now, going up to bed after his arrival late last night. Far from dying long before his time, he's very much alive and in excellent health. I'm sorry his appearance at my window gave your wife a bad shock. The reason he was raising my blinds was because I'd overslept and he had kindly brought me a cup of coffee. Now, if you'll excuse me, I must go and do the washing up.'

When she returned to the kitchen, Hawk was buttering the last of the rolls.

'Could you hear that conversation?' she asked.

He nodded. 'You should have said you had to do the dishes. On this side of the Atlantic, to wash up means to wash oneself.'

She drew in a sharp, angry breath; the ire felt last night rekindling.

'You are an exasperating man! You don't seem to care a hoot that you've probably ruined my reputation in the eyes of the entire town!'

'As you'll only be here a short while, does it matter what they think?'

'On the contrary, I intend to be here a very long time. I'm planning to live here,' she informed him.

The announcement surprised her more than it seemed to surprise him. Yet a second later she knew the decision had been germinating at the back of her mind from within a few hours of her arrival.

'And just as I couldn't stop you from moving *in* here, you can't make me move *out*,' she added, lifting her chin.

He regarded her thoughtfully for a moment. 'The practicalities may defeat you, Caroline. You haven't thought your plan through. It's a pipe-dream which may not work when you try to put it into practice.'

'I don't see why not. I——'

He interrupted her. 'Last night you said you weren't short of money but that you had none to waste. When we talked on the telephone, and I asked you if you worked, you didn't answer. I assume you live on an allowance. It had better be a large one if you're going to keep a house this size up. The exterior urgently needs painting. The old boiler needs replacing with an immersion tank, which means having the house wired. There are taxes you will have to pay. I don't believe you've considered any of those problems.'

'No, I haven't—not yet,' she admitted. 'But in the same way you were mistaken about my relationship with Robert, you're wrong if you imagine I'm someone who has never done anything but enjoy herself. Girls like that don't exist any more. I've worked for my living for six years, and it isn't because I'm no good that I'm out of work at the moment. My boss was axed too, and he was a senior executive. If I hadn't lost my job, perhaps I might not have come to Nantucket. But I have come and I mean to stay—whatever the problems involved. I'll find some way round them.'

He rose, beginning to clear the table. 'I won't argue with you now. Later today I shall be in a better position to make you see sense. Why not go up and clean your room while I do the dishes? Then we'll go down to A. & P. and buy some groceries.'

'Very well. Shall I make your bed, too?'

'It's made already,' he answered.

It would be, she thought, a bit grimly, as she left the kitchen. Clearly he was super-efficient; a man of great energy and drive who expected everyone around him to match the exacting standard of his own performance.

She was efficient herself—during her working hours. But she felt that, at home, it was possible to be too much of a perfectionist. It didn't apply in her mother's case because Barbara Halland had staff to relieve her of the household chores, but Caroline had had a school friend whose mother's mania for tidiness had made her family's life a misery. As a guest in that immaculate household where nothing was ever out of place, Caroline had resolved never to become like that herself.

As she climbed the stairs to her room, wondering if Hawk was going to turn out to be a male version of her friend's mother, she remembered that less than half an hour earlier she had been concerned about losing her heart to him.

The fact was that, very foolishly, she had done what teenagers did with pictures of movie and pop stars. She had let herself make-believe that the man in the portrait in the parlour had possessed all the qualities she hoped, one day, to find in a real man.

Probably James Starbuck had been nothing like her idea of him. He couldn't have been or he wouldn't have left his bride behind. He would have taken her with him and made passionate, demanding love to her in the privacy of the Captain's quarters. How could any redblooded man leave the girl of his choice on a voyage which might last several years?

Probably, taking advantage of the double standard of his day, he had expected Damaris never to glance at another man during his long absences, but had himself enjoyed as many pretty South Sea Island girls as came his way.

It was only a few minutes' walk from Captain Starbuck's house to the Pacific National Bank, the handsome brick building, erected in 1818, which dominated the upper end of main Street Square.

Caroline had been inside the bank to change a travellers' cheque, and had seen the large murals depicting the island in the heyday of the whaling era. But she hadn't known, until Hawk told her, that from the roof of the bank, in October 1847, a Nantucket woman, Maria Mitchell, had discovered a previously unknown comet which had made her famous not only in her own country but throughout the world.

'She became the first professor of astronomy at Vassar which, as you may already know, is one of our leading women's colleges,' he said, as they passed the bank. 'For such a small island, Nantucket has produced quite a number of outstanding people. You've heard of Macy's in New York, the world's largest department store?'

'I spent a week in New York at the start of my trip. I looked round Macy's and Gimbels.'

'The man who founded the store, Rowland Hussey Macy, was the son of a Nantucket sea captain. He went whaling himself, as a young man. Then he tried his luck in California during the Gold Rush, as a lot of Nantucketers did. But it wasn't until he opened a small store on Fourteenth Street that he began to make his fortune.'

His knowledge of the island's history—which was not necessarily known to all its inhabitants—prompted her to say, 'You said on the telephone that you had no desire ever to live here again. But now that you're back for a visit, don't you feel *some* response to the charm of the place? Surely it must be unique? Or are there other towns in America where the atmosphere of the past is as pervasive as here?'

They were about to cross the mouth of Orange Street. As Hawk's palm cupped her elbow, he said, 'They say this street here is unique in housing one hundred and twenty sea captains in the space of a century.'

But he chose not to answer her first question.

They had come to the shop with *Mitchell's Book Corner* on the fascia spanning the width of the two twelve-paned windows displaying a selection of new books. No longer holding her arm, Hawk checked his stride to look at the volumes on show. In doing so, he passed Robert's test of a civilised man. In her brother's estimation, anyone who could pass a bookshop without pausing to look in the windows was not worth knowing.

'This is an excellent shop. Was it here when you lived here?' she asked.

'No, it opened the year after I left. But someone wrote me about it. It was started by a couple from New York who had been vacationing here for a number of years and thought they would like to retire here, but still have some occupation. Now it's run by their daughter, I'm told.'

As they walked further down the street, past the newly-opened ice-cream parlour, Caroline wondered who it was who had written to him. One of his many girl-friends, perhaps.

Even as the thought crossed her mind, a woman's voice called out, 'Hawk! It is you. For a minute I thought I must be hallucinating. When did you get back?'

Both Hawk and Caroline turned in the direction of the voice. It belonged to an attractive woman in her late twenties or early thirties. She was casually dressed in a pink shirt and matching pants, and was carrying what Caroline recognised as a Nantucket lightship basket.

These oval wickerwork baskets, their lids ornamented with small ivory carvings of whales or seagulls on a wooden plaque, were on sale in most of the towns gift shops. They were extremely expensive. Prices seemed to start at four hundred dollars, rising to several thousand for a large basket with an elaborate piece of modern scrimshaw on the lid. Caroline thought the baskets delightful, but over-priced to the point of absurdity. However, she had noticed that many of the local women, as opposed to the day visitors, carried baskets which had clearly been in use for a long time, and which probably hadn't cost a fraction of the price they fetched now. It was such a basket—the wicker weathered from a pale colour to a much darker tone—which the woman in pink had on her arm.

She said, 'Hawk, you look great. So tanned! I can tell *you* didn't spend most of the winter shovelling snow. Oh, it's so good to see you again!'

As she reached up to kiss his cheek, he bent his tall head to receive her affectionate greeting. 'It's good to see you. How are you?'

The woman stepped back, her eyes twinkling. 'I don't believe you know who I am. I saw that blank look in your eyes.' She laughed and, turning to Caroline, said, 'It's a terrible moment when someone greets you, and you don't have the faintest idea who they are. Have you had that experience? I have.' She turned back to him. 'But sixteen years is a long time, so I'll forgive you, Hawk. I'm Nancy Lake Allen. I hope that rings a bell.'

'My God! Little Nancy Lake, all slimmed down and grown up and gorgeous! No wonder I didn't recognise you. The last time we met you weren't looking like this'—his glance skimming her excellent figure.

She gave an exaggerated shudder. 'Don't remind me. Is this your wife?'—with another smiling look at Caroline.

'No. This is Caroline Murray, who sounds British but is American.' He left their connection unexplained, asking, 'Do I know your husband, Nancy?'

She shook her head. 'No, he's from off. We're only here for the weekend. I must run—the family is waiting for me to get back. We're taking a picnic to Quidnet. Why don't you and Caroline stop by for a drink this evening? I can't ask you to dinner without consulting my mother, but I know she and Dad would be delighted to see you, Hawk. Say around six?'

'Can we take a rain-check on that, Nancy? I'd like to meet your parents again—and the lucky Mr Allen—but we already have a date tonight.'

'Oh, too bad. Maybe next weekend, then? Chuck and I only live sixty miles away, and the kids just adore it here. Unless there's a terrible weather forecast, we come most weekends. It was nice meeting you, Caroline.'

She hurried away in the direction of Murray's Toggery Shop. They strolled towards Nantucket Looms where Caroline had already admired the designer-quality tweeds woven on looms in back of the elegant showroom.

'What is our date tonight?' she enquired.

'I felt it might be better to avoid contacts with local people until we've come to an agreement about the house,' he told her.

The lower end of Main Street Square was known as Lieutenant Max Wagner Square in honour of a young officer killed during the American involvement in the Philippines in 1899. The drinking fountain for horses in the centre of the cobbles was a reminder of the time when Nantucketers had tried to opt out of the automobile age. It had not been until 1918 that, by a narrow margin of votes, they had allowed cars to supersede bicycles and horses.

Dominating the lower end of the square was a building of mellow pink brick with the date 1772.

'That was originally the counting house of William Rotch, a Quaker whaling merchant,' Hawk told her. 'Later on it became the Pacific Club, a meeting place for shipmasters. From that building, they cleared *Bedford* for her voyage to London. She was the first ship to hoist the American flag in the Thames after the Revolutionary War.'

Glancing up at his hard, sun-tanned face, Caroline sensed that, although he might not acknowledge it, the island and its contribution to America's maritime history had been a strong formative influence on him.

The A. & P. was a supermarket close to the waterfront, not far from Straight Wharf where Caroline had landed. Apparently many changes had taken place there since Hawk's time. Before they went shopping he had a look round the area which now combined modern boat basins and shingle-clad summer cottages built over the water on piles where, before, there had been only run-down fishing shanties and coal sheds.

Most of the craft using the new berths that weekend were expensive motor cruisers equipped for game fishing. But Hawk made her see the waterfront as it had been in the great days of whaling; a forest of tall masts and, ashore, sail lofts, rope walks, warehouses piled high with casks, coopers' shops, chandlers and the heavy whale oil drays which, had Main Street not been laid with cobbles, would have reduced the road to muddy sand.

Inside the supermarket, he took charge of the cart and began selecting groceries in the manner of someone well accustomed to doing the catering when necessary.

Caroline had fallen a short distance behind him when someone close behind her said, 'Good morning. I was coming to find you as soon as I'd finished shopping. What are you doing in here? Aren't they feeding you properly?'

As she turned to find Todd Blackwell smiling at her, she realised that although she had spoken about him to the proprietress of the guesthouse, since moving to Captain Starbuck's house she had forgotten his existence. Moreover, instead of feeling pleasure at seeing him again, her reaction was close to dismay.

'Todd . . . hello,' she said, mustering a smile. 'When did you arrive?'

'This morning. Sometimes I get down on Friday night, but last night I couldn't make it. When did you get here?'

She told him, conscious that Hawk had noticed her in conversation and was returning to join them.

She introduced them. 'Todd, this is Captain Lowell . . . Todd Blackwell works in New York and comes here for weekends, Hawk.'

The two men shook hands and exchanged civilities, although, as she had anticipated, Todd did not look enthused at finding she wasn't alone.

'Your first visit to Nantucket, Captain Lowell?' he asked. 'In a place this size, most regular visitors know each other, if only by sight.'

'I've been here before, but not for a long time,' Hawk answered. 'How do you two come to know each other?'

Caroline felt certain if he discovered the circumstances in which they had become acquainted, he would have some sardonic comments to make.

She said briefly, 'We met in New York,' and went on to give Todd a brief account of where she had been since last seeing him.

This was cut even shorter by Hawk, who said, 'Excuse me, Caroline, but I think it would be better to postpone this conversation until we've finished our shopping. More people are coming in now, and we should move on or we'll cause a bottleneck. Why don't we meet outside and have coffee somewhere?'

'Come to my place for coffee,' Todd suggested. 'It's right around the corner.'

'All right—fine. We'll see you in a little while,' she agreed.

As she turned away to resume her inspection of the well-stocked shelves, she guessed he was wondering why she was shopping with Hawk.

After studying a wide choice of fruit-flavoured yogurts, she decided that none of them would be as nice as natural yogurt with fresh fruit.

Todd's arrival was going to complicate an already fraught situation. It wasn't the moment for analysing the reason why she felt thus; but she knew there was definitely no future in the tentative relationship begun on the bus to Boston.

Somehow she had to convey that certainty to him before his feelings were hurt. Unless it turned out that, seeing her again, he revised his first favourable opinion. She hoped very much that it might be so. For Todd to feel a warmth towards her which she couldn't reciprocate would give her no satisfaction. Some girls seemed to enjoy being pursued by men for whom they cared not a jot, but Caroline shrank from the prospect.

His place turned out to be the white-balconied upper floor of a house on the wharf called Old North, once the headquarters of packets running to Baltimore, Norfolk and even to New Orleans.

A grocery bag under each arm, Todd led the way up the outside staircase to the landing outside his door. Today he was casually dressed in a madras cotton shirt and very pale pink canvas pants with cuffs at the ankles.

'Are those trousers Nantucket Reds?' Caroline asked, coming up the weathered treads behind him.

'Yes, I bought these the first year I came here. They wear for ever. Have you invested in a pair?'

'No, I thought they were only for men. I haven't been into Murray's Toggery yet, but I heard some people at the guesthouse talking about them as one of the good things to buy here.'

'I think they're a much better souvenir than those lightship baskets which only the nouveau riche buy now,' he said, dumping his bags down in order to unlock the door. 'These pants are brick red when they're new. Breton red, it's called. The colour and the hard-wearing canvas were worn by fishermen in Brittany in northern France, and then by international yachtmen, some of whom used to come to

Nantucket. Back in the Fifties, the man who owned the store wanted to stock these pants, but at that time they were only made in Britain. So he had an American company copy some for him, and since then Murray's is said to have sold thirty thousand pairs. Now, each year, the present Mr Murray has between five and ten thousand yards of the stuff specially woven for him. The women's pants don't have cuffs. My sister bought a pair recently. They were twenty-five dollars, which is a lot better than those crazily expensive baskets which, according to her, aren't as useful as a shoulder bag anyway.'

'I agree with your sister—the lightship baskets would be fun if they were a reasonable price. But when I was exploring the Lower East Side of New York, I saw an alligator bag for less than four hundred dollars. Besides, I'm worried about the ivory decoration on the lightship baskets. Where is the ivory—Oh, Todd, what a lovely room!'—this as she crossed his threshold and saw golden reflections of sunlit water gleaming on the walls and ceiling of a room furnished in the colours of a beautiful old Canton platter which hung facing the doorway.

'Thank you. I'm glad you like it. Please sit down and make yourselves comfortable while I unload this stuff and fix the coffee.'

'First, I want to look at your pictures,' she said, turning to the wall on which were massed various studies of the waterfront and the town. Pen and wash, watercolour, pastel—Todd had used almost every medium to capture the place in all its aspects.

As Hawk joined her in looking at them, she explained how their host made his living.

'What does your title signify, Captain Lowell? Are you a Navy man . . . an airline pilot?' Todd asked, from behind the breakfast counter which marked the boundary of the kitchen area.

'I'm the Master of a cruise ship.'

'Not a liner . . . a sailing ship,' Caroline amplified.

Then she wished she hadn't, because Hawk's dark brows drew together in a way which made her feel she had spoken out of turn.

She was glad when Todd said, 'You were talking about ivory, Caroline. That was something which worried Julie . . . my sister. She has strong views on wild life preservation. According to her, America banned all imports of ivory, whalebone and tortoiseshell in 1980. She spoke to a number of shopkeepers who told her that the carvings on the baskets and the scrimshaw piece were made from ivory which the carvers had had in stock at the time of the ban. But Julie wasn't convinced that they would have had such large amounts on inventory. She thought a lot must be smuggled, and that anyone who buys ivory souvenirs is encouraging the slaughter of African elephants.'

'I see you have a piece of scrimshaw,' said Caroline, picking up a whale's tooth with an elaborate design scratched in the surface of the ivory.

'I bought that tooth in a yard sale when I was a kid. I think it cost a quarter,' said Todd.

'May I see?' Hawk took the piece from Caroline and turned it between his strong fingers to examine the design scratched in the surface of the ivory.

'It's an unusual piece. When colouring is used, other than black, it's usually dark blue or red. This sepia colour comes from tobacco juice,' he told her. 'This is an example of what collectors call "original scrimshaw" which means it was made by a Yankee whaleman during the Golden Era between 1826 and 1865. It's been estimated that, during that period, up to two hundred thousand men passed the time at sea making things like this.'

'Are you a collector?' she asked, remembering Kiki's minor bequests to him.

'I have a small collection—yes.'

Todd said, 'It's America's only important indigenous folk art, apart from Indian art. But I didn't know that when I bought the tooth. I'd never heard of scrimshaw at that time; it was only an interesting object. Had you heard of scrimshaw before you came to Nantucket, Caroline?'

'Yes, I had, as it happens. I've seen pieces in museums in England. What sort of scrimshaw did Kiki leave you in her will, Hawk?'

'It's a busk which, as you probably know, is a strip of bone intended to stiffen the front of an old-fashioned corset. They were often beginners' pieces, but this one is particularly well designed and it has a verse on it: *In many a gale has been the whale in which this bone did rest. His time is past, his bone at last must now support thy breast.*

'How many teeth does a whale have?' she asked.

'Some don't have any. Some whales have plates of baleen which act as a strainer to separate the organisms they feed on from a mouthful of water. Baleen is what's usually called whalebone. It's not bone, it's more like horn, but very flexible. I remember reading somewhere that at one time oil and whalebone brought back from the Pacific by Nantucket ships "lit the lamps and laced the ladies wherever there was civilisation." '

He put the tooth back on the shelf from which she had removed it. 'That tooth belonged to a sperm whale which, if it was a big one, would have had about fifty. They range from four to ten inches long. As well as being left whole, like that one, they were cut up for much smaller objects such as umbrella handles and bodkins.'

They continued discussing scrimshaw, the original work and its modern imitations, while drinking coffee. Presently Hawk stood up, saying, 'I'm going to take the groceries back to the house, and then I have a couple of calls to make. I'll rejoin you in about an hour, Caroline.'

'He has a house here?' asked Todd, when he was alone with her.

'*We* have a house here.' She explained Kiki's will.

'Are you related to each other?' was the next question.

'Only in the sense that we were both part of Kiki's adopted family. I don't know the full story yet, but it seems she was in love with Hawk's grandfather when she was a girl. Her connection with my family began when she and my mother's mother made their debut together at the Assembly in Philadelphia. They wore long white kid gloves and pearls, as girls did in London at one time when they were presented at Court. But all that has died out in England. I expect it has here.'

'I believe it's still quite an important ritual in the South, but less so here in the north-east. I don't know too much about it. My family was never on the Social Register. Captain Lowell could probably tell you. Lowell ... Winthrop ... Cabot ... Forbes ... Adams ... those are all V.I.P. names in Boston, like Coffin and Hussey in Nantucket.'

Caroline forbore to mention that Hawk's middle name was Cabot.

'Although being captain of a cruise ship seems an unlikely occupation for a Boston Brahmin,' Todd went on. 'But I guess if it's a *sailing* ship that makes it okay.'

'A Boston Brahmin?' she queried.

'It's a name for Boston's upper crust. The Brahmins are the highest caste among the Hindus. Get it?'

'Yes, of course. Slow-witted of me not to get it in one.'

'How come Captain Lowell's wife wasn't shopping with him? Is she sick?' he asked.

'He's not married. He doesn't want to keep the house, but I do. Neither of us can sell without the other's consent, but on the other hand I don't know that I could support myself in Nantucket. I should think the openings for P.A.s and secretaries must be strictly limited. Anyway, I don't feel I want to go on working in an office.'

In spite of her immediate reaction on meeting Todd in the supermarket, it was good to have someone with whom she could discuss her problem. They were still talking it over when Hawk returned.

He was not alone.

The front door was standing wide open. As the sound of his voice made them look towards the doorway, the person to whom he was speaking came into view.

She was a very pretty girl, younger than Caroline, with a spectacular figure emphasised by a tight white tee shirt—but no bra—and a white skirt split up one thigh.

CHAPTER THREE

TODD had already risen to his feet when the girl in white paused on the threshold, looking from him to Caroline with a shy expression which didn't accord with her head-turning outfit.

Her hair was a wild mop of curls, dark brown with henna-red glints. She had brown eyes, and sun-tan which made Caroline conscious that, although her own exposed parts were browner than when she left London, she was still pale under her clothes.

'Emerald, this is Caroline ... and Todd,' said Hawk, speaking over the girl's shoulder while at the same time propelling her forward. 'I thought you wouldn't mind my bringing Emerald back with me, Todd. She's come over for the day from the Cape, and she's on her own.'

'Not at all. Glad to know you, Emerald. Let me fix you a cold drink,' said Todd, shaking the girl's hand and giving her his friendly smile.

Caroline felt certain he must be thinking, as she was: What an astonishing person for Hawk to pick up!

However, as Todd had, she kept her surprise to herself, saying warmly, 'Hello, Emerald. You've been on a spending spree, I see.' For not only was the girl laden with parcels, but Hawk was carrying a couple of the largest ones for her. 'What nice things have you been buying?'

'Oh ... you're English.' The girl looked pleased. 'I come from Yorkshire. Where are you from?'

'London.'

As Emerald was visibly delighted at finding herself in the company of someone she imagined to be a compatriot, Caroline decided to postpone her usual explanation until later.

'Yes, I think the shops here are super,' the girl said, in answer to her question. 'I bought myself two or three outfits, and a couple of the lightship baskets—one for me, and a bigger one for Mum—and a miniature gold lightship basket to wear as a pendant. It's lovely, it really is. Have you been staying here long? have you seen them?'

Caroline shook her head. Remembering what Todd had said about the baskets being bought mainly by the nouveau riche nowadays, she was careful to avoid catching his eye.

Emerald rummaged in her white shoulder bag for a small package which she unwrapped to reveal a jeweller's box. Inside was a tiny replica of a lightship basket without a lid. It was a well made little bauble and obviously expensive.

'It's charming,' said Caroline politely, although it was not an adornment which she would have bought, even if she could have afforded it.

Her own taste was for classic pieces—gold chains and

bangles, gold hoop ear-rings—or inexpensive fun things such as the twisted ribbon and chiffon necklet she had bought from a craft stall in the Sunday market near Columbia University in New York.

'It's cute, as they say here, isn't it?'

Taking the pendant between a frosted-pink fingertip and thumb, Emerald held it against her golden skin. It was a gesture which drew attention to the vee of her tee-shirt and to the bouncy young bosom outlined by the flimsy cotton.

It was not a provocative gesture, Caroline felt sure. In spite of the way she was dressed, there was nothing deliberately seductive in Emerald's manner. The fact that she had plumped herself down on the sofa next to Caroline, rather than choosing to perch on a stool at the breakfast bar, the better to display her legs, was evidence that the impression she gave at first glance could be misleading.

But even if, by holding the pendant an inch or two above her cleavage, she had not intended to draw the men's eyes to her breasts, her action had that effect.

Glancing at Todd, who was coming towards them, a tall glass in either hand, Caroline saw that his eyes were on Emerald's bust, albeit with a hint of amusement. Hawk, too, was eyeing her curves and clearly visible nipples. However, as Caroline looked at him, he shifted his gaze to her face, meeting her eyes with an inscrutable expression which she could not interpret.

How in the world had he and this naïve little piece of Yorkshire cheese-cake got involved with each other? she wondered, for the second time. She had no doubt he had the aplomb to pick up a dowager duchess if he wanted to; but Emerald seemed the kind of girl who would view with suspicion an approach from a stranger so much older than she was.

'Oh, ta . . . I mean thank you.' Her cheeks flushed with embarrassment at having let slip the idiom of her native county, Emerald accepted the drink Todd offered her with one hand, while putting away the pendant with the other.

'It hasn't got vodka in it, has it?' she asked, before tasting it. 'I can't drink vodka—it gives me a headache. As for those Bloody Marys which everyone drinks where we're staying, *one* of them makes my head spin. Have you tried them, Caroline?'

Again, Caroline had to shake her head. 'I usually stick to wine or spritzers.'

'There's nothing alcoholic in that,' Todd assured Emerald. 'What about you, Captain Lowell? Will you have a beer or something stronger?'

As Caroline was wondering why he persisted in being formal when Hawk addressed him by his first name, Emerald turned to her and said, 'It was such a surprise meeting Hawk here. When we went on a cruise on his ship, I used to call him Captain Lowell, but he says I'm to call him Hawk now. Dad was still alive then. In fact the cruise was his idea. Mum didn't really want to go because she gets seasick easily. But it isn't rough in the Caribbean. The sea was like glass. It was super. We went to the island of Mustique where Princess Margaret has a house. She lets people rent it, you know. Dad was going to do that the next year, but he had a heart attack and died.'

'I'm sorry,' Caroline said gently, seeing the way the girl's pretty face fell at the memory of her father's sudden death. 'Are you here in America by yourself, Emerald?'

'Oh, no—I shouldn't like that. I'm with Mum, but she's still not too well and she didn't feel up to coming today. Last winter we rented a lovely house in Florida. Then I wanted to look at New York, so we took a flat there for a month. Then Mum caught the 'flu. When she didn't pick up, the doctor suggested the air on Cape Cod might be better for her. So now we're renting a house in Hyannisport. It's where President Kennedy used to have a home. It's given her ever such a thrill to stay near where he lived.'

By now it was clear that Emerald's father had left his widow and child in extremely comfortable circumstances. Caroline wondered if Mum was as naïve as her daughter.

Yorkshire people had the reputation of being warmhearted, down-to-earth and, in matters relating to money, shrewd and thrifty. Judging by Emerald's purchases within a short time of arriving on the early ferry, thrift was not a dominant factor in her youthful outlook on life. But it could be that her father had been so rich that the purchase of two lightship baskets, a gold pendant and more than one 'outfit' would make a negligible hole in the fortune he had left his widow.

'Where are you going to go next?' she asked.

'I don't know. We haven't decided. Mum still isn't really well yet.'

'Perhaps she's homesick for Yorkshire,' Caroline suggested.

'No, I don't think it's that. She loves America—or she did before she had the 'flu. I think not having to stay in the house where she and Dad lived together has helped her get over it faster. She hasn't the memories here that she would have had, staying at home.'

Hawk had moved from a chair to the breakfast bar where he and Todd were discussing the redevelopment of the waterfront.

Glancing over her shoulder and seeing the two men engaged in a separate conversation, Emerald said confidentially, 'She'll be thrilled to hear I've met Hawk. He was ever so nice to us on the cruise. Some of the passengers were a bit stand-offish and snooty. Once or twice Dad almost lost his temper. He didn't mind people not being friendly to him. 'Stuck up blighters. I can buy and sell them twice over,' he'd say to Mum and me. But it made him ever so annoyed if he thought the women were being bitchy to her. Captain Lowell—Hawk, I should say—had a way of smoothing Dad down before he got really stroppy and came out with something he shouldn't.'

She leaned closer. 'To tell you the truth, I had a crush on him. I was only eighteen then, and he looks even more good-looking when you see him in uniform, with gold braid on his cap and on his epaulettes. He looks smashing, he really does!' She rolled her eyes upwards and licked her lips, at the same time giving a shiver of simulated ecstasy.

Caroline couldn't help smiling, which made Emerald say, 'Don't *you* think he's dishy? Or do you prefer the other one?'

'They both seem very nice, but I've only just met them,' was Caroline's guarded reply.

'I think it's Fate,' Emerald said earnestly. 'I think we were fated to meet again. It was in my forecast for this week. *By reviving an old acquaintance you may find you have a great deal to gain on a long-term basis. This is a good week for getting out and about and for taking a break from routine. Try to find time to do the things you really enjoy.* That's what it said in my horoscope. I'm Aries. Which sign are you?'

'Libra,' said Caroline, who admired the skill with which

horoscopists worded their predictions, but who didn't take them too seriously.

Clearly Emerald did. She said, 'That's Mum's birth sign. Your horoscope for this week was: *Careful handling of a relationship is necessary if you wish to keep the peace. Try not to let the situation upset you, and avoid arguments with a partner or colleague if you can.*'

The first part was certainly applicable, thought Caroline, glancing at Hawk's tall figure standing by the bar with his back to them.

'What time are you leaving Nantucket?' she asked Emerald.

'I'm on an Extended Day Round Trip, which means that I can stay till the last boat if I want to. That doesn't leave here till twenty-five minutes past eight, but I think perhaps I ought to take the three-fifty. It'll be almost six o'clock by the time I get back to Hyannis—say six-thirty to get to our house—and that's a long time for Mum to be on her own. I left at eight-thirty this morning.'

Caroline looked at her watch. 'If you only have a few hours here, it's a pity not to make the most of them. Why not leave your parcels here—I'm sure Todd won't mind—and walk up to the Three Bricks.'

'Three Bricks? Just three ordinary bricks? That doesn't sound very interesting,' Emerald said doubtfully.

'It's the local name for three identical brick houses which Joseph Starbuck built for his three sons. Directly opposite them are two magnificent white mansions put up by his son-in-law. They're the most astonishing buildings to find in a small town like this. They make one realise how rich the whaling merchants were. You should see them, Emerald.'

'Oh, all right, if you think so—but couldn't I get a taxi instead of walking?'

'It's no distance from here; not five minutes' walk, I shouldn't think. Although your heels are rather high for sightseeing,' Caroline conceded, looking down at the thin white straps which encased the girl's baby-plump feet and looked as if they were already causing her some discomfort.

'I don't usually do much sightseeing. Mum and I don't really care for museums and churches and suchlike. We prefer to look round the shops and have a nice meal. Where's the best place to eat, would you say? I thouht Cap'n Tobey's Chowder House looked quite nice.'

'I don't know. I haven't eaten in any of the restaurants yet. Todd will know.' Caroline took Emerald's empty glass and carried it to the bar. Waiting until there was a pause in the men's conversation, she said, 'Todd, where's the best place to eat?'

'The Chanticleer over at 'Sconset, but there are some good places in town. I was hoping you'd have lunch here. You, too, Emerald—if you'd like to,' he added, smiling across the room at her.

'Yes, I'd love to,' she answered, with a beam. Coming to join them, she looked up at Hawk. 'Have you been to these houses Caroline says I ought to see?'

A few minutes later—Todd having said it would only take him half an hour to throw a salad together—all four of them strolled up the Square to where the Pacific Bank separated the beginning of Main Street from the bottom of Liberty Street.

More precisely, three of them strolled while Emerald took short, jerky steps on her high, spindly heels. This time it was she whom Hawk steered across the side-roads, an attention which obviously gave her a great deal of pleasure.

Caroline, walked behind them with Todd at her side, saw the glowing upward looks which Emerald gave her tall companion whenever he took her by the elbow. She found herself feeling an almost maternal concern for the younger girl's artless vulnerability—as if she were twice Emerald's age instead of a mere four years older.

Could the little thing—for without those ridiculous heels she would be about five feet two—really believe that she and Hawk were destined for each other? To Caroline they seemed to have nothing in common, either physically, mentally or socially.

I hope she doesn't take it into her head to come over here every day, she thought. If she does, she'll be inviting a painful setdown. I'm sure as soon as Hawk realises what's in her mind, he won't hesitate to send her packing—and perhaps not as tactfully as he handled her father on their cruise. He had been dealing with a passenger then. With his crew, and in his private life, he might not mince matters.

On the other hand, Emerald is an exceptionally pretty girl with a stunning figure. Maybe he won't mind her chasing him.

Maybe he'll take her to bed—but not in my house, she added mentally—and then silently laughed at herself for sounding like a strait-laced landlady.

A landlady!

That's the answer, she thought, assailed by a brainwave which all at once seemed so obvious an answer to her problem that she couldn't imagine why she hadn't thought of it before.

She had always liked cooking. Even housework wasn't the bore to her that it was to some of her friends. To turn the Captain's house into a guesthouse was the perfect solution. She would even call it *Captain Starbuck's House*. and perhaps have his portrait copied for an inn sign to swing above the door.

'A moment ago you were looking worried. Now you're smiling to yourself. What's going on in that blonde head?' Todd asked, catching hold of her hand, not because they were nearing a crossing but as a gesture of companionability.

'Oh, I just had a bright idea. I'll tell you about it later on, but this isn't the moment,' she answered.

It was then, as they were walking with linked hands, that Emerald paused to look at something in a shop window, something she must have missed on her first tour of the Square. Hawk also paused, glancing back at the couple following behind.

Why his glance should make Caroline want to snatch her hand free from Todd's light clasp, instead of freeing it more casually as she had intended to in a moment, she didn't know. But that was the effect it had; and when he turned away she felt a pang of vexation that he had happened to look back at that particular moment.

The cobblestones covering the square continued up tree-lined Main Street, although its name was misleading as it wasn't a shopping street but an avenue of elegant houses. Soon, by the corner of Pleasant Street, they came to the two white mansions, each with four massive columns rising from porch to roof level and supporting a classical pediment.

Caroline, who had walked past it several times, already knew that the mansion nearest the corner, now known as the Hadwen-Statler Memorial and open to the public, had been built by William Hadwen, a silversmith who had come to the island in 1820. After his marriage to Eunice Starbuck, he had made investments in whaleships and later gone into partnership with Nathaniel Barney, the husband of Eunice's sister, Eliza. Soon, as majority shareholders in the ships *Enterprise* and *Alpha*, the two men had made their fortunes. In the 1840s, William had spent part of his on erecting the great white house inspired by the Temple of the Winds.

'I think what makes it more striking is its being so close to the street rather than at the end of a long drive as houses of this size usually are,' she remarked, as the four of them stood on the brick path between the cobblestoned street and the white balustrade surrounding the mansion's small front garden.

'Who does the other belong to?' asked Emerald, looking at the neighbouring building, almost a twin to the Hadwen house except that it had a hedge instead of a balustrade, and the capitals at the top of its columns were in the Corinthian style whereas those on the Hadwen house were Ionic scrolls.

'The Hadwens had no children of their own. They adopted a niece, Amelia Swain. William built the house next door for her and her husband, George Wright,' Hawk told her. 'It's known as the Wright Mansion and it's still in private hands, although the present owners aren't Amelia's descendants. These two houses are sometimes called the Two Greeks because of their neo-classical style. It's said that Hadwen wanted to outdo the Three Bricks built by his father-in-law across the street.'

'Later on, they were both outdone by Jared Coffin whose mansion is now a restaurant,' put in Todd. 'Personally I prefer the earlier houses built when the Quaker influence kept ostentation in check. But these two are impressive symbols of what in whaling days was called "greasy luck".'

They went up the steps to the entrance and Hawk paid the fee for admission. Two pleasant middle-aged women were on duty to guide visitors round and point out the most interesting features of a house filled with fine old furniture, portraits, chandeliers and antique needlework.

When Caroline entered the room to the right of the hall and saw that it opened into a second room which led to a third, with a view over the large garden at the rear of the house, it was easy for her to imagine the parties and other entertainments which would have taken place there. Having grown up in a house built even earlier than this one, she could readily visualise the clothes and manners of past generations.

However, she noticed that Emerald was not really paying attention to their guide, and that her brown eyes spent more time studying Hawk's dark features than the portraits on the walls.

'It must have been terribly dull in the evenings without television,' was her comment to Caroline, as they left the house.

'They had books and embroidery and conversation and music. I shouldn't think they were bored,' said Caroline. 'Have you any hobbies, Emerald?'

'I used to like drawing at school, except that they always gave us dull things to draw. Boxes to teach us perspective, and bottles and old boots . . . things like that.'

'What would you have liked to draw?'

'People. I like drawing faces, but it's difficult to get anyone to sit still long enough. I'd love to draw Hawk,' she murmured, in a lower tone. 'I did some good sketches of Dad, but his face was fat, you couldn't really see the shape of it. It's the same with Mum. She was always plump, and she's put on weight since he died. Hawk's face is more bony.' She looked sideways at Caroline and giggled. 'He's got ever such a sexy mouth. Have you noticed?'

'No, I can't say I have,' Caroline answered, rather shortly.

She was torn between being touched by Emerald's naïveté and finding her immaturity irritating. In many ways she was more like a girl of sixteen than one of twenty.

In case she had sounded too crushing, she added, 'You should talk to Todd about sketching. He's an artist—a very good one. What did you do when you left school? I gather you've given up work to travel with your mother.'

'Oh, I never worked,' Emerald said airily. 'Dad said it would be silly when he had plenty of money to keep me until I get married. I didn't do very well at school so I wouldn't have been able to get an interesting job. I wouldn't have minded going to art school. But my headmistress—a proper old dragon she was—said I wouldn't get a place. Anyway, I like being with Mum. We're like sisters really—except that I'm an English size ten and she's an eighteen. I might bring her over next week. Will you still be here?'

'I shall, but I don't know that Hawk will.'

Back at Todd's place, Caroline helped him to prepare the lunch while the others sat on the balcony drinking Bloody Marys, the one Todd had made for Emerald having less than the statutory two fingers of vokda in it.

In addition to the salad ingredients he had bought at the A. & P., his refrigerator was stocked with good things to eat from a SoHo delicatessen.

'I keep my weekend clothes here. The only luggage I bring is a cool-bag,' he explained.

Emerald looked doubtfully at some of the unfamiliar delicacies he served with the salad, and at the dark pumpernickel bread. It seemed that she and her mother, although they liked eating, had yet to sample the delicious foodstuffs and dishes brought to America by each successive wave of immigrants and now melded into an exciting international cuisine which had its apogee in the restaurants and delis of New York.

There was just enough room on the balcony for the four of them to eat there. By the time they had had coffee, and then more coffee, it was time for Emerald to think about catching her ferry back to the Cape.

Evidently she hadn't said anything to Hawk about bringing her mother to see Nantucket. While the boat was discharging its incoming passengers, he said, 'If you're not doing anything tomorrow, I'll come over and see your mother, Emerald.'

'That would be super. She'd love to see you again. We often talk about our cruise.'

'Give me your number. It might be as well to call you beforehand. If she hasn't been well lately, she may not want a visitor tomorrow.'

'She'll want to see you,' she assured him.

When the outgoing passengers had boarded, Todd said, 'I know you two have a lot to discuss concerning this house you've inherited, but I was wondering if you'd mind if I took Caroline to dinner this evening, Hawk.'

'Not at all, but shouldn't you find out how she feels about it?' the taller man said dryly.

'Yes, you're right.' Todd looked slightly embarrassed. 'Would you care to have dinner, Caroline?'

She smiled at him. 'As Hawk cooked my breakfast and you organised my lunch, why don't I cook dinner at our place? You'd like to see our house, wouldn't you?'

'Yes, very much, but——'

'In that case I'd better hurry home and put on an apron. We'll see you at seven-thirty.'

'I don't know the address.'

Caroline told him how to find the house.

After Todd's way home had diverged from theirs, Hawk said, 'Was that invitation a polite way of sliding out of a dinner à deux? Do you want to keep him guessing a while longer? Or did you feel it might be impolite to desert me on my second evening here?'

'I didn't have any of those reasons in mind,' she said lightly. 'It just seemed a good idea to return his hospitality, show him the house, and do my share of the catering. You never finished teling me about Kiki and your grandfather. You had got as far as 'Sconset becoming an actors' colony in the 1890s, and then we were interrupted by Mr Bailey.'

'Kiki's father was a theatrical director. Her mother was an actress with the same upper-crust background as Katharine Hepburn's, hence Kiki's début with your grandmother. She started coming to Nantucket at about age three, at which time my great-grandfather on the Chase side was making a living as a gardener, working mainly over at 'Sconset in the gardens of the rich summer people. When Ben Chase wasn't at school, he would help his father and that's how he and Kiki got to know each other—as kids before the first World War. I guess her parents should have foreseen what would happen and put a stop to it earlier. But they didn't—not until Kiki and Ben were in love and planning to marry.'

'Was he still his father's assistant?' asked Caroline.

'No, his father had died by that time and Ben was carrying on the business and doing well at it. He was a hard worker and determined to recoup the family fortunes. You might think that no one ever made much money gardening. But your friend Todd was telling me this morning that Mrs Walter Beinecke Senior is rumoured to have paid ten thousand dollars a year to have her garden on Sankaty Avenue at 'Sconset kept in good order. He mentioned it à propos her son, Walter Beinecke Junior, the man responsible for rebuilding the waterfront area and backing a lot of other preservationist projects.'

Caroline had not missed his reference to Todd as 'your friend Todd', implying that there was something more between them than friendship at its most casual level. She supposed that was the result of his seeing them walking with clasped hands.

'However, it wasn't only because Ben was a working gardener as opposed to a landscape designer that Kiki's parents broke it up,' he went on. 'They felt—rightly, as it turned out—that she had a big future in the theatre or the movies. She suggested to Ben that they postpone their engagement for two years, but he wouldn't agree. It had to be now or never as far as he was concerned. It was foolish to make her choose between him and the exciting career prospects her family were dangling in front of her.'

'How old were they then?'

'They were both nineteen—a crazy age to marry in any circumstances. Twenty-one isn't much better, and that's when Ben married my grandmother. Kiki's parents had sold their house here, but somehow she got wind of Ben's wedding and came running over to beg him not to go through with it. She was ready to give up her career for him. He said he couldn't back out and make my grandmother a laughing-stock. I suspect she was already pregnant. My mother was supposed to have been a premature baby. Maybe she was, maybe not. Anyway, she wasn't the son Ben had wanted, and his wife didn't have any more children. She was only twenty-six when she died.'

'By which time Kiki had married the first of her husbands, I suppose,' said Caroline.

'That's right. After turning down innumerable proposals, she had finally succumbed to the most persistent of her suitors, the man who gave her black pearls and had Addison Mizner design Casa Romantica for her.'

'She left the pearls to my mother. I wonder who has inherited the Palm Beach house? Have you been there?'

'Yes, I've stayed there a couple of times. The house itself is delightful. It has lawns running down to a private beach of fine white sand. You can lie in a hammock strung between two Royal palms and watch the pelicans diving into the ocean. Mizner also designed the interior. To achieve perfection down to the smallest detail, he had a factory built. It was called Las Manos—the hands—because all the ceramics and metal and woodwork were handmade to his designs.'

'The beach sounds gorgeous. But Kiki never sunbathed, did she? She always sat in the shade and wore hats or carried parasols. I suppose that's why she still had a perfect complexion even in her eighties.'

'I imagine a couple of face-lifts and a lot of expensive beauty treatments were contributing factors,' he said dryly. 'Ben knew her before she had acquired the star image. She was lovely, but not a glamour girl. By the time she was in her late twenties, she had become a different person. Her appeal was mainly to women. She represented their idealised vision of themselves, which isn't the same as a man's idea of the ideal woman. I was fond of the Kiki I knew. But, judging by photographs I've seen, I shouldn't have lost my heart to her when she was a younger woman.'

'As you're still unmarried, presumably you've never lost your heart,' said Caroline.

'Not irretrievably—no,' he agreed.

They had reached the gate leading into the garden. As he pushed it open and stood aside, Caroline said, 'Thank you. Tell me now about your parents. You said this morning they were victims of the same situation as Kiki and Ben, but in reverse.'

'In their case it was my father's family who tried to put a stop to it,' he said. 'They had a summer house on Hulbert Avenue, and my grandfather gardened for them. The Lowells had three daughters and one son. The two married daughters used to come down from Boston with their small children and the children's nurses. One time one of the nurses was sick, and Mrs Lowell asked my grandfather if he knew of a reliable local girl to substitute for her. He suggested his daughter, Maria, and that's how she and Skip Lowell, my father, met each other.'

He took out his keys in readiness to unlock the back door. 'After losing her mother, my mother had been very sheltered ... not allowed to play with other kids except in school ...

made to spend all her free time studying. I don't know why Ben suggested her for the job at the Lowells' place, unless it was for the money. She was starting college that fall and he had been losing customers. He was what Nantucketers used to call "wadgetty", meaning irritable. A free-lance gardener needs to be a good-humoured man.'

'If your mother was going to college, she must have been clever,' said Caroline.

'Not clever enough to realise that my father's parents would never accept her as a daughter-in-law,' was his sardonic reply. 'They already had a bride lined up for him—Alice Adams, one of the Boston Adamses who all claim descent from our second President, John Adams.'

'But even so your mother *did* become their daughter-in-law?'

'Yes. But with the result that my father was disowned by his parents, and Ben told her never to come back here because she wouldn't be welcome.'

'How could he be so cruel?' she exclaimed distressfully. 'After suffering the same thing himself?'

'He was an embittered man. Bitterness is a canker which eats into people's souls and makes them cruel. My mother wasn't blameless. She didn't tell him what she was planning to do. He learned that she had eloped from a letter she wrote him, knowing what a shock it would be and that she was the only person he cared for. It was an act she regretted later on.'

'And which she made you atone for by coming to live with him after she died,' said Caroline, trying to visualise him as a boy in his early teens; already taller than his contemporaries but without the proportionate breadth of shoulder he had now, and certainly without the air of total self-assurance which emanated from him today.

'I had nowhere else to go,' said Hawk, shrugging. 'It could have been worse. I was only here on vacation. Most of the time I was at school.'

'At one of the best in Massachusetts, according to Mrs Batson. How did that come about?'

'My youngest aunt was particularly fond of my father, and she had some money of her own. She saw my parents occasionally, and she paid for my education, thinking my grandfather would eventually relent. He did. When I graduated, he offered me a place in his bank. Even if I hadn't found my vocation by then, I shouldn't have gone to work for him. A man who disowns his only son for making what he considered a mésalliance has his priorities wrong.'

They had entered the house and Caroline went directly to the kitchen to start preparations for the evening meal. As she washed her hands, she said, 'You mentioned that your father had a drinking problem. Do you know why that started? Did your parents seem to get on well when you were a small boy?'

'I believe so. They didn't have rows. But I think my father would have done better to marry the Adams girl. He'd been raised in a certain milieu. When he found himself excluded from it, he went slowly to pieces.'

'Your mother's illness can't have helped,' she said sympathetically.

'No.' For a moment his lips were compressed and she thought his whole face seemed to harden. Then he said, 'That's enough of my life history. Let's think about dinner.'

'Leave me to think about dinner. You relax in the parlour, or go out and work up an appetite. I like to have the kitchen to myself when I'm cooking something special.'

'Are you sure you can cope with that stove?' he asked. 'Do you have the ingredients you need?'

'I think so. If I haven't, I can always pop down to A. & P. The stove is no problem.'

'Okay, I'll leave you to handle it, while I do some work in the yard. The path to the back gate needs clearing. I'll be in around six to freshen up and fix you a cocktail.'

By now it was half past four, which gave her three hours before they sat down to eat. During that time she had not only to prepare and cook the food, but also to find and clean the necessary cooking pots and three place settings.

Up to now she had managed with a minimum of kitchen equipment and very little china and silver. But tonight she was particularly anxious to produce a simple but perfectly cooked meal and serve it with style. Why it was so important to do the thing well was something she hadn't time to analyse.

When Hawk strolled into the house a little less than two hours later, he found Caroline on her way upstairs.

'Everything is under control. I'm just going up to change,' she told him, her calm smile giving no hint that more than one moment of panic had been weathered in his absence.

The Portuguese bell in the South Tower had chimed seven o'clock when he joined her in the parlour, the clothes he had worn during the day exchanged for the shirt and grey flannels in which she had first seen him.

She had decided to put on a dark red skirt of finely pleated wool crêpe with a silk shirt to match. A wide belt cinched her slender waist, and there had been time to put her hair up.

Hawk's blue gaze took in the details, including the sheer pantyhose and the classic black patent pumps.

Silghtly to her disappointment, he didn't say anything complimentary, but merely asked, 'What can I get you?'

'I needed some wine for the cooking. The rest is in the decanter over there.' She indicated the drinks tray set out on a side table. 'I'll have a glass of that, please.'

After he had gone out for his walk, she had noticed a carton of liquor on the kitchen dresser. He must have bought it and carried it home during the morning.

The red wine she had bought, the day she moved in. She had needed something to revive her at the end of her stints of spring-cleaning. It was the bottle she had opened this evening which had caused her some hassle earlier on. The only corkscrew in the house was an old-fashioned gadget with which she had bungled the uncorking. The cork had split. The only solution had been to push it down into the bottle, decant the wine into a jug and fish out some crumbs of broken cork. Then, because the jug wasn't the kind in which wine could be served, she had had to search for a glass decanter. Fortunately there had been several on the top shelf of a cupboard. Although some had had a film of irremovable-looking residue in them, one had needed only a rinse with hot water to make it presentable.

'Oh, lord! There's no ice for your drinks,' she exclaimed, in abrupt dismay.

'Yes, there is. Seeing Todd's refrigerator this morning reminded me there's a primitive but usable ice-box down in the basement,' Hawk told her. 'I put a large bag of cracked ice in it, and a couple of bottles of white wine as I heard you say you liked spritzers.'

'How thoughtful of you. You had a busy time in town this morning.'

'And learned something to our mutual advantage. Excuse me while I fetch some ice, then I'll tell you what I found out.'

In his absence, Caroline sat down and sipped her wine, first raising her glass to Captain Starbuck and wondering if he would disappove of having a copy of the portrait displayed outside his front door.

In England, innumerable inns had been and still were named after kings, queens, dukes, admirals and generals. However, first she had to sell the idea to Hawk, and tonight's dinner would—she hoped—be a practical demonstration of her ability to feed her paying guests well.

Her eyes on the stern, black-browed face in the heavy gilt frame, she found herself remembering Emerald's murmured aside about Hawk's mouth.

There was nothing to suggest an amorous nature in the cut of Captain Starbuck's lips. Both were thin; the line between them straight. Nor had he, she noticed, the deeply engraved laughter lines which furrowed Hawk's cheeks when he grinned.

A moment later he re-entered the parlour with a small polystyrene tub for ice which must be something else he had bought that morning.

She looked at his mouth—and could see what Emerald had meant. Both lips were fuller and more curved than those of his ancestor. Taken out of the context of his other features, they might have had the decadent sensuality of Lord Byron's mouth.

Set between the strong, high-bridged nose and the square-boned jut of his chin, the impression was sensual but not dissolute. Caroline was startled to find herself wondering what it would be like to be kissed by him.

'After I'd been to the liquor store, I called at a couple of real estate offices,' he said, as he put some chunks of ice into a glass and poured rum over them. 'What would you judge the value of this house to be as the market stands at the moment?'

'I really have no idea. I don't know how American house prices compare with those in England. This place needs such a lot doing to it. I don't think it can be worth much with no power and only one bathroom.'

Hawk strolled across to the fireplace and rested one arm on the mantel.

'Because it's in a particularly good location, and was built by one of the island's outstanding whaling captains, this house—as it stands—is worth upwards of a quarter of a million dollars,' he told her.

Caroline did a swift mental calculation to convert dollars into pounds. The result was startling.

'A quarter of a million? It can't be!' she exclaimed, aghast.

'Check it out for yourself on Monday. Or buy a copy of *The Inquirer* and look at the ads. Houses in the historic part of town don't change hands too frequently, and a lot of rich people from the mainland would like to retire to Nantucket. According to one realtor I talked to, in the years since I left Nantucket prices have soared to the extent that if the island needs to bring in a coof to fill some specialised vacancy—say, a teacher or a nurse—they have a problem finding affordable accommodation for them. A coof is Nantucket slang for an off-islander,' he added.

Caroline was still stunned by the value he had placed on the property. She was accustomed to the astronomical prices of houses and apartments in London. She also knew that in Guernsey and the Isle of Man prices were artificially high because both places were tax havens.

However, as far as she knew, people who came to Nantucket didn't escape American taxes. She had heard that some years ago there had been an attempt to secede from the Commonwealth of Massachusetts—jokingly known as Taxachusetts—at the time when the state legislature had first moved to do away with the island's individual representation. At that time there had been some Nantucketers who had talked of seceding from the United States and setting up an independent government.

However, the Massachusetts sales tax which made almost everything she bought slightly more expensive than the price on the tag was proof that even Nantucketers had not been able to throw off the controls ordained by Boston and Washington D.C.

'Supposing we take a conservative view and say that the

house fetches only a quarter of a million,' Hawk continued. 'Your split would be one hundred and twenty-five thousand dollars which, at present rates of interest, could be invested to yield an income of about nine thousand pounds sterling per annum. I suspect that's a good deal more than you earned before losing your job.'

'Yes, it is—much more,' she admitted. 'But I was paying tax on my income, and the tax on unearned income is higher. At least it is in England. I expect it's the same here.'

'True: but even after tax you'd be left with a comfortable allowance—enough to support you if you managed it wisely.'

'But my capital would be depreciating every year. The house is an asset which should appreciate.'

'Not necessarily at a better rate than an investment. The place could be rented, of course, but not without a substantial outlay of capital for modernisation.'

'People who rent houses don't always take care of them properly. They put glasses on polished tables and let cigarettes fall out of ash-trays. I should hate all this lovely old furniture to be left to the mercy of renters. If the house were sold, as you suggest, what would become of its contents?'

'We'd get someone from Sotheby's in New York to come and appraise them. They should also fetch a good price. Some of the furniture is older than the house. Starbuck must have inherited pieces. The curly maple highboy in the room above us looks late eighteenth century to me. It must be worth at least thirty thousand dollars.'

'But it's an heirloom,' she objected. 'A family thing handed down by generations of your forebears. You can't sell things like that. It's sacrilege. They should be treasured for your heirs.'

Hawk drank some rum. 'I live on board a ship—remember? I don't need a houseful of heirlooms—or even half a houseful. My heirs—if I have any—may not care for these old things. They may prefer modern furnishings. Making plans for the next generation is a futile exercise, especially a generation which doesn't yet exist, and may never do so.'

Caroline gave him a long thoughtful look, her clear grey eyes troubled.

After a pause, she said, 'I should have thought your job would carry a very good income. But perhaps you have some special reason for needing the money this house would fetch?

is that why you're anxious to sell? Are you in pressing need of funds?'

He did not answer immediately. Then: 'If I were, would you agree to sell?' he asked.

'It would depend on the circumstances. No, probably not; because if you had a good reason for needing a lot of money quickly, we could raise a mortgage on the house.'

'How would you suggest we repay it?—If you have no job, and I am already short of cash?' was his dry enquiry.

'I—I don't know,' she confessed. 'But if one is desperate enough, there are usually ways and means to do things. It depends how much money you need. Perhaps we could raise it by auctioning a few pieces of furniture. At a pinch, I would sell the diamond brooch Kiki left me. I would rather not, but I don't suppose I'll wear it very often. What about your collection of scrimshaw? Have you thought of raising money on that?'

'Certainly not,' he said adamantly. 'I intend to add to it, not dispose of it. When I asked if you would sell the house to help me out of a difficulty it was a theoretical question. I could use more money. Who couldn't? But I learnt very early in life to adjust my needs to my resources. It was generous of you to contemplate selling your brooch, but that sacrifice won't be necessary. I'm not in any urgent need of funds.'

She felt a surge of relief. She had thought he was going to produce a reason which would make her feel morally obliged to concur with his wish to sell the house. But in the absence of any such pressure . . .

She said, 'In that case, I'll repeat what I said this morning. I'm going to live here.'

'Caroline, you're talking nonsense,' he said, in a patronising tone.

She was not in the habit of losing her cool. She rarely had cause to be angry; and the teenage years of tempering her personality to the pattern prescribed by her mother had been an excellent training in never allowing her temper to rise above simmering point.

However Hawk's casual put-down was more than she could endure. Springing up from her chair, she said hotly, 'Oh, am I indeed? We'll see about that. Captain Lowell, I am not a member of your crew! The sooner you get back to Baltimore and start giving orders to people who are paid to say "Yes, sir—no, sir—three bags full, sir," the better it will be for both of us.'

For an instant the vivid blue eyes held a gleam which made her quail slightly. But he only said softly, 'Well . . . well. So there's a spitfire lurking behind that cool blonde image you present to the world. I had a feeling there might be.'

Leaving his drink on the mantel, he crossed the short distance between them.

'This is not a docile girl's chin,' he said, putting his clenched fist beneath it and tilting her face slightly upwards. 'Nor a puritan's mouth,' he added—a second before he bent to kiss it.

As a way of extinguishing the sudden flare of her temper, it couldn't have been more effective. Rage gave place to the paralysing incredulity of being kissed by a man she had known less than twenty-four hours.

Nor was it a fleeting caress. He touched his lips softly to hers and she felt his warm breath on her mouth and smelt the tang of the rum and a faint aroma of shaving cream.

But that was only the beginning. An instant later, not only had his fingers opened to take her lightly by the throat, but his lips were pressing more firmly, confidently exacting a response from her.

At twenty-four, Caroline had been kissed many times and in many ways. But never like this. Never with an insolent authority which took her surrender for granted.

And, to her subsequent chagrin, she did respond. She couldn't help it. The feel of his thumb gently stroking the side of her neck and the sensuous movements of his mouth made her react in a way she had never experienced before, or not with such shattering intensity.

With one kiss—and he didn't even have his arms round her—Hawk made her whole body tremble with a wild, almost frightening excitement.

She was so far gone she didn't even hear the sound which made him raise his head and say calmly, 'Our guest has arrived. I'll go and let him in.'

As he left her and went into the hall, she had the curious floating sensation she associated with drinking too much wine. Not that she had much experience of that condition. Once, five years ago, when she and another girl had given a party at the flat they had shared at the time, after the last guest had gone they had finished up a jug of Sangria which still had several glassfuls left in it. Later, for the first and only time in her life, she had gone to bed slightly tight, and woken with a headache and a determination never to repeat the mistake.

But she hadn't known, until now, that kisses, like wine, could go to the head and leave one out of control. It seemed there were kisses and kisses.

Some were like spritzers; enjoyable, even euphoric, but unlikely to become intoxicating. And some—such as Hawk's startling kiss—were as dangerously heady as Sangria when the wine was laced with Spanish brandy.

Trying to recover her sangfroid, she listed to the men greeting each other.

'This is a fine old property you have here,' she heard Todd say.

'Yes, but in a bad state of repair. It's going to cost the next owners a lot of money to put it in order.'

'You're definitely going to sell it?'

'My co-owner is resisting the idea at present. She'll come round.'

The casual arrogance of this statement was precisely what Caroline needed to pull her together. It did more than that; it rekindled the anger she had felt a few minutes earlier when Hawk had told her she was talking nonsense.

Forgetting her intention to keep her relationship with Todd on a low key, as he entered the parlour she gave him a radiant smile.

'Hello, Todd. Welcome to Captain Starbuck's house. This is the Captain'—with a gesture at the portrait, as if she were introducing them.

Todd, who was carrying something swathed in white paper, looked up at the painting and, taking his cue, gave a bow as he said, 'Good evening, sir.'

He did a double-take. 'Good God! What an amazing likeness!' His glance travelled swiftly back and forth from Hawk's face to that of his ancestor. His trained eye spotted the differences much faster than hers had. 'The eyebrows are different, and the mouth, but otherwise it's a fascinating example of heredity.' He remembered the thing he was carrying and handed it to Caroline.

It was, as she had guessed, a pot plant—a white azalea.

'It's lovely. Thank you very much, Todd. I hate to disappear the moment you've arrived, but there's something on the stove which needs my attention. I'll be right back.'

She stayed away from the parlour for ten minutes, partly because she did have things to do in the kitchen and dining-room, and partly to compose herself.

However outrageously Hawk had behaved, there was no reason for her to follow his example. For the next few hours her first duty was to make Todd feel at home and give him an enjoyable evening with no inkling of what had been happening when he arrived, or that a fierce row would break out soon after he left.

When she returned, Todd was talking about the street parking restrictions which would come into force from mid-June until mid-September but which didn't prevent the centre of town becoming choked with traffic to the detriment of its present tranquillity.

'That's a beautiful colour you're wearing tonight, Caroline,' he said, as she picked up her glass. 'And very becoming to your colouring.'

'Thank you.'

As she had not sat down, both men were still on their feet. She said, 'Would you like to have a quick tour before we eat?'

'Very much. Shall I bring my drink with me?'

'Why not?' She led the way into the hall. 'You'll see the dining-room presently, so we'll start upstairs. You'll notice that we have a mortgage button'—tapping it with her finger as she passed the newel post.

'So far I've only cleaned the parts of the house which I use. The rest is still thick with dust, although not as musty as it was the day I first came here,' she explained. 'This is the bedroom I'm using.'

'You mean you're sleeping *here*—not at the guesthouse?' Todd asked, looking taken aback.

'I only stayed there a few nights. It was very nice, but this is nicer. Isn't that a beautiful quilt? I wonder who made it.'

'That's the Mariner's Compass,' said Todd, looking at the

red motifs on the quilt's white ground. 'It's supposed to be the hardest of all the designs because of the difficulty of sewing all these sharp, narrow points. I'm no expert on quilts, but I used to have a girl-friend who was. I went to quite a few exhibitions with her.'

'She would have liked this house. All the beds have lovely old quilts on them, and there are several spares in a chest. Come and see if you recognise the pattern on the quilt in the other front bedroom.'

Hawk had remained in the doorway while the other two entered her room. Now, as she turned to leave it, he did not at once step aside but remained standing on the threshold, the top of his dark head very close to the lintel and his powerful shoulders almost filling the space between the jambs.

For the first time since he had kissed her, she was forced to look at him; her grey eyes cool as they met the faint glint of amusement in his.

'Excuse me.' The polite hint for him to move held an edge of antagonism which she was unable to control.

He looked so damned pleased with himself. As if he knew what had been going on inside her while his mouth was on hers; as if he could do it again, any time he pleased.

But he wouldn't catch her off guard a second time. She was going to make certain of that, she thought furiously, as he stood aside and she was able to sweep past him.

Having shown Todd all the principal bedrooms, she said, 'Now I must go back to the kitchen. It'll be about another ten minutes before dinner is ready, if you'd like Hawk to show you the view from the walk on the roof.'

As she went down the stairs, she wondered if Hawk would also show the other man his sleeping quarters, and what Todd would make of the set-up. Would he share the Baileys' disapproval? Or, being of a different, less convention-trammelled generation, would he think nothing of it?

She wondered if the antique quilt expert had been a live-in girl-friend who had shared his SoHo loft with him. There must have been women in his life. It would be unnatural for a nice-looking man of his age not to have had at least one or two close relationships.

Most people would probably consider it strange for a girl of her age to be inexperienced. However, curious as she was to know whether physical love was all it was cracked up to be, she knew that for her the state of being in love was an essential prerequisite to making love. And she never had been in love.

Until now.

The thought was as petrifying as if, in a room where there was no one but herself, someone had spoken to her.

For a fraction of a second before she realised the source of the thought, she almost glanced round the empty kitchen. Then she knew that it was her own mind—at an almost subconscious level—which had presented her with this unwelcome suggestion.

Don't be ridiculous. You can't love a man you don't know, she apostrophised herself. He's a stranger. This time yesterday you hadn't met him.

But Kiki had known him well. She had known them both, and she must have had a reason for leaving them each a half share in the house. Could it be that Robert had been right when he had suggested that the old lady had had it in mind to do, as her brother had put it, a spot of posthumous matchmaking?

If that had been her intention, why leave it till after her death? Why not bring them together in her lifetime?

A more plausible explanation of her unusual bequest was that, wanting Hawk to inherit the house, but knowing that the place had unhappy associations for him, she had cast about for a way to prevent him from selling his inheritance. Her solution had been to include someone else in the bequest.

Knowing me, she probably guessed I should love the house and want to keep it; but it would have been a lot simpler to leave it to him with an entail which prevented him from selling it, ever—thought Caroline as she halved the avocadoes which, with a home-made shrimp dressing, were to be the first course.

To her relief, the meal was a success. The arrangement of the table wasn't perfect because there hadn't been time to find and launder the damask napkins which she felt sure were somewhere in the house. Nor had she found a pepper mill which, at home, she used both for cooking and on the table.

But apart from these two deficiencies, the table looked very handsome set with white and gold china, old silver and antique wine glasses. She had found enough flowers in the garden to make a low centrepiece, and on future occasions she would have candles to light as it grew dusk. For there was going to be a future—of that she was fiercely determined.

The avacadoes were followed by chicken cooked with wine and mushrooms, and accompanied by baked potatoes with herb butter and a side salad.

At the end of the first course Todd has asked if she would like help bringing in the next one, but she had smilingly refused his offer, saying she preferred to manage single-handed.

'You're a Cordon Bleu cook, Caroline. The chicken was——' He made a circle with his forefinger and thumb to express his enjoyment.

'Thank you. But I can do better than that with more notice and a better equipped kitchen. When I'm more settled in, I'll cook you one of my specialities,' she promised him, wondering if Hawk would make any comment on this statement.

He chose to let it pass, saying only, 'Yes, if the old saying is true, you shouldn't have any trouble finding your way to a man's heart, Caroline.'

'I don't think she'd have trouble even if she couldn't cook,' Todd added.

It was said in a tone of lighthearted gallantry, and she laughed, saying, equally lightly, 'You'll turn my head if you aren't careful!'

Having no dishwasher in her tiny kitchen in London, she was accustomed to doing the dishes by hand. Long ago she had worked out a system whereby, while her guests were too busy chatting to notice a short delay between courses, she would quickly wash the dishes from the previous course. It meant that, at the end of the evening, she didn't have to tackle a drainer stacked high with plates, either then or the following morning.

If there had been time to make pastry, she would have given them the pudding which most Englishmen loved above all others—old-fashioned treacle tart. But pastry baked in an unfamiliar oven could be a disaster. She had settled for another favourite male dish; baked apples stuffed with raisins and served with sour cream. She had baked five, hoping the men would be able to manage two each.

'Do you know what I'd do if this were my house?' said Todd, piling cream on his second apple. 'I'd retire from the New York rat-race and open a guesthouse—not year round, in the summer only. In winter I'd paint. Of course the success of a guesthouse depends on how good·the food is. I can only do steaks and salads, so I'd have to hire a cook. But you would only have to hire help with the cleaning, Caroline. You mentioned this morning you were tired of being an office worker. Why not try your hand at being an innkeeper?'

She could have jumped up and embraced him, but instead she said, in a calm tone, 'That idea had occurred to me, too. Do you think there's scope for another guesthouse in town?'

'Definitely. There's always scope for anything first-rate. With the kind of food you've served tonight, and this authentic whaling era atmosphere, I don't see how you can fail. What do you think, Hawk?'

'I think running a guesthouse is no sinecure; and I'm not sure the guests would appreciate the authenticity of waiting in line to use the one and only bathroom,' Hawk replied dryly.

'Sure, you'd have to install more bathrooms, but that's no real problem.' Todd turned to Caroline. 'With this house as collateral, the bank would lend you the money to modernise. You'd need a couple of ads in *Town and Country* and maybe *The Connoisseur* to attract your first guests. The word of mouth would do the rest. You remember what Emerson wrote? Oh, no, maybe you wouldn't, as you grew up in England.'

'Were you going to quote—*If a man write a better book, preach a better sermon, or make a better mousetrap than his neighbour, though he build his house in the woods, the world will make a beaten path to his door*?' she asked.

He smiled at her. 'Clever girl! I thought Emerson might not be read much in England.'

'He's one of my brother's favourite philosophers. It was Rob who said I must go to Concord and see Emerson's house and his grave.'

Todd said, 'But you must be an admirer, too, or you wouldn't be able to quote him. A girl with your looks, who can cook, and is also an intellectual, is a *rara avis*, in my experience.'

This time he was not being playfully gallant. Both his tone and his look made it clear that he spoke with sincere and serious admiration.

Conscious of Hawk looking on—probably with a sardonic gleam in his eyes—she said, 'My brother would fall about at the thought of my being classified as an intellectual! I think moderately intelligent would be a more realistic rating.'

'Brothers are notoriously unappreciative of their sisters' qualities. I would say "very intelligent",' Todd amended.

'I would disagree,' Hawk said casually. When Todd looked surprised and put out by this intervention, he added, 'Any girl who gives serious consideration to the idea of starting a guesthouse in a house which if it were sold, would provide her with a reasonable income, is not even moderately intelligent. She needs her head examined.'

Caroline saw Todd's mouth tighten.

She said hurriedly, 'I don't think we should embroil Todd in our argument, Hawk. If you two will adjourn to the parlour, I'll bring the coffee there.'

Hawk pushed back his chair. 'I'll make the coffee. You've done enough work this evening.'

This was not the way she had planned it. While the coffee was percolating, she wanted to wash the dessert plates and the serving dish, leaving the kitchen tidy so that, as soon as Todd took his leave, she could go directly to bed and avoid another tête-à-tête. If Hawk was capable of behaving outrageously at the beginning of the evening, there was no telling what he might do late at night, with a stiff rum, several glasses of wine and perhaps some more rum under his belt.

'Yes, come and keep me company while he does his share of the work,' the younger man urged her.

Realising that she didn't *have* to clear up in the kitchen before going to bed—tomorrow was Sunday and, even if it had been a weekday, for the time being she was no longer one of the world's workers—Caroline acquiesced.

As soon as they were alone in the parlour, Todd said, 'I feel Hawk's approach to your difference of opinion about this property is arbitrary, to say the least. Maybe I shouldn't say this, but I didn't like the way he talked to you just now. You said you were not related except by your connection with Kiki

Lawrence. Have you known him all your life? Is that why he feels free to talk to you that way?'

As she felt that sooner or later he was sure to find out that she and Hawk were virtually strangers, she said, 'No, as a matter of fact we met for the first time last night. I thought it was an intruder moving about down here and was very relieved when it turned out to be him. He had seen the light on in my bedroom and thought I was an unofficial tenant.'

'I don't like you being alone here at night. I think you should have stayed where you were,' he said, with a frown.

'I'm not alone now. Hawk is staying here. Didn't he show you his room up on the top floor?'

'No, he didn't!—And I can't pretend that reassures me. Does it reassure you?' Before she could answer, he went on, 'For Pete's sake, Caroline, he could take advantage of this situation. You say he's not married. At his age that means he's either gay or a womaniser.'

'That's overstating it, Todd—like calling me an intellectual. You're not so much younger than Hawk. How would you like it suggested that you came in one of those categories? There are other reasons why men of your age, and his age, aren't married yet.'

He did not reply for a moment or two, and then he surprised her by saying quietly, 'I should have been married four years ago. My fiancée and her father were killed in a highway accident a few weeks before our wedding day.'

'Oh, Todd—how dreadful for you! I'm so sorry.'

They were sharing the mahogany sofa and, instinctively, she reached out to lay her hand on his arm.

He covered her fingers with his. 'It was bad at the time, but I'm over it now. I loved Louise very much, but I can't spend my life in mourning for her. I didn't believe I would ever love anyone else. For all of us there is more than one person in the world with whom we could live in harmony.'

There was a look in his eyes as he said this which made her feel deeply uneasy. She attempted to withdraw her hand, but, to her dismay, he lifted it from his forearm and raised it to his lips.

He was kissing the back of her hand when Hawk walked in.

CHAPTER FOUR

CAROLINE felt her cheeks flame under the mockery of his stare.

'I hope I'm not intruding,' he said blandly.

Todd released her hand and stood up. 'Of course not,' he said, somewhat brusquely.

Hawk said, 'The coffee will be ready in a few minutes. Meanwhile let me get you a drink.'

'I haven't finished my wine yet,' said Caroline, indicating the glass she had brought with her from the dining-room.

'What about you, Todd? Brandy?'

'No, thanks. No more for me. I'm not much of a drinker.' He turned to her. 'It was a drunken driver who was responsible for that accident I was telling you about.'

As Hawk poured himself a glass of brandy, he said, 'People who drink too much are a menace. On the other hand, I've never met an abstainer who wasn't an odd fish. I'm in favour of enjoying all the pleasures life has to offer—including butter on my potato rather than margarine and, when I'm ashore, a brandy or two after dinner.'

'Don't you drink at all on board your ship?' she asked.

'Not when I'm in command of her. As I told you, sometimes the first officer is in charge.'

'But only when you are on leave, I thought?'

'Sometimes I don't take shore leave. I stay on board. Many of our passengers are extremely interesting, influential people with whom it's rewarding to mix. In fact if it wasn't necessary to come ashore from time to time, I could happily stay on board for years—as he did'—looking up at his ancestor. 'Excuse me. The coffee should be ready by now.'

As soon as he had left the room, Todd said, 'If he's going over to the Cape tomorrow, why don't you and I take a lunch to one of the beaches? The sea won't have warmed up enough for us to swim yet, but we can sunbathe. Or, if you prefer, we can go for a walk on the moors.' Taking her assent for granted, he asked, 'What time shall I pick you up? Would ten o'clock be too early?'

Caroline had reservations about spending a whole day in his company. The scene which Hawk had interrupted had revived her worry about encouraging Todd to think she felt as warmly towards him as he seemed to feel towards her.

She said, 'Twelve would be better. I must do some more cleaning and sorting out tomorrow morning. There's no inventory of the contents of the house, and I think there should be.'

'Can't the sorting out wait till Monday? I shall be catching the Wall Street on Monday morning, and I won't be back until late Friday night or Saturday. You'll have all week to work hard. Sunday should be a day of rest.'

'I'll enjoy the afternoon more if I've done something useful before lunch. Come at twelve, Todd. What is the Wall Street?'

'It's the seven a.m. flight to New York. I don't know of anyone here who commutes to the city every day, but there are a lot of Mark Cross briefcases on that first flight on Monday.'

Hawk returned with the coffee. They drank it in silence until, in an effort to keep a conversation going, Caroline said, 'To revert to your passengers, Emerald was telling me this morning that you were good at smoothing her father's ruffled feathers when the other passengers upset him. Did he take umbrage unnecessarily? Or were there some who were unpleasant to him and his wife?'

'Emerald's father had a genius for making money, but he found it difficult to learn the rules of the world his money enabled him to enter,' said Hawk. 'The first rule being that it's not done to brag about one's riches. Albert Wigan was a kind, generous man who never advertised the fact that he gave a lot of his money to public and private charities. Unfortunately he never stopped boasting about his expensive possessions. That, combined with his loud voice and smoker's cough, made him less than popular with a lot of the other people on that cruise. Mrs Wigan has a weight problem and an unfortunate partiality for fluorescent colours. But she's a nice person. Would you care to come over and meet her tomorrow?'

'Todd has invited me to go on a picnic to one of the beaches.'

'I see.'

There was another silence.

Earlier in the day, and at dinner, the two men had got along well. But since Hawk's remark about Caroline needing her brains tested, and Todd's discovery that the other man had moved in, that friendliness had evaporated.

Todd's hostility was now almost tangible; while Hawk, she felt sure, was saying nothing because he derived a perverse amusement from watching her discomfiture.

As captain of a cruise ship, he must have an extensive repertoire of conversational gambits, she thought vexedly. He was just not making any effort.

'Tell us about some of your other passengers. Have you had any famous people on board?' she asked.

'Yes, many internationally-known people have cruised with us. But I make it a rule never to discuss them. Gossip spreads faster than fire, and one of a captain's duties is to be discreet.'

'Can you ensure that your crew is equally discreet?'

'They know that if they aren't they'll soon be looking for another berth,' was his dry reply. 'Of course I have no jurisdiction over the passengers. If we have a celebrity on board who causes gossip among the passengers, that's his or her lookout. But what anyone does in the seclusion of their stateroom—or someone else's stateroom—isn't leaked to the gossip columns by any member of the ship's complement.'

When he paused Caroline thought that, unless she prompted him with another question, the conversation would collapse again.

However, to her relief, he went on, 'The trickiest part of my job is striking a balance between giving the passengers a taste of the thrill of sailing in a square-rigger, and not making people such as Mrs Wigan uncomfortable or, worse, seasick. That's why I enjoy the tall ships races, because then we have no one on board who isn't prepared to be seasick if necessary, and we can sail her as she was meant to be sailed, often with her full spread of canvas.'

'How many sails does a tall ship carry?' she asked.

'It depends on her rig. *Damaris* is a four-masted barque with twenty-nine sails, making a total of more than three thousand square metres of canvas.'

'*Damaris*? Didn't you say that was the name of Captain Starbuck's ship?'

'Yes, it was. The present *Damaris* was built in 1929 at the Castellamare di Stabia shipyard in Italy. She was built for and named after an opera star of that period. The company which owns her now decided to re-name her. Ships, as you know, are female, and I suggested *Damaris* as a pretty name, with historic associations. I was, and hope to remain, her first American master.'

He looked at Todd. 'Enough of my job. What about yours? You spoke of retiring from the New York rat race. I would have thought your work must be extremely interesting.'

'There's a great deal of pressure involved—as there is in any occupation which is governed by a deadline. Like most artists, writers and musicians, I would prefer to do my own thing. But that might not pay the rent, and my muse isn't strong enough to make me prepared to starve for my art,' Todd answered.

Plied with questions by Caroline, who was dreading the moment when he would leave her alone with Hawk, he talked at some length about the demands of his job. He was interesting, as any man talking about his work was interesting. Yet somehow she didn't find the insight into the workings of a weekly news magazine as exciting as the concept of living aboard a great sailing ship.

Perhaps it was that, as Todd himself had admitted, he was not doing his own thing and was therefore not totally fulfilled.

Hawk was a man who had realised a boyhood dream. The ship of which he had command meant so much to him that he stayed aboard her even when he was on leave. He had said that if he married his wife would have to live aboard with him—and share his heart with the vessel which was his other, perhaps his primary passion, she thought.

'You're tired, Caroline. I must leave and let you get to bed,' said Todd.

Embarrassed that she had let her inattention show, she said hastily, 'No, no ... it's early yet. Have some more coffee. Change your mind and have a small brandy. I'm going to now.'

He shook his head. 'It's an hour past the old-time curfew and I know you're an early riser,' he said, standing up.

'Thank you for a delicious dinner. I've enjoyed this evening very much.'

She rose. 'Thank you for the gorgeous azalea.'

'My pleasure. I'll be back at noon tomorrow. I'll take care of lunch.'

Hawk was also on his feet. It was he who opened the front door to let their guest out.

After they had said goodnight, Caroline lingered at the top of the steps, watching Todd walk along the quiet, well-lighted street.

Behind her, Hawk said, 'Oil from whales caught by Nantucket ships was lighting the streets of London before the end of the eighteenth century, but it never lit these streets. That would have been an extravagance, and the Quakers didn't approve of extravagance. Did you know that for a long time they were the leading sect here?'

It was a question which suggested he was no longer in the mood to repeat his behaviour before dinner.

Relieved, she turned to go in, saying, 'Yes, my guide book mentions them briefly, but I don't know a great deal about them. Why were they called Quakers? Their proper name is the Society of Friends, isn't it?'

'Yes, but their founder, George Fox, is supposed to have told a magistrate to quake at the word of the Lord, and that led to their nickname. As religions go, I think their ideas make more sense than most, but the Nantucket Quakers were a law unto themselves. Instead of saying thou, as Quakers did everywhere else, here they said thee. And they were particularly severe about disowning members who disobeyed the rules. They not only disowned all the forty-seven Quakers who fought in the Revolutionary War, but they also chucked out a man who went on board an armed ship to negotiate an exchange of prisoners. That's carrying pacifism to the point of absurdity.'

'I knew they were pacifists, but what other beliefs did they hold?'

'They thought women as well as men were entitled to preach if they felt like it, but that silent meetings were the proper form of public worship. Your friend Emerson would have approved of that. Wasn't it he who wrote—*I like the silent church before the service begins better than any preaching?*'

'I don't know. If he did, I agree with him. Which reminds me, Todd told me to look at the Tiffany windows and Erica Wilson needlepoint in one of the churches here, and I've forgotten which one.'

Hawk had locked the door and was following her into the parlour as he said, 'I don't think you should flirt with him, Caroline. He could get serious about you. The harm may already be done.'

She had been collecting the coffee cups. On her way to the tray, with a cup and saucer in each hand, she stopped dead.

'I have *not* been flirting with Todd! I—I barely know him.'

In the act of picking up his cup, Hawk slanted a mocking glance at her. As he placed it on the tray, he said, 'You barely know me, but you let me kiss you before dinner.'

'*Oh*!' Her cheeks flamed with angry colour. 'I didn't *let* you. You . . . you forced that kiss on me.'

He arched a dark eyebrow. 'Forced? I don't recall using force. As I remember it, I walked towards you, like this, and I tipped your chin up a little and—whoops!'

The exclamation came after her hasty step backwards had dislodged one cup from its saucer. Before it could hit the floor which, just there, had no rug to cushion the impact, he caught it.

'If you don't want to spoil the set, you'd better put those down,' he suggested, the lines round his blue eyes crinkling with maddening amusement.

'And you'd better keep your hands off me!' she told him furiously. 'This is valuable porcelain. If you come any nearer I'll throw it at you. You know damn well you forced that kiss on me. I think it was absolutely contemptible!'

'You seemed to enjoy it at the time. I certainly did. That luscious mouth isn't just window-dressing. It feels as good as it looks. Soft . . . warm . . . delicious,' he told her, his gaze fixed on her lips. 'Even now, when you're grinding your teeth, your mouth looks ineffably kissable. If I had been Todd, I wouldn't have wasted time kissing your hand—or not the back of it. As I'm sure you know from experience, a kiss on the palm produces much more reaction.'

Caroline's rage was exacerbated by the fact that merely by

looking at her mouth and talking about kissing her palm, he was making her pulses race and causing a flutter of excitement in the pit of her stomach.

'Englishmen don't have the gall to kiss people who don't want to be kissed,' she told him frostily.

'How do they know unless they try? Don't tell me they ask permission. That I don't believe,' he said, smiling. 'And although you may not have wanted to be kissed—or not consciously—before it happened, if we hadn't been interrupted we might still be kissing—probably under the mariner's compasses by this time.'

At first this last remark was lost on her. Then, as she remembered Todd telling her the name of the pattern on the antique quilt on her bed, fresh colour swept up from her throat.

'That's insulting!' she flared, her grey eyes sparkling with anger.

He said mildly, 'It may be more precipitate than an Englishman's approach to the matter, but there's nothing intrinsically insulting in telling a girl that you find her very attractive and would like to go to bed with her. It's what your English men friends would have been thinking from the outset, even if they took longer to get around to telling you. Anyway, you're an American. If you're going to stay here you'll have to adjust to American ways.'

'Speak for yourself, Captain Lowell. I'm sure very few Americans share your conviction that you're one of God's gifts to women and none of them can resist you!'

He laughed, showing his sound white teeth.

'A crushing indictment—but not true. It was because I wasn't sure of my ground that I put it to the test by kissing you. Up to that point I hadn't been certain if the feeling I had was mutual. When we kissed I knew it was. We are *both* quite powerfully attracted to each other, Miss Caroline Murray'—a teasing riposte to her icy formality—'And if you're going to tell me that what you felt was revulsion, I won't believe you. You enjoyed that kiss and you know it.'

What could she say? She could deny it, but not with conviction. The lie direct had always been impossible for her; even an indirect untruth made her feel uncomfortable, unless it was the only way to avoid wounding someone's feelings.

But although it would have given her great satisfaction to puncture Hawk's amour propre, she could not look him in the eye and refute his claim. She would remember his kiss all her life—and not only for its effrontery, but for the slow frisson of pleasure which had radiated through her body as, with a light hand on her throat and the pressure of his mouth, he had held her captive for several minutes.

'Good! I don't mind a little feminine prevarication, but I don't like a liar,' he said approvingly. He picked up the tray. 'Put those things on here. They won't protect you, and you don't need protection from me. I don't take kisses or anything else by force—or not more than a woman enjoys.'

As, feeling that her face must be almost as red as her shirt, she put the two saucers on the tray, he said, 'How about that brandy you were going to have? Shall I make some more coffee?'

Caroline swallowed. Without looking up at him, she said, 'N—not for me, thank you. I don't want any brandy either. I'm going to b—to my room.'

As she turned towards the door, he said, 'In a straightforward world I'd come with you, and we'd both sleep a lot more soundly than we will staying on different floors. But I guess it won't hurt to delay things if it makes you feel better.'

She looked at him then. 'I'm not delaying. I'm saying no. Not tonight . . . not ever.'

As his mouth took a quizzical twist, she went on, 'If you think that's a challenge, it's not. If it will bolster your ego, I'm prepared to admit that I did enjoy it when you kissed me. I'm a normal girl and you *are* a very attractive man. But I haven't spent the past five years resisting other men's passes to hop into bed with you, Hawk. I'm not looking for kicks, as you are. I'm waiting till I meet someone who will be my best friend as well as my lover. I don't want a man who tells me I need my brains tested. I want one who treats me as an intelligent person whose ideas deserve a fair hearing— not lordly dismissal. You told me that Nantucket women were ahead of their time in taking responsibilities and making decisions which would normally have been a male prerogative. By birth I'm a Nantucket woman, and I'm not about to let the side down by letting you treat me as a plaything to take to bed, but not to take seriously downstairs. Goodnight!'

She was awake half the night, tossing and turning, wondering how it would have been if she had let Hawk spend the night with her.

Bliss? Or a disappointment?

Was he as restless as she? Racked by unsatisfied desire? Somehow she couldn't imagine Hawk losing sleep over anything—least of all a girl. Clearly he was a man who had enjoyed a great many women, and who had taken for granted that she was far from inexperienced.

Now he's probably decided I'm under-sexed, she thought unhappily.

But the memory of his kiss on her lips, and the aching longing it evoked, was proof that it wasn't an innately unpassionate nature which had made her resist, for so long, the casual amours indulged in by many of her contemporaries.

She was longing for love, eager for it. But she wanted that rare form of love defined by Jane van Lawick-Goodall whose study of apes Caroline had read in her last year at school. In the same year, the senior girls had been encouraged to start a common-place book of things they wished to remember. After school she had kept up the habit and now possessed several notebooks filled with snippets of poetry and prose. The night before she left London, she had skimmed through the pages of the first book, refreshing her memory of what had impressed her at seventeen. Not that she had ever forgotten the words which had formulated the most important of all her youthful ideals. They were engraved on her heart.

It may be that what we think of as true love—an emotion which embraces both the body and the mind of the beloved, which mellows with time and brings about harmony of living, which removes any needs, in the man or the woman concerned, for another sexual partner—is one of the rarest of human heterosexual relationships.

Although, before saying goodnight, she had more or less accused Hawk of having a mind which repelled her as much as his body attracted her, that was not strictly true.

She had several reasons to believe that mental rapport was not impossible between them. She had liked the way he had spoken of 'your friend Emerson', showing that he understood the sense of communion one could feel with a favourite writer—even one who had died a century ago.

She liked him for taking the trouble to visit one of his former passengers who was now a widow and not well. By the sound of it, he and Mrs Wigan had very little in common, but he was prepared to spend four hours on the ferry to give her the pleasure of talking about her late husband to someone who had known him. That was an act of unselfish kindness which went a long way to counterbalance the arrogance of his attitude towards herself.

She wondered if, as he had yesterday, he would waken her with a cup of coffee. After lying awake even longer than she had last night, it was likely she would oversleep again. Last night ... it seemed unbelievable that Hawk hadn't entered her life until the last hours of the day before yesterday.

When she went downstairs the next morning, the kitchen table was laid for breakfast for two, but he wasn't there.

A few minutes later she saw him striding across the garden with what appeared to be several newspapers under his arm.

Finding her in the kitchen, he said pleasantly, 'Good morning. I've been down to the Hub to pick up a *New York Times*.'

'Good morning.'

She watched him unfold the bundle of newsprint and separate it into sections, arranging them in a neat row at the empty end of the large table.

'Take your pick,' he invited. 'I'm going to fry bacon and eggs.'

Caroline had watched some television newscasts since her arrival, but she hadn't bought any papers. In England, when she spent the weekends at Thornbridge Manor, there was a choice of Sunday papers to read, but none had more than three or four sections and a colour supplement. However, she soon realised that much of the bulk of this Sunday edition of the *New York Times* was either advertising material or news, such as sports, of no interest to her.

By the time Hawk sat down to eat she had looked at the

main news and was ready to hand over that section and look at another.

For the most part they breakfasted in silence. It wasn't until they were clearing the table that he said suddenly, 'Let me get something straight. When you said last night you had spent the past five years resisting passes, did you mean you had never let anyone make love to you?'

Before meeting him, she couldn't remember the last time she had blushed. Now, all at once, she was blushing as often as a selfconscious teenager.

She nodded. 'Does that make me a freak?'

'Not a freak. It must be unusual—particularly for a girl with your face and figure.' His glance skimmed her slender shape. 'You must have had to resist a hell of a lot of guys. Why? I'd like to know why.'

'I told you that last night—I'm waiting for Mr Right,' she answered lightly.

'Do you expect him never to have slept with anyone else?'

'No . . . what happened before we met each other wouldn't be my concern. I'll wash the dishes this morning. Which of the ferries are you catching?'

'There's one which leaves at a quarter after eleven. I'll be back here soon after eight and we'll eat out tonight.'

'Todd may ask me to have dinner with him.'

'Tell him you're sorry but you and I have business to discuss. Which we will have. When a Nantucket woman demands to be taken seriously, it takes a braver man than I to defy her,' he said with a grin. 'After you'd gone to bed, I thought the situation over, and maybe a compromise is possible. But we'll thrash out the details over dinner at the Woodbox, which Todd says is one of the better restaurants. I'll reserve a table for the second sitting at a quarter of nine.'

'What sort of compromise had you in mind?' she asked warily.

But Hawk was not to be drawn.

After he had left the house, giving her an hour and a half to spare before Todd's arrival, she could not resist going up to the top floor to see which room he was using.

All the doors on that floor were wide open, and several windows were propped on the lower notches of their sticks.

The once-white muslin curtains were stirring slightly in the breeze.

In his room the curtains had been removed and put elsewhere. Caroline decided to take them all down and leave them to soak in cold water to loosen the accumulated grime which made them look grey.

But before she tackled that task, she stood on the threshold of his room which was now swept and dusted. There were two small closets, probably full of the accumulated belongings of many generations. The hanging bag which seemed to be his only piece of luggage, and the clothes it had contained, were suspended from knobs attached to a long strip of wood spanning one wall. These hanging strips seemed to be a feature of the house. She had noticed them in other rooms and in the large walk-in closets.

She was surprised to see that, as well as the clothes he had arrived in, he had brought a well-cut grey suit and a tropical dinner jacket. She would not have expected him to possess one. If she had thought about it, she would have assumed he would have a dress uniform for formal wear on the cruises; and that, when he was ashore, he would move in circles where a coat and tie in the evening were sufficiently formal.

She had the impression that, in America, black tie events were confined to the very richest strata of society, stage and screen premières, and political galas. Why Hawk should consider it necessary to bring a dinner jacket to Nantucket was a puzzle. Unless he was going somewhere else before rejoining *Damaris* at Baltimore.

There were two books on the table by the bed. Although she felt she ought not to be looking round his room in his absence, Caroline succumbed to the temptation to see what they were.

The uppermost volume had no dust jacket and looked as if it might be at least as old as she was. The title was *Sailing Eagle*. The author was Alan Villiers, a name which would have meant nothing to her before her visit to the town of Plymouth on the mainland. There, visiting the modern replica of *Mayflower*, she had learned that her master during the voyage from England to Plymouth had been an internationally famous mariner, Alan Villiers; a man who had gone to sea as a boy of sixteen and tried every kind of sea-life from

Portuguese cod-fishing in the Arctic to trading between the Persian Gulf and Zanzibar.

Clearly a man like that would be one of Hawk's heroes. But his interest in the other book was harder to understand. The title was *Corporate Cultures: The Rites and Rituals of Corporate Life*. Why he should want to read about that world was a puzzle. Unless the book had been left on board *Damaris* by some top-level executive and he had picked it up out of idle curiosity about the world of boardrooms and power struggles.

She was wearing a bikini under her shorts and shirt when Todd came to pick her up. He had brought a map of the island so that she could see where they were going.

'As you'll notice, all the place names are Indian. Wauwinet . . . Pocomo . . . Madaket,' he said, as she spread it on her lap. 'There were Algonquin Indians here long before the first European settlers arrived. In 1659, two of the sachems or chiefs sold the rights to most of the land to an English colonist, Thomas Mayhew, and his son. They paid twelve pounds down and fourteen pounds the following summer. Which, incidentally, is a lot more than was paid for another Indian island—Manhattan!'

'Are the names only names? Or do they have meanings?' she asked.

'Nantucket means The Faraway Island which, way back then, it was. Not any more. I think Yesterday's Island is more apt. That's the name of a souvenir newspaper which is given away free to visitors. I don't know who thought up that name for Nantucket, but it's certainly—to adapt a French expression—*le nom juste*. In many ways time has stood still here. In certain parts of town, you get the feeling that, if you closed your eyes, you might open them and find yourself back in the 1880s or the 1780s. It's a shame the place gets so crowded in July and August. It's nicer now, out of season.'

Caroline was only half listening.

'Yesterday's Island . . . where I want to spend my future,' she murmured dreamily, looking at the fine old houses on both sides of Pleasant Street which was their route out of town.

She turned to Todd. 'By the way, after you left last night, Hawk and I had a verbal sparring match. This morning he

said we might be able to reach a compromise. But he wouldn't
tell me what he had in mind.'

'I don't know, but I can guess why he's gone to the Cape to
see Mrs Wigan. For Emerald to buy all the stuff she took
back with her, they must be loaded. Two lightship baskets,
for God's sake! And the largest and fanciest at that. If Hawk
is so short of cash that he's ready to sell his family home,
he may find it easier to sweet-talk Emerald and her mother
than to persuade you to sell your share. The girl is already
dazzled by him. She's a pretty kid. If he married her, he could
quit his job as a charter captain and have a big yacht of his
own.'

'Oh, Todd, that's a crazy idea,' she expostulated. 'Hawk
loves what he does for a living. It's more than a job, it's a
vocation. I don't think he's short of money. He wasn't happy
when he lived here with his grandfather, and he has no need
for a house. He told me that, if ever he marries, his wife will
have to go to sea with him. As for marrying Emerald, that's
ludicrous. She's much too young for him and she's . . . well,
not his kind of person. On his father's side he is what you said
he might be—a Boston Brahmin. Emerald is a dear little
thing, but she's right at the other end of the social scale. She
doesn't dress or behave in the way expected of a captain's
wife. She wouldn't be at ease in that situation.'

'She's young enough for him to mould her any way he
wants her—and obviously she has enough money to buy
clothes from the best designers if someone pushed her in their
direction. Or if she went to the fashion director of one of the
top New York stores and said, 'I have X-thousand dollars to
spend. Make me elegant. Give me style,' they would do that
for her. No problem.'

'Yes, they could make her look the part. But her manner
would still be very gauche. Anyway, I'm positive that,
whatever else he may be, Hawk isn't a fortune-hunter. He's
not the type. By the time he left Harvard, his Lowell
grandfather was prepared to have him back in the clan from
which his father had been excluded. He could have had a job
in the bank, married some rich Brahmin girl, and been set up
for life. He didn't want that.'

'Maybe not then. He might now. That must have been ten
years ago or more. People change in less time than that. When

I was fresh out of college, I was going to be an independent artist by the time I was thirty. I'm not going to make that ambition. In the meantime, I've realised I don't have enough creative energy to hold down a demanding job and also cut back on sleep to spend more time on my own work. Also I'd like a wife and children, and they'll have a more secure future if I stick to being a design director than they would if I went free-lance. But if I were a different kind of guy, and a millionaire's daughter took a shine to me, I might consider resigning. I might jump at the chance.'

'How do we know Emerald's father was a millionaire? He may have been a moderately rich man whose wife and daughter have already squandered a great deal of what he left them.'

They had reached a traffic circle on the outskirts of town. Todd took a road which had a bike path alongside it. Presently they turned off to the left on another road signposted Polpis.

'Tell me more about the early history,' Caroline suggested, wanting to turn the conversation from the disquieting idea that Hawk's motive for going to the Cape today might not, after all, have been the disinterested kindness with which she had credited him. 'Were Thomas Mayhew and his son the first two First Purchasers?'

'No, after the Mayhews had settled up with the Indians, they then re-sold most of the island to nine other men. The price was thirty pounds and two new beaver hats for Mayhew and his wife. Those nine were the First Purchasers, and they were followed by the half-share partners, who were mainly the craftsmen which the settlement needed. The undeveloped land on the island is sometimes referred to as the moors, and sometimes as The Commons, from when the first settlers agreed that it should be shared pasture for their cattle and sheep. In a little while I'll park the car and we'll walk along one of the dirt roads which cross The Commons.'

There was a wild, windswept beauty about the interior of the island which contrasted sharply and pleasingly with the tall trees, green lawns, brick sidewalks and white picket fences in town. Here there were only a few isolated houses in a terrain inhabited by rabbits and pheasant, birds and butterflies.

'In the fall, the colours are superb. But you have to watch

out for poison ivy,' said Todd, as they returned to the car to drive on to 'Sconset.

There they had their lunch on the beach and afterwards lay down and sunbathed. Because she had had a poor night, Caroline fell into a doze. When she woke up she found Todd at work with pen and sketch pad.

'Don't move for a minute,' he said, as she opened her eyes.

She realised he had been drawing her as she lay on her back, one arm cradling her head, the other lax at her side.

Had it been Hawk who had been studying the contours of her almost naked body—the lime green cotton bikini she had bought in France the previous summer had white cord ties at the hips and a white cord halter—she would have ignored the instruction and sat up at once. But even though she suspected that Todd felt a warmth towards her which very soon she must make clear she could not reciprocate, he did not look at her in the unnerving way which Hawk did. With him, she was always aware of being shorter, curvier, physically weaker than he was; and that he was much taller, his long bones armoured with muscle and his shoulders almost twice as broad as hers.

She had never seen him without his clothes, but she guessed from the way he moved and carried himself that his body must have the lithe symmetry of Michelangelo's *David*.

Todd was above average height and looked fairly well built with his clothes on. Without them, his arms had a softness which she found less attractive than Hawk's tanned and sinewy forearms; and although he couldn't help being pale-skinned at this early stage of the summer, he had an under-exercised look which, in a few years' time, could deteriorate into flabbiness.

Caroline was no athlete. At school she had detested organised games. But for the past couple of years she had realised that her mainly sedentary life at the office could damage her looks if she didn't do something about it. Now, three evenings a week, she attended an exercise class at a work-out studio. The other four days she jogged round the park before breakfast. It was an effort, but it made her feel great afterwards.

She could tell that, although he had drunk more last night than Todd, in general Hawk took better care of his body.

How he managed it, living aboard ship, she had no idea. Maybe *Damaris* had a gym, and most of the time she would be sailing in waters where swimming, snorkelling and windsurfing were possible.

'Okay, you can relax now,' said Todd.

As Caroline bent her knees, clasped both hands behind her head and rolled into a sitting position, she remembered the strain of doing sit-ups when she had started exercising. Her tummy had always been flat, but now it was firmer and the obstinate pads of puppyfat at the tops of her thighs had disappeared.

'May I see?' she asked.

He handed her the drawing.

It confirmed her fear that she was doing him a disservice by spending most of the day alone with him. Only a man in the grip of what she hoped would prove to be a transient infatuation could have flattered her to this extent.

She had no illusions about herself. She was slim, fit, passably nice-looking. Todd had drawn a girl who was beautiful.

Somehow without enlarging her breasts or changing the shape of her hips and thighs, he had given her the voluptuous quality which she recognised in Emerald but had never seen when she looked at herself in the mirror.

'It's marvellously flattering. Perhaps instead of drawing drop-outs, you ought to be making your fortune doing portraits of rich women. May I keep it?'

'No, I want to keep that one. But I'm hoping to do a lot of sketches of you this summer ... maybe even a full-scale portrait.'

'If I can get Hawk's consent to the guesthouse idea, I shall be too busy for any more lazy days like this, Todd.'

'You'll have to have some time off.'

'Not very much, the first year. I expect to have to work very hard to make a success of the project. I'm longing to get at the job of scraping off all the old paint which spoils the front of the house. I wonder if it was always white. I'd like to restore it to exactly the way it was in Captain Starbuck's day.'

'Dull red was a popular colour at one time, but only for the windows surrounds, not for a whole façade, I wouldn't think. There's a book you ought to get hold of. It's by an architect who lives here and has made a study of Nantucket houses. His name is Duprey. I borrowed the book from the library when I first had a place here. Have you been in the library yet?'

Caroline shook her head. She had passed the handsome Greek Revival edifice with ATHENEUM written in gold above the Ionic columns and below the fine double pediment, and had thought it yet another of the architectural marvels of a unique small town which had once been described as an 'unknown city in the ocean.'

'I'll go in tomorrow,' she answered. 'Now can we look round 'Sconset?'

Todd took her to see the old village pump, no longer used to draw water from the well dug in 1776 but preserved by the Nantucket Historical Association. Then they walked to the little cedar-shingled cottage called Auld Lang Syne which was the most ancient of the original fishermen's cottages, having been built before 1700. The street in which it stood was called Broadway, a name given to it by the theatrical people who had summered in 'Sconset long ago.

Caroline thought of Kiki who had come here from childhood to the brink of womanhood, never guessing there was heartbreak in store, and fame, and three husbands who between them had given her everything a woman could want—except the capacity to love them.

For the first time it struck her that she didn't know how Kiki and Hawk had become acquainted. She must remember to ask him tonight.

She wondered what she should wear, regretting the limitations of her wardrobe and wishing she had brought the apricot chiffon short summer evening dress which Kiki had insisted on buying for her in an expensive boutique. But who would have thought she would need a knock-out dress in Nantucket?

Why *did* she need it? she asked herself.

The answer was no longer one from which her mind could shy away. She was in love with him. Even though her intelligence told her that love couldn't come into being as quickly as this, her heart told her that it had.

'You're very quiet. You don't have a headache, do you, Caroline?' Todd asked concernedly.

'No, I'm fine ... just woolgathering. It's one of my bad habits, I'm afraid,' she answered lightly.

He smiled at her; a smile of such patent affection that she longed to say—Don't, Todd. For you to love me is as hopeless as for me to love Hawk.

But how could she warn him off except by avoiding his company after today?

Later, on the drive back to town, she thought about why she felt loving Hawk was a foolishness which could never have a happy outcome. She supposed it had to do with her feeling that he didn't take women very seriously; that only *Damaris*, the great square-rigged ship he commanded, had a lasting hold on his heart.

It was on the drive back, moments after a private aircraft had flown overhead on its way to land at the airport, that Todd said, 'I thought of taking you to the Brotherhood of Thieves tonight. It's a strange name for a restaurant, isn't it? As you probably know, the Quakers were always against slavery. In 1841 they had a three-day anti-slavery convention in Nantucket. One of the speakers was Frederick Douglas, an escaped slave, and another was Stephen S. Foster—*not* the Stephen Foster who wrote *Swanee River*—who denounced the churches for not taking a strong enough lead against slavery. Later on, he wrote a pamphlet called *The Brotherhood of Thieves: A True Picture of the American Church and Clergy*, and that's how the restaurant got its name.'

'Todd, I'd like to go there, but I can't tonight. Hawk wants to discuss this compromise he's thought up, and he's booked a table at the Woodbox. I'm sorry.'

'Oh ... I see,' he said disappointedly. 'I assumed he wouldn't be coming back until late. How about next weekend?'

'Could we leave it open for the moment?'

'Okay,' he agreed reluctantly.

'If you've been coming here for several years, you must have made quite a few friends, haven't you?'

'I know several people ... acquaintances rather than friends. I get along with people all right. At work, I have to. But, aside from the demands of my job, I'm not basically very outgoing. Parties bore me. I prefer a quiet dinner such as we had last night—and I should have enjoyed it even more had there been only the two of us,' he added.

One of Caroline's closest friends in England was a former school friend, now assistant to the Personnel Director of a large London store. She had told Caroline that a good way to smooth an antagonism between two employees was to take each one of them aside and tell them how highly the person they disliked thought of them.

Even when it's not strictly true, it works like a charm, Suzy had told her. *It's hard to sustain a dislike of someone who thinks you're the tops.*

Caroline felt this was a good moment to try out Suzy's technique. She said, 'It's kind of you to say so, but I know Hawk wouldn't have enjoyed the evening half as much if you hadn't been there. He's very impressed by the paintings we saw at your place, and by your achievement in reaching your present position before you're thirty.'

'Oh, really? Maybe I got a little too hot under the collar about what he said to you at dinner. It could be he didn't mean it the way he sounded. I guess any kind of ship's captain has to make a lot of fast, one-man decisions rather than working in consultation with other people. That could account for his seemingly overbearing attitude. But if you stood up to him later, and this morning he seemed more co-operative, maybe you can work something out.'

Inwardly amused by his more conciliatory attitude, she said, 'I certainly hope so. I feel he has much more right to the house than I have, but already I love the place. I felt at home there the moment I stepped inside, and it's not only the house. The town as well seemed . . . to embrace me. That may sound silly and fanciful. It's a difficult feeling to explain. Perhaps it has something to do with knowing that my father loved Nantucket. I've always suspected that I'm much more like him than like my mother; and yet, because she's seldom spoken of him, he has always been slightly mysterious. I think my curiosity about him has been what adopted children feel about the natural parents they can never trace. But somehow, being in Nantucket, I feel I have traced him.'

'Do you have a photograph of him?'

'No, I haven't. I wish I had. Unfortunately after I was born there was an estrangement between my mother and his. His father was already dead. After Mummy remarried, she and her first mother-in-law had nothing more to do with each other. I once thought of writing to my grandmother and asking her for a photograph, but I didn't know her address, and anyway it would have seemed disloyal to Mummy. I'm sorry . . . I'm rambling on about something which is only of interest to me.'

'On the contrary, everything about you interests me. Maybe you could get hold of a photograph of your father even now. Did he have brothers and sisters?'

'Yes, two sisters. Kiki told me that. But they both married men whose careers took them overseas. Goodness knows where they are now.'

By this time they were back at the house. Although she felt he was hoping to be asked in for tea or a drink, she said, 'Thank you for a very nice picnic, Todd. I have no idea what the situation will be by next weekend, but you're always welcome to drop in.'

She disliked having to give him even the gentlest brush-off. But it would be even more unkind to allow him to hope that she might be beginning to feel more than liking for him.

Having plenty of time before Hawk came back, she washed her hair and decided to wear it loose for a change. Luckily it had plenty of natural movement and, not being able to plug in her portable dryer, she sat in the evening sun on the back steps, letting her hair dry naturally and encouraging it into a good shape with her comb and her fingers.

She was ready by eight o'clock, wearing the same clothes as the night before, but having taken extra care with her make-up and nails. Last night, producing an appetising meal had been her chief concern. Tonight she wanted to look what Kiki had used to call *soignée*—a term used by her generation to denote perfect grooming.

At eight-thirty, when there was no sign of Hawk returning, she checked the timetable she had kept since her own crossing. The six-ten p.m. from Hyannis should have docked at eight-ten and the ferries weren't usually late. The walk from Straight Wharf to the house couldn't take more than ten minutes, especially on Hawk's long legs.

They were due at the restaurant in fifteen minutes. Where was he?

She remembered what Todd had said to her before lunch. *The girl is already dazzled by him ... If he married her, he could quit his job as a charter captain and have a big yacht of his own.*

There was a later ferry which left the Cape at seven-thirty p.m. and reached the island at nine forty-five. Could it be that Hawk had decided to spend extra time with the Wigans? Perhaps to stay overnight?

But surely, having no way of letting Caroline know of any alteration in his plans, he wouldn't just leave her to stew?

Wouldn't he? How did she know what rules of conduct he lived by in his private life?

For the next fifteen minutes she stood at the parlour window, peering down the street and experiencing, for the first time, all the agonised suspense she had watched her girl friends endure during their love affairs.

By a quarter to nine she had made up her mind to go to the restaurant by herself. In the unlikely event that the ferry had been delayed, he could join her there. She would leave a note on the hall table. If he had left her in the lurch, she was not going to spend the evening gnashing her teeth over a solitary pot-luck supper. She might as well go out and enjoy someone else's cooking.

Fortunately the restaurant was among those listed in her New England guide book, otherwise she would have had no idea where to find it. It was on Fair Street, not far. On the way there she passed the Ships Inn, a house not unlike hers and Hawk's except that the exterior was in better repair and there were four dormer windows projecting from the roof, presumably a modern addition to the original structure.

At the Woodbox she was shown to a table for two and, having explained that her companion might not be able to make it, was given a menu.

Asked if she would like a cocktail, she said, 'No, thank you, but I'd like to see the wine list.'

Having chosen her meal, she ordered a bottle of French wine. It was fairly expensive and, if Hawk failed to turn up, she wouldn't be able to drink it all by herself. What was left, she would have to take home.

She was not expecting the meal to make a hole in her

budget. He had suggested they should dine here. If he stood
her up, the least he could do was to offer to pay the bill—an
offer she would have no compunction in accepting, she told
herself.

By the time she had drunk half a glass of Burgundy—
having asked them to bring it straight away—the soothing
effect of good wine, and the pleasant early Colonial style of
the restaurant, had gone some way to calm her vexation.

Yesterday, she would have tried to delude herself that it
was disappointment at the postponement of their business
discussion which had made her angry. Today she could admit
that it was dining *à deux*, as much as hearing what he had to
say about the house, to which she had been looking forward.

'Sorry I'm late, Caroline. I was unavoidably detained. Did
you think I'd missed the boat?' Hawk took his place on the
opposite side of the table.

Had her face lit up at the sight of him? Hoping her pleasure
and relief were not too apparent, she said, 'Yes, I did. Was it
late arriving?'

'No. I'll explain in a minute'—this as the waitress
approached and said, 'Good evening, sir.'

'Good evening.' He took the menu she handed him. But his
quick eye had already noticed the bottle of wine. 'You've
ordered, I expect. What have you chosen?' When she told
him, he said to the waitress, 'I'll have the same as Miss
Murray.'

'No, the ferry wasn't late,' he went on, when they were
alone. 'But there was an old lady on board whose friend
hadn't turned up to meet her. As the friend was also an old
person, who might have been taken ill, I felt I ought to check
it out rather than leaving her in the hands of a taxi-driver.
We'd been talking most of the way over, and it seemed
discourteous to say goodbye and walk away. You may think
that was being inconsiderate of your feelings, but I felt my
being late for our date wouldn't upset you as much as she was
upset.'

'I wasn't in the least upset. I merely assumed the ferry had
broken down or something,' she said casually. 'Was the friend
all right?'

'Yes, there'd been some minor catastrophe which had
delayed her. Nothing serious. I wondered if I might find Todd

here. When I didn't turn up on time, you didn't think of asking him to join you?'

'No.'

'Enjoy the picnic?'

'Very much, thank you. How was your day with Emerald and her mother?'

'They've agreed to my suggestion. In fact they were already thinking of coming over here before I suggested they should stay with us.'

'With us?' she echoed, her eyes puzzled.

'Before giving you my backing in the guesthouse project, I think you should have a trial run. Mrs Wigan and Emerald are willing to be your paying guinea-pigs, as it were. Their present lease ends in two weeks. They'll then come here for a month. If you can cope with them, you'll have proved your potential capacity to handle a houseful of people.'

Her immediate reaction was to tell him he must be mad: the house couldn't possibly be ready for guests in two weeks' time, and expecting her to cater to the Wigans—people accustomed to every comfort—in the building in its present state was expecting the impossible.

However, as she drew breath to expostulate, it struck her that more than once her ex-boss had expected the impossible of her. It had never occurred to her to remonstrate with him.

Hawk had no power of hire and fire over her; but he was in a position to frustrate her wish to keep the house. Therefore, instead of being instantly up in arms, she would serve her purpose much better by reacting as if he were her boss.

'Very well,' she said levelly. 'If Mrs Wigan and Emerald are willing, I have no objection to that.'

It seemed to her that, for an instant, his astute blue eyes held a warmth she had not seen before; a look which had nothing to do with her being a young and not unattractive female with whom he might amuse himself.

But perhaps she only imagined it. Seconds later he was looking at her hair, saying, 'You should wear your hair like that all the time. The way it was last night is too severe. I like this better'—as if he had a right to approve or disapprove of her hairstyles, and to let his gaze rest on her mouth as if he would like to be kissing it.

She ignored the flutter inside her and, studying the colour of her wine, said, 'Of course you've warned Mrs Wigan that we only have oil-lamps at present? If Emerald uses lots of electrical gadgets—heated rollers for her hair, and so on—she won't be able to with us.'

'As soon as they agreed to the scheme, I called various people I used to know. Work on the wiring, and on improvements to the kitchen, will be starting first thing tomorrow. By the time Emerald gets here, the house should have plenty of power for her stuff, and for your kitchen equipment.'

'In two weeks?' she said, with raised eyebrows. 'I should have thought that ... unlikely'—substituting this last word for her first choice which had been 'impossible'.

'It's amazing what can be done if you have the right contacts—and if you're prepared to pay for immediate service.'

'I don't doubt it—if money is no object. But I can't afford to pay a high premium for speed. Surely the usual procedure is to ask for several quotations and accept the most competitive one?'

'Don't worry. I'm prepared to pay all the bills at this stage of the operation. If the scheme works, you can pay me back out of profits. If it doesn't, we can add the cost of renovations to the selling price. I'll also arrange for a telephone to be installed as soon as possible, and for the exterior to be painted.'

She said, 'That was something I was planning to do. I like painting. I could be doing up the outside while the electricians are busy inside.'

'At the top of a twenty-foot ladder? I think not,' Hawk replied firmly. 'You can do some interior painting and decorating, if you like, and I think you should make an inventory for insurance purposes.'

By this time they had finished the first course and the waitress was serving what in America was called the entrée, although in England that term meant a dish served between the first and main courses.

As the days passed, Caroline was discovering more and more linguistic differences between the two countries. Most were unimportant; some could cause misunderstandings and perhaps give unintentional offence.

From a menu of classic dishes she had chosen the duck *à l'orange* and, for some minutes after its arrival, they concentrated on their food.

'What I don't see,' she said, at length, 'is how you benefit from the scheme? Are you expecting to share the profits of the guest house? If I'm going to do all the work, I don't feel inclined to share the proceeds. They're not going to be very large for the first year anyway. At the same time you're giving up the income which you would have had if I had been willing to sell the house.'

'But retaining a property which should appreciate in value and—I hope—keep pace with inflation,' was his reply. 'To answer your question: No, I don't expect to share the profits. I won't even press you to repay your share of the renovation costs until you're comfortably established. If, in fact, you get to that point,' he added, with a hint of scepticism.

'If you're not completely confident that I shall, why agree to my plan in the first place?'

'Complete confidence is over-confidence. One of the things I've learned from associating with top level businessmen is that they always assess what they stand to lose if an investment is a flop. The majority of unsuccessful businessmen have only thought about what they stood to gain from a venture. In this instance, I've nothing to lose and perhaps a great deal to gain.'

He raised his wine glass to his lips and drank from it, his blue eyes narrowed and enigmatic as they met her look of enquiry.

'In what way?' Caroline asked him eventually, when it seemed he didn't intend to enlarge on his statement.

Her puzzlement seemed to amuse him. 'At this stage I'm not ready to say. Ask me again in a few weeks. By then I should know for sure.'

'You're talking in riddles. I'm baffled,' she said, with a shrug. But the germ of a nasty suspicion was lurking at the back of her mind.

'One good thing has already emerged. You are happier now, and less hostile. Shall we drink to the success of your venture?' As he spoke, he refilled their glasses.

'I think it would be better to wait until the end of my

probationary period to do that,' she said cautiously. 'Have you discussed terms with Mrs Wigan? Are they expecting full board, or bed and breakfast only?'

'They may want an occasional evening meal, but in general they like to eat out at night. They expect a cooked breakfast and a light lunch.'

When he told her the terms he had given them, Caroline did protest. 'But that's outrageously expensive! They could stay at the Ritz Carlton in Boston for that amount, I should imagine.'

'Very possibly; but so can anyone who can afford it. Your place will be far more exclusive. With only eight bedrooms, you should aim at being able to pick and choose your guests.'

Seeing that she wasn't convinced, he went on, 'We live in a world where a great many people believe that the more a thing costs the better it must be. It's not always true, but it's what they think, and you should take advantage of that belief.'

Caroline finished eating, touched her napkin lightly to her lips and leaned back in her chair.

'All right: so there are plenty of idiots who think that if anything costs an arm and a leg it must be better than something less expensive. But I'm not sure I want them in my guesthouse. I'd rather cater to the more intelligent types who want really good value for money and don't go in for conspicuous extravagance.'

'Then you'll never make your fortune,' Hawk said dryly.

'That isn't the object of the exercise. I only want to preserve a lovely old house and be gainfully and happily employed. You'll have to tell Mrs Wigan you made a mistake. Perhaps you could say you gave her the rate for full board in the high season. Even so it would be extortionate. *I'll* tell her what my rates are . . . when I've worked them out.'

'As you wish, but you'll be a fool if you give yourself too little profit. Agnes Wigan is a very rich woman. She's used to paying top dollar for everything and may feel she should move elsewhere if you make your charges too low.'

'How much is a cruise on your ship?' she asked.

'At present, one of the staterooms used by the original owner and her guests is twelve thousand dollars for one week's cruise for two people.'

'My God! You can buy a car for that!' Caroline exclaimed.

'Our passengers already have all the cars they need.'

'What do they get for their money? Caviar at every meal?'

'They get a king-sized bed, antique furniture, gold-plated faucets, the best food and wines and well-organised, interesting shore excursions. When we went to Barbados recently, we arranged to borrow a Palladian-style mansion built by Sir Ronald Tree on the west coast about forty years ago. It's a magnificent house with a fine garden and we laid on a supper party there. You don't get that sort of thing on the regular Caribbean cruises.'

After a pause, he added, 'Nor does an ordinary cruise liner look like *Damaris* with her masts and rigging alight and reflected in a flat calm sea. When she's lit up at night, she's almost as beautiful as she is under sail by moonlight. Sometimes, when she's ghosting, I take a few of the passengers out in one of the launches and show them the view from ahead of her.'

'The wondrous sight of the ivory Pequod bearing down upon her boats with outstretched sails, like a wild hen after her screaming brood,' she quoted.

It was a passage she had read that afternoon, while drying her hair in the sun.

'You've read *Moby Dick*?' For the second time since his arrival, it seemed to her that his eyes held a friendly interest which held nothing predatory in it.

'I haven't finished it yet. I found a copy in the house. It has your name in it.'

'I have another one now. It's a book which bears more than one reading. What do you think of it?'

'Dull in places ... riveting in others. What does the term ghosting mean?'

'It means when there's almost no wind and the ship is gliding along at two or three knots. If you hadn't committed yourself to this guesthouse project, you could have joined us on the voyage from Baltimore to Newport. The staterooms aren't normally used when we're taking part in a race. You could have had one of them—free.'

Caroline felt a pang of regret that she wouldn't be able to avail herself of the opportunity.

'What would the owners have to say if they found out you were letting someone enjoy all that *grand luxe* for nothing?' she queried.

'They allow me absolute discretion.'

She couldn't help wondering if she was not the first girl he had invited to sail on *Damaris* when she wasn't cruising, and if there were certain strings attached to such an invitation.

'Is Baltimore her home port now?' she asked.

'No, she's registered in the Cayman Islands, if you know where they are?'

'Somewhere in the Caribbean, aren't they? I'm not certain where.'

'West of Jamaica, which used to administer them. Since she became independent they've been a British Crown Colony with their own tax rules, and therefore a haven for companies which can think of better things to do with their profits than handing them over to governments to be spent on stockpiling bombs and building fall-out shelters for bureaucrats.'

'How many philanthropic projects does the company which owns your ship support?' she asked, with a rather sceptical smile.

'At the moment, every cent of their profits is spent on restoring another barque. It's a costly business to recommission an existing vessel. To lay the keel of a new one—which is what they hope to do next—is a multi-million-dollar investment.'

It was about half past ten when they left the restaurant. Hawk suggested they should cut through Martin's Lane and Plumb Alley to stretch their legs in a walk round the waterfront.

Some of the yachts and cruisers which had been there the day before had returned to the mainland, but others were still at their moorings with their owners and guests relaxing on deck, or strolling about the catwalks.

Caroline could not fail to notice the interested glances which her tall companion attracted, especially from women. She sensed that some of them were wishing themselves in her place, and probably wondering why he was not with a girl of as striking appearance as his own.

Near the Pacific Club there was a restaurant called the Club Car which was housed in an old railway carriage.

'Nantucket used to have a railroad,' Hawk told her, when she remarked that it was a strange thing to see on a small island thirty miles off the mainland. 'The first line ran from here out to Surfside, over on the south coast, and the first run was made on the Fourth of July in 1881. That was also the year of the great Coffin Family Reunion—five hundred of them, all descended from Tristram Coffin, one of the first Purchasers, and his wife Dionis. They had a party which lasted for three days, with a clambake and speeches and photographs. It must have been quite an occasion.'

As their leisurely, roundabout route brought them nearer to the house, Caroline began to wonder if he would kiss her.

If they hadn't been sharing a house, she would have liked him to kiss her. However, she felt that, in the circumstances, once he started kissing it might not be easy to stop him.

He was an experienced man, accustomed to going all the way. But she wasn't ready for that yet. Being in love with him wasn't enough. She had to know that he cared for her before she could give herself to him.

They entered the house by the front door, leaving it open so that the street lighting illumined the hall while he lighted an oil lamp. As its soft radiance fell on the glossy patina which strenuous rubbing with wax polish and soft clothes had restored to the furniture in the hall, he said, 'Shall we have some more coffee?'

She shook her head. 'If we're going to have workmen arriving first thing tomorrow, I think I'll turn in. Would you light my candle for me, please?' She would have done it herself, but he was still holding the box of matches.

'Surely.'

He did as she asked. There was nothing in his manner to prepare her for what happened next.

As she moved near the table to pick up the old-fashioned candlestick with its drip tray and ring-shaped holder, Hawk intercepted her hand. His other arm slipped round her waist, pulling her to him.

As she drew in her breath, excited but also apprehensive, he looked down at her quivering lips and unsure grey eyes.

'I would rather light the fire inside you,' he told her softly.

His arms tightened, pressing her closer. His hands

drew hers upwards, uncurling her fingers, exposing her small, soft-skinned palm. He stroked it gently with his thumb, the light sensuous touch sending a delicious sensation streaking along the whole length of her arm. When he held her hand to his mouth, and she felt the warm pressure of his lips against her palm, and the hardness of his jaw beneath her fingertips. every nerve in her body vibrated in response.

He laid her hand against his chest. Then, with both arms round her, he bent his tall head towards hers.

'Shall I do that, Caroline?' he murmured huskily.

CHAPTER FIVE

WITHOUT giving her time to reply—which she couldn't have done, being hypnotised by the undisguised flare of desire in the narrowed blue eyes looking down at her—Hawk kissed her.

It was a different kind of kiss from yesterday's. Not only was she locked in his arms, but there was a fiercer demand in the way his mouth moved upon hers. As well as her own rapid heartbeats, she could feel the racing of his blood.

When at last he released her mouth, it was only to trail his lips across the smooth skin of her cheek to the soft place under her ear and, from there, to the base of her throat.

Caroline made an indistinct sound and her head sank backwards against his supporting hand as his warm lips explored her slim neck. The pleasure it gave her was almost painful in its intensity. Her own hands wandered over his shoulders, feeling their solid strength beneath the cloth of his blazer.

When his mouth returned to her lips, they were open in a soundless cry of ecstasy. She felt his powerful frame shudder, and the arm round her waist gripped more tightly, straining her to him. For an instant, she was afraid of the blaze of passion which her parted lips seemed to have ignited. And then, just when she thought his feelings were out of control and she'd have to fight her way free—if she could; if, indeed, she wanted to—he jerked up his head and put her away from him.

'No . . . I think not . . . not yet,' he said thickly.

They stared at each other for a moment. She could see the effort it had cost him to stop kissing her; and the iron control he was exerting not to snatch her back into his arms.

Thrusting the candlestick towards her, he said, 'Go to bed. Goodnight, Caroline.'

When they met for breakfast the next morning, his manner was casually friendly, as if their embrace had never happened; or had happened but didn't change anything.

Before they had finished doing the dishes, the electrical contractor and several workmen arrived. During the morning Caroline sorted out a cupboard in which she found a set of five open-topped baskets, their sizes graduated to allow them to fit together and form a nest.

When, at lunchtime, she showed them to Hawk, he said, 'They look as if they're some of the original lightship baskets made in the last century by the crew of the South Shoal Lightship.'

He had spent most of the morning conferring with the contractor about how the old house could be wired efficiently but unobtrusively. Once or twice they had canvassed her opinion on the placing of sockets and switches.

After lunch, she decided to take a couple of hours off to visit the Peter Foulger Museum to see if they had an exhibit of authentic lightship baskets. At the museum, she found that Nantucket basket-making had a history which went back much further than the nineteenth century. Splint baskets with woven bases had been made by the Indians. The collection included baskets made by Abram Quayr, the last descendant of the Algonquins who had inhabited the island long before the settlers' arrival.

The introduction of cane to replace hickory splints had been a spin-off from whaling. Nantucket's close contacts with the Pacific had brought the new material directly to the island. Gradually a distinctive type of basket had evolved; made on a wooden mould, and with a wooden base to anchor the ribs and produce a strong, durable container with many uses.

It was from this workaday product that the modern

handbag had evolved. First a basket-maker called Mitchie Ray, the grandson of a lightship captain, had devised the lidded basket. Then, after the second world war, Jose Reyes, a Philippines-born Harvard graduate who had wanted to live on the island but had failed to get a teaching job there, had made some more covered baskets and found such a ready sale for them that he had made a career of it.

The final development had been the addition of ivory latches and pins, ivory dowels to attach the wooden handles, and ebony and ivory carvings of whales, dolphins, seagulls and scallop shells on the wooden piece in the centre of the lid.

One of the finest carvers had been a woman, Aletha Macy, whose tools with some of her work were on display in a glass case. Caroline gazed with delight at a pair of ivory ear-rings in the form of tiny whales.

However, they didn't tempt her to look for a similar pair in the gift shops. At the time Miss Macy had been carving, and when Jose Reyes had first popularised the Nantucket basket as a chic accessory among Ivy League wives and daughters, there had been less widespread concern about the extinction of whales and the indiscriminate slaughter of elephants. Nor had the production of baskets become as over-commercialised as it was at present.

Caroline had moved away from the basket section, and was looking at a pair of silk stockings bought in Paris in 1832 by Henry Coffin for his fiancée, Eliza Starbuck, when Hawk appeared.

The sight of him, unexpectedly, made her heart give an odd little lurch.

He said, 'I've had a telegram from Baltimore. My bo'sun is seriously ill, and I have to fly back there immediately. There's a taxi outside. Come to the airport with me, will you? I'm in a hurry, but I want to talk to you before I leave.'

She followed him out of the museum.

'Do you know what's the matter with him?' she asked, as the taxi pulled away from the kerb.

'Peritonitis. Thank God it flared up now, not at sea. Even so it sounds touch and go. If they can't pull him through, I shall have lost one of my best officers and a valued friend,' he said heavily.

'I'm not sure what a bo'sun does,' said Caroline.

'He's the officer—or sometimes a seaman—responsible for the maintenance of a ship's boats, and her sails, rigging, cordage, cables and anchors. On a sailing ship, he plays a key role. I don't know how long I'll be gone. You'll have to cope as best you can.'

'Of course . . . no problem,' she assured him.

'No, most likely there won't be; but if anything should crop up which you feel you can't handle, I can be reached at this number.' He gave her a card. 'It may not be too much longer before you have a number I can call.'

He put his hand over her wrist. 'I want your promise that you'll have a careful check round the whole house every night from now on. Whenever there are workmen in a place, there's always a risk that one of them will be careless with a cigarette butt. I don't think that's likely to happen—most people here are fire-conscious—but it only takes one dummy to start a blaze. I'm not concerned about the house. I'm concerned about your safety.'

The tone in which he said this, and the way his fingers tightened on her wrist, made her disappointment at his going change to a sudden surge of happiness.

'I'll be careful,' she promised. Struck by a thought which she knew should have occurred to her before, she asked, 'Is there any insurance cover? I forgot to ask the lawyers about that.'

'I didn't. Yes, the place is covered, although not to the extent it should be in view of its current market value. If it's okay with you, I'll call my insurance brokers and get them to cover the house and its contents. When you've finished making the inventory, my brokers will probably want to send one of their experts to check the value of all the antiques, and they may insist we have special locks fitted. A more immediate concern is the choice of new kitchen fitments. I shall have to leave that in your hands. My feeling is that, although it should include all the latest equipment, the kitchen ought not to look like the inside of a space capsule.'

'I agree. An ultra-modern kitchen wouldn't be appropriate. I know just how it should look. Don't worry; I shan't make a botch of it.'

'I'm certain you won't. Your good taste is obvious,' he told her.

His praise made her flush with pleasure. 'What time does the New York plane leave?' she asked, with a glance at her watch. It was clear that the driver of the taxi had been asked to go as fast as he could.

'I'm not going via New York. I'm flying directly to Baltimore. Luckily there's a plane here I can rent for as long as I need it.'

'You don't mean you're going to fly yourself there?'

'Why not? It's the quickest way.'

'I suppose so. When did you learn to fly?'

'A long time ago. It seemed a useful thing to be able to do, as is proved by the present emergency.'

It was only a five-dollar ride from town to the airport and, at the speed they were travelling, it didn't take long to arrive.

'No need for you to get out, Caroline,' said Hawk, as the vehicle drew to a halt. He handed the driver some money. Then he turned back to her. 'Goodbye. Take care of yourself.'

'You, too.'

Her reply was husky, for she found she had a lump in her throat.

He leaned towards her and kissed her lightly on the mouth—a fleeting brushing of lips which nevertheless made her heart give a convulsive leap. An instant later he was on his feet outside the taxi.

She watched him stride away and disappear into the airport building. Then she noticed the driver watching her in his rearview mirror and realised that her own vision was blurred.

'Okay to go back now?' he asked.

She blinked away the foolish tears. 'Yes, please.'

But had she been driving herself, she would have waited to see Hawk's plane take off. How far away was Baltimore? She knew it was somewhere along America's eastern seaboard, but she had no idea how many miles south of Nantucket.

When they were back in town she asked the driver to drop her at the Atheneum. She had been planning to join the library before long, and now it was a matter of urgency to look at an atlas and start improving her knowledge of the geography of her homeland. From now on, it was going to be that in every sense of the word.

Presently she found that Baltimore was situated at the inner end of Chesapeake Bay, about a hundred and fifty miles from the ocean, and not far from Washington, D.C. Taking a direct line, it seemed to be about three hundred and seventy miles from Nantucket.

She wondered how long it would take him to reach there, and wished she had some means of knowing he had arrived safely. No doubt he was an excellent pilot, but not all the other people flying small aircraft—and in America, she knew, it was a much more common form of self-transport than in Europe—might be as careful as he was.

She left the library with an armful of books and a card signed by the librarian which read *This card certifies that Caroline Murray is entitled to the privileges of this institution.* It was the first tangible evidence that this was where her future lay.

But did it?

Now that she had fallen in love with Hawk, her future was no longer in her control. It depended on him; on the possibility that he might reciprocate her feelings.

He had admitted to being powerfully attracted to her. The fact that last night he could have gone much further but hadn't, and today had expressed concern for her safety in his absence, seemed to predicate a growing affection.

Long after he had sent her to bed on her own, she had lain awake knowing that, if he had chosen to seduce her, she would not have resisted.

Why had he suddenly stopped kissing her? What had he meant by: *No . . . I think not . . . not yet?*

She could only assume it was because she had admitted to being inexperienced that he hadn't followed through his advantage.

Maybe it was a matter of principle with him never to be a girl's first lover. Not that it was a circumstance which was likely to arise very often now that he was well into his thirties. No doubt there were other girls of her age who, for various reasons, had never made love; but certainly they were a minority, and most of the virgins he encountered would be too young for him.

On the other hand, if a man were beginning to fall in love, sex was not his primary objective. It was part of love, an important part. But real love—the kind which lasted a lifetime—could wait for physical fulfilment. Perhaps that was what distinguished it from infatuation.

With these thoughts and hopes in her mind, Caroline cooked herself supper, and later obeyed Hawk's instruction to look round the house and make sure the electricians had left everything in good order. They had worked late. She wondered how much it was costing to have them do a rush job.

The next day another team of men began work on the redecoration of the exterior. This raised the first decision she had to make on her own. The man who employed the painters wanted to know what colour scheme she had in mind.

By this time she had read part of the Atheneum's copy of *Old Houses On Nantucket*, the book recommended by Todd.

Referring to the exterior of a typical Nantucket house of a somewhat earlier date than Captain Starbuck's, the author, Kenneth Duprey, had written: *The shingled walls are usually left to weather, their colour varying with the weather. After a driving north-easter they are almost black, and when they have been dried by the sun they become a soft, silvery gray. The trim is usually painted, although the present habit of painting the trim white is a fairly modern innovation. Originally the trim was a dull red or was often left to weather like the shingles.*

She thought it a pity James Starbuck had not had the façade of his house shingled to match the sides and back. She could then have revived the dull red trim of earlier eras. However, as he had preferred a clapboard front, she decided to have it re-painted pale primrose yellow—a colour which looked well on several other houses in town—with white windows and a white front door.

For the rest of that week nearly all her time was devoted to sorting and listing. But every afternoon she allowed herself some time off to pay further visits to the fascinating miscellany of objects in the Foulger Museum, or to continue her exploration of the environs.

One day, wandering among the early headstones in the old north cemetery, she came upon a horizontal slab inscribed with a memorial verse. The names of the occupants of the grave had gone, but one or both of them had been only twenty years old.

Standing beside their last resting place, wondering why they had died so young, Caroline read:

spotless honor and unsullied truth
smiling innocence and blooming youth
female sweetness joined with manly sense
and winning wit that never gave offence
modesty that never wore a frown
and goodness that may claim a Heavenly crown
if virtues such as these deserve a tear
here pour thy grief for they are buried here!

The cemetery reminded her of her father, although she knew she wouldn't find his grave on the island. When the sea had given up his body, it had been taken to the mainland for burial, Kiki had told her.

That night she wrote to her mother, breaking the news that she meant to remain in America; and also to her brother, asking him if he could spare a weekend to pack up her most personal belongings and arrange for her bed and other furniture to be returned to Thornbridge Manor.

With Hawk away in Baltimore, and Mrs Wigan and her daughter arriving in two weeks, I can't possibly leave here at present, she wrote to him, having previously explained the guest house plan. *I know it will be a nuisance for you, but I should be so grateful if you could handle it for me. What news of your legacy? Have you heard who has inherited the Villa des Anges?*

Kiki's house in the south of France had taken its name from a piece of mediaeval stone carving, depicting a pair of winged angels, which had been built into the structure above the main entrance.

The next morning Todd reappeared. Inevitably, he was astonished to find the refurbishment of the house already advanced when the Sunday before the scheme had still been in the air.

Caroline had expected him to be delighted that Hawk had agreed to her wishes. Instead his reaction was lukewarm. Very soon it was clear there was something worrying him.

'What's the matter, Todd? What's on your mind?' she asked him, at length.

He frowned. 'I don't like running anyone down, Caroline, but the fact is I've found out some things about Lowell which make me wish you weren't in any way involved with him.'

'What sort of things? You mean he isn't who he claims to be?'

'Oh, yes, he's everything he says he is. I had him checked out by a journalist friend who came up with an article about him, or rather about his ship and the kind of people who can pay twelve thousand dollars for a week of high living at sea.'

'What did it say about Hawk that you find disquieting?'

'That although he was a first class captain, he was also one hell of a stud where women were concerned. The writer gave a list of passengers—actresses, models and other good-looking women—whose names have been linked with his. One or two of them virtually admitted that a shipboard romance with the captain had been the best thing about the cruise, and the writer of the article hinted that Lowell is more familiar with the king-size beds in the staterooms than with the single bed in his own quarters.'

'It sounds libellous to me. What rag was this article in?' was Caroline's first reaction.

'No rag. It was a feature in one of the top glossies.'

'Did your friend get a copy of it for you? Did you bring it with you?'

'No ... no, I didn't. This was published more than a year ago. I know someone in the magazine's New York office, and they arranged for me to look through their file of back numbers. You don't imagine I'd make up something like this, do you? I can get a copy to show you if you want proof of what I'm telling you,' he said, in an injured tone.

'No, I know *you* wouldn't make it up. But it sounds as if the writer of the article might have exaggerated Hawk's amorous propensities. I shouldn't have thought a ship's captain would have time for intensive womanising. If he isn't always on duty, he's certainly always on call.'

'It's a cruise ship, not a Navy ship. I doubt they'd disturb him at night except for a major emergency.'

Caroline said lightly, 'Okay, so Hawk is, or has been, why my old Nannie would call a ladykiller. Most attractive men are—until they find the right girl. If a beautiful actress made it clear she was willing to have a fling with you, what would you do? Turn her down?'

'Maybe not, but there's a difference between having

some relationships with women and getting around the way he does. What concerns me is that sooner or later he may try making it with you.'

'I doubt it. I'm not a famous beauty, I'm not throwing myself at him, and we're involved in a business venture together. Business and pleasure don't mix. I'm sure Hawk knows that,' she said, trying to sound cool and detached.

But even as she stated the reasons why Todd's anxiety was unnecessary, she couldn't help wondering if it was the third reason which had caused Hawk to break off the embrace which might otherwise have developed into a heavy and successful pass at her. Had it been, as she wanted to believe, a chivalrous desire not to take advantage of her inexperience which had made him stop kissing her last Sunday? Or had it been only self-interest? Because, for him, there were plenty of other pebbles on the beach, and he could afford to pass up an opportunity which might complicate their association as co-owners.

To her relief, Todd let the subject drop.

'Are you shopping at A. & P. this morning? If so, I'll help you carry your groceries home,' he offered.

'Thanks, but as they stay open late I did my weekend shopping last night to avoid the Saturday morning crush,' she explained. 'I am going into town this morning, but only for a few odds and ends. I forgot to buy toothpaste yesterday, and I need some postcards and stamps.'

'If you're on your own this weekend, maybe you'd like to come to a party tonight?' he suggested. 'The hosts are New Yorkers who spend a lot of time here. They have a large shingle-style house on the north side of town, and they give a lot of good parties. They left a note under my door inviting me along, and saying I should bring my house-guest if I had one. They'll be delighted to meet you, and you'll enjoy yourself. They have a heated swimming pool, and there'll be dancing, and Janie puts on a great buffet.'

Had he asked her to dine *à deux* she would have demurred. But a party was another matter, and she saw no reason to turn down an opportunity to widen her acquaintance on the island.

'Thank you, Todd, I'd like to come with you.'

'Great! I'll pick you up at seven.'

They walked into town together.

'I'm going to ask the bookshop to order me a copy of the Duprey book,' she told him. 'It's the kind of book you want to own rather than borrow, and also I think a good guesthouse should have a collection of books for the use of visitors who are interested in Nantucket's history.'

However, although Mitchell's Book Corner had a room at the back of the shop devoted to the island's literature, she was told the title she wanted was at present out of print.

'Is there anywhere I might get hold of a second-hand copy?' she asked.

'You could try the Island Attic.'

When she asked for directions, Todd said, 'I know it. I'll take you there, Caroline.'

They walked down to the bottom of the square and round the corner of the building which had a large compass painted on the side of it, with the distance from Nantucket to cities all over the globe. Presently they came out on Washington Street, close to the southern shore of the huge landlocked harbour.

Since Hawk's departure, Caroline hadn't bought any newspapers and, without television or radio, had been out of touch with world events. As they walked, Todd brought her up to date. Although she didn't say so to him, she found she wasn't much interested in the latest disasters and crises.

How much happier people must have been in the days when news travelled slowly, and wars and rumours of wars weren't a daily diet, she thought to herself. In Nantucket, by ignoring the media, it was possible to recapture the mood of earlier times when people had only had to grapple with their personal problems and not take all the world's troubles on their shoulders.

Presently the tarred road swung inland and the shore route became a dirt road. This led to a large barn-like structure, its stoop crowded with second-hand furniture. The interior reminded her of an English junk shop. There were shelves of books near the door, including some about the island, but not the one she was looking for.

When she asked if they had ever had a copy of it, the person in charge said, 'Yes, we've had it, and we have a lot of enquiries for it. But the second-hand copies are much more expensive than the book was originally. They're around fifty dollars or more.'

'Oh, in that case I can't afford it,' Caroline said regretfully.

As they walked back the way they had come, Todd said, 'Why don't I give you a hand with your back yard? I used to earn money gardening when I was a kid. I know which are weeds and which aren't. In fact, if you'll fix me some lunch, I'll get started on it right away.'

It was difficult to refuse the offer, especially as the garden behind the house was urgently in need of attention. Apart from the work Hawk had done in clearing the path, the garden was a wilderness of long grass and overgrown shrubs.

'I can hire someone to clear the garden. You have better uses for your time. You should be painting, or just relaxing.'

'I can use the exercise. It will be good for my waistline. I'd like to feel I'd done something to help you get started.'

With some reluctance, Caroline accepted his offer. She wasn't easy in her mind about it. But, short of being pointedly cool towards him—and she couldn't bring herself to be that—it was difficult to see how she could discourage him from visiting her and being supportive.

From the time they returned to the house until six in the evening, with about an hour's break for lunch and a shorter break at four, Todd toiled in the garden. Before a mower could be used on it, the tall grass which had once been a lawn had to be slashed down with a long curved blade which Hawk had found and sharpened the Saturday before.

She had an uneasy feeling that, unaccustomed to manual labour and not being as fit as Hawk, Todd would pay for his afternoon's exertions with aching muscles and ligaments. However she failed to persuade him to stop work earlier. When he went home to shower and change, although he looked hot and his shirt was drenched with sweat, he did not seem unduly exhausted.

An hour later he was back, refreshed and spruce, wearing his Nantucket reds with a pink shirt and a navy blue blazer similar to Hawk's.

As he had said the party would be very informal, but there would be dancing, she had put on a dress bought at Mary Farrin's shop in South Molton Street, a fashionable street in London. In England Mary Farrin's knit dresses were recognisable by the airy texture of the fabric—sometimes as

soft and fine as a Shetland christening shawl—and by the
subtlety of the designer's colours. Caroline's dress was the
same smoky grey as her eyes. She had changed the narrow
cord belt for a wider band of pewter ribbon fastened with an
eighteenth-century shoe-buckle. This she had bought for a few
pounds in a country antique shop because its companion was
missing.

Her ear-rings were more flamboyant than her everyday gold
hoops. They had been a present from Rob: pieces of turquoise
and coral interspaced with small silver beads.

'You look gorgeous,' said Todd admiringly.

'Thank you.'

As they set out, she couldn't help wishing it were Hawk
who was taking her to the party, and wondering how he was
spending this Saturday evening. Perhaps at the bedside of his
friend, if the man had recovered; perhaps with the bo'sun's
widow, doing what he could to comfort her.

When Todd had referred to their hosts' house as shingle-
style, what he had meant, she discovered, was that it was
cladded with cedar shingles but was otherwise larger and freer
in form than the houses in the historic area of town with their
pitched roofs, Georgian windows and the extensions called
warts at the side of the original buildings.

Like the other large houses in the neighbourhood, the one
where the party was taking place had been designed to
accommodate an affluent family and their staff at the turn
of the century. If, today, the staff had been replaced by
modern gadgets and outside caterers, the air of affluence
remained.

Todd received a vivacious greeting from his hostess. When
he introduced Caroline, Janie made her feel she was the most
welcome and interesting newcomer to their circle in several
years.

She herself was a slim, grey-haired woman dressed in an
emerald silk shirt and a skirt patterned with emerald, lime
green and yellow on a white ground. During the evening
Caroline saw several women wearing dresses and skirts in
equally striking combinations of vivid colour Later she learnt
they were all designs by Lilly Pulitzer of Palm Beach.

'It's an unusual name. Is there any connection between her
and the Pulitzer prizes?' Caroline asked the woman whose

scarlet and hot pink pants she had admired.

'Yes, the prizes were endowed by Joseph Pulitzer, the proprietor of the *New York World*. Lilly's first husband was his grandson. She didn't start out to be a designer. Her stepfather was Ogden Phipps, the thoroughbred owner, and she went to Miss Porter's School in Farmington, Connecticut, with people like Jackie Onassis. Her marriage to Peter Pulitzer didn't work out, although they had three lovely children, and after a doctor had advised her to find something to do, she got into designing by accident. Now her annual gross is around fifteen million dollars a year, and you never go to a country club or a yacht club without seeing someone in her clothes. These pants I have on are two years old, but, because they're lined with white batiste, they wash and wear forever.'

'They're stunning,' Caroline told her.

'Thank you. Most of her prints have her signature *Lilly* hidden in the pattern. I guess the reason this print doesn't is because the pink flowers are lilies.'

'Can you only buy them in Palm Beach?' asked Caroline, wondering why Kiki had never worn them. Then she remembered that her benefactor had adored flowered English and French chintzes for slip-covers, and flower-sprigged porcelain and flower paintings. But on herself she had worn only solid colours.

'Goodness, no! You can buy them everywhere. Except in New York, oddly enough. I think she has thirty shops, mainly in resorts like Newport. You can buy them here at Murray's new branch at the Harbour House, and sometimes they have them at close-out prices at Murray's warehouse outlet on New Street. But the Lillys there tend to be in very big sizes, and you're an eight, I imagine?'

Caroline was about to say that she was an American ten when their clothes-chat was interrupted by a man who, having been introduced to her, began a lighthearted flirtation.

He had only been with her a few minutes when Todd reappeared and swept her off to have supper. He performed this manoeuvre with less aplomb than she would have expected of Hawk in similar circumstances. She didn't mind being retrieved—the other man had been too pleased with himself to be likeable—but the possessive way Todd took her arm to steer her to the buffet table was a little worrying.

The large Roman-shaped swimming pool which was the focal point of the garden was surrounded by a wide paved deck furnished with many comfortable blue-cushioned loungers and groups of white upright chairs arranged around circular tables with sunbrellas fitted to them. The low walls which separated the deck from the lawns provided additional seating and, as it was a fine, mild night, most people chose to eat their supper out of doors.

There was only a thin crescent moon in the cloudless sky, but the lights beneath the surface of the pool, and cleverly concealed flood-lamps among the trees and shrubs, provided plenty of illumination. Taped music, not too loud, was a pleasant background for the murmur of conversation punctuated by bursts of laughter.

Todd and Caroline shared a two-seater white cane sofa which probably belonged in the glass-walled garden room which, for tonight, had been cleared of everything but the buffet tables.

There were two canvas directors' chairs close to the sofa. Presently a couple they hadn't talked to before came and sat down and introduced themselves as Chip and Martha. The girl was Janie's niece and had been coming to Nantucket since she was a child. Chip was her bridegroom of six months.

By the time they had finished eating, Caroline could tell Todd was tired. Twice she noticed him stifling a yawn and guessed that the hours he had spent in her garden were beginning to catch up with him. However, when she remarked that after an arduous afternoon he wouldn't feel like staying up late, he denied his fatigue. To prove his energy, he was among the first to start dancing when the background music changed to something livelier.

Caroline had always loved dancing. She had a strong sense of rhythm and dancing had a champagne effect on her. After one dance she was more relaxed; after two she was beginning to sparkle in a way which surprised people who thought of her as a quiet, rather serious girl—a good listener, and nice, but a little lacking in bezazz.

When she and Rob danced with each other, other people on the floor stopped to watch them. They were both crazy about old tap-dance movies starring Fred Astaire and Gene Kelly, and had picked up a few of the routines which, when they were dancing together and the music was right, they would try out, just for the fun of it.

At first, moving to the music with Todd, she watched to see what kind of dancer he was. There was no way of telling beforehand. She could think of a friend of her stepfather, a burly man in his fifties, who was a better dancer than his sons.

Todd seemed to be about average. When, after a couple of fast numbers, the tempo changed to something slower and sweeter, he drew her close, she realised that this, for him, was the real purpose of dancing—the chance to hold a girl close and press his cheek against hers. Perhaps it wasn't always his object; but it certainly was tonight.

Had it been Hawk who was holding her, the slow music could have gone on for ever. With Todd it lasted too long. She couldn't relax in his arms for fear of giving him the impression that she was enjoying the contact as much as he seemed to be. At the same time she couldn't hold herself away from him too noticeably. Striking a balance between yielding and straining away was as tricky as dancing with a much shorter man and having to sag at the knees in an effort to reduce her own height.

To her relief the smoochy number was followed by the livelier beat of one of her favourite South American songs, *The Girl from Ipanema*. Free of Todd's encircling arms, she surrendered to the lilting beat of the bossa-nova.

The soft folds of her skirt swirled into fullness as her slim hips swayed to the rhythm. Her feet flew over the polished stone surface of the dance floor. Every part of her body—her shoulders, arms, hands, even the swing of her hair—expressed her response to the music. Unaware how much of her inner self was revealed by the fluid movements, the perfect timing and the glow on her face, Caroline let the music sweep her away.

'My God, you really can dance! Did no one ever suggest you should do it professionally?' Todd asked her afterwards, as they went to the bar where two white-coated waiters were kept busy replenishing glasses.

'You must be joking,' she answered. 'If I'd suggested dancing as a career, both my school and my parents would have done everything to discourage me. I did think about it at one stage, but not until I was fifteen or sixteen, by which time it was too late. Anyway, I'm not that good.'

'I think you're terrific—and so did a lot of other people.'

To confirm his opinion, Janie came up behind them, saying, 'You didn't tell me Caroline was a dancer, Todd.'

'She isn't, but you're right—that's what she should have been.'

Their hostess stayed chatting to them for several minutes. Presently he said, 'Janie, it's a great party, but we have to slip away early tonight.'

'Must you? That's too bad.'

After Caroline had made some complimentary remarks about the delicious supper and the attractions of the garden, Janie moved away to speak to other guests.

'You don't mind leaving early, I hope,' said Todd when, having finished their drinks, they made an unobtrusive departure. 'I guess I am a little tired now.'

'I don't mind at all,' she assured him.

As they drove the short distance back to Captain Starbuck's house, she wondered if he meant to kiss her goodnight. She hoped not but, if he did, she would have to make it clear there could never be anything but friendship between them.

However whether Todd had been intending to end the evening in that way was something she never found out. When the house came into view, the parlour windows were alight.

For an instant Caroline wondered if they were about to surprise a burglar at work. Then she realised that no thief would have lit the lamps and left the blinds up so that he could be seen from the house across the street.

'Hawk must have come back!' she exclaimed excitedly.

Todd muttered something under his breath which suggested that he didn't share her pleasure at this turn of events.

When the car stopped, she didn't wait for him to come and open the door for her. She opened it herself, swinging her feet to the ground before asking, 'Will you come in for a nightcap?'

'I don't think so, thanks. Not this time.'

'Thank you for taking me to the party—and for all your hard work in the garden today.'

'My pleasure.'

'Goodnight, Todd.'

'Goodnight.'

He waited until she had climbed the steps and turned to give him a final wave before he drove away. She couldn't be certain, but she suspected he was annoyed by the unexpected return of a man he distrusted.

As she expected, the front door was unlocked. With a swift glance at her reflection in the mirror above the hall table—she would have liked to retouch her lipstick but didn't want Hawk to come into the hall and catch her at it—she opened the door of the parlour.

He was seated in the high-backed winged chair on the far side of the fireplace. He had been reading and kept the book, closed, in his hand as he rose to his feet when she entered.

But her smiling 'Hello, Hawk' was met with a grim expression which she assumed must be caused by an unhappy outcome of his trip to Baltimore.

Her smile fading in the face of his sternness, she said, 'If I had thought you might come back, I shouldn't have gone out this evening. What time did you arrive?'

'Before dusk.'

'Have you eaten?'

'Yes. When have you been?'—eyeing her dress and the light-reflecting buckle on the velvet belt.

'To a party. It was given by some friends of Todd's. He thought I might like to start getting to know people. We came away early because he's been clearing the garden most of the day and I think he's pretty tired.'

'I shouldn't have thought a little gardening would have exhausted him,' he said sardonically. 'Perhaps he hoped to continue the party here, but hadn't bargained for my being around.'

'Todd did more than a little gardening. He worked hard for five or six hours. That's a long stint for anyone who isn't accustomed to physical work.'

'Exactly. Which might make a less naïve girl ask herself what reward he had in mind,' he said cynically.

All her delight in his return dashed by his unpleasant attitude, she retorted, 'It may be hard for *you* to believe, but there are people whose actions are prompted by disinterested kindness!'

'There are also girls who don't encourage expectations which they have no intention of fulfilling,' he returned. 'I would have said you were one of them. Maybe I was wrong.'

Beginning to be angry, she said, 'I have never encouraged Todd to expect anything from me but friendship. Anyway, I can't see that our relationship is any of your business.'

The instant she had said this, she regretted it; realising that what she longed for above all things was for everything about her to be a matter of the deepest concern to him.

Hawk gave her a long, hard look. 'Perhaps it isn't,' he said coldly. 'If you'll excuse me, I'll say goodnight.'

In stricken silence—at this moment it was hard to believe he had kissed her goodbye—Caroline let him stride past her into the hall.

Then, knowing she couldn't bear to go to bed with this wall of hostility between them, she called, 'Hawk ... please ... wait a minute!'

He was five or six steps above her when she followed him into the hall.

'Yes?' Both the upward flick of his eyebrow, and his tone, denoted impatience.

'Your bo'sun ... is he all right?'

He didn't answer her immediately. She had a sinking feeling it would have been better not to ask.

Then, his tone a little less clipped than when he had bade her goodnight, he said, 'He's alive. He's still ill. Unfortunately they had to give him gentamicin—it's an antibiotic which is known to cause damage to the ears which can upset or even destroy a person's ability to balance. How severely Nils will be affected we don't yet know. It could mean he'll have to give up the sea, which, for him, would be like taking away his freedom.'

'I'm sorry,' she said sincerely. 'It must be very worrying for you—both as his friend and his Captain. Will the company pay for him to have the best possible treatment?'

'Yes, that's no problem.'

'Are you going back to Baltimore?'

'Some time on Monday. I came back to check how things were going along here. Have you had any problems?'

She shook her head. 'Not so far. Are you sure you wouldn't like a hot drink before you go up? I'm going to have one.'

'No, thanks, Caroline. I'll see you at breakfast. Goodnight.'

He continued his way up the staircase, leaving her to go to the kitchen where she made herself a cup of coffee, feeling a little less cast down than she had a few minutes earlier.

She could see that if Hawk had flown all the way from Baltimore to make sure that her project was progressing smoothly, it must have been more than a little exasperating to arrive and find the house empty. But why hadn't he sent a telegram to say he was coming? It was rather unreasonable to assume that, even at the weekend, she would spend every evening at home.

At breakfast the following morning they again shared the *New York Times* and had little conversation until Hawk said suddenly, 'It looks like a good day for you to start learning to sail. Unless you've already made other plans?'

'No . . . . none. I'd love to go sailing. Do you know where to hire a boat?'

Less than an hour later, with Hawk carrying the cooler containing their picnic lunch, they walked down towards the waterfront.

Loath to risk disrupting this morning's harmony, but feeling that good manners obliged her to take that chance, Caroline said, 'If you don't mind, I should have a quick word with Todd. He may be thinking of doing some more work in the garden, and I should tell him we're going to be out today.'

Hawk's reaction was enigmatic, but at least he didn't look as thunderous as he had the night before.

He was at her heels as she climbed the stairs to Todd's door. She was slightly surprised to find it closed. On their previous visit, it had seemed that he usually left it open to let in more sunlight.

For a few moments after she knocked it seemed there was nobody there. She knocked again. This time there was a sound like a groan, followed by some inaudible words.

When, after further delay, the door opened, it was immediately obvious that Todd had been woken up and was not at his best. Not only was he unshaven, with tousled hair, but he looked heavy-eyed and his posture was stooped like that of an elderly man.

'Caroline!' He looked taken aback and embarrassed at finding her on his doorstep.

'I'm sorry if I've dragged you out of bed, Todd. The thing is that Hawk is taking me sailing and I thought I ought to stop by and tell you, in case you were thinking of coming up to see us today. Are you all right?'—this because, while she was speaking, he had pulled himself upright with an involuntary grimace.

'Yes, yes—I'm fine. A little stiff in the shoulders, that's all. A hot shower will loosen me up. Hi!'—with a nod to Hawk which made him wince again.

'Goodness, you are stiff,' said Caroline. 'I should never have let you go on working so long yesterday. Now your Sunday is spoiled. It is a shame.'

Presently, when they had left him, Hawk said drily, 'Don't let his aches blight your day. They're at least sixty per cent self-inflicted.'

'You mean because he overdid the gardening?'

'No, because he overdid the liquor. How much did he have to drink at the party?'

'Very little. Not more than two or three lagers.'

'Judging by the half empty bottle which I noticed on a table in there, he had more than a couple of vodkas before he turned in last night. You may not recognise a hangover, but I do. That guy was feeling like hell. Even the sun was hurting him.'

She had to concede that Todd had seemed glad to say goodbye and retreat into the dimmer light of his curtained room.

'He did *look* rather bleary,' she agreed. 'But somehow I can't see him as a solitary drinker.'

He shrugged. 'How long have you known him?'

Caroline didn't want to be drawn into another verbal skirmish over Todd. Seeking a way to avoid that, she said lightly, 'Longer than I've known you, but he doesn't have Kiki's seal of approval, as it were. How did you and she meet? Not through your grandfather, presumably?'

'No, we met by chance in a restaurant in the south of France. She stopped at my table and said, "Young man, whether you know it or not, you must be descended from

Captain James Starbuck of Nantucket." Naturally I knew who she was, but only her public persona. Ben had never mentioned her to me. She told me that story, later on.'

'How long ago did you meet her?'

'About ten years ago. I was second officer on a German millionaire's super-cruiser. Have you ever seen pictures of Adnan Khashoggi's *Nabila*?'

She shook her head.

His mouth twisted sardonically. 'Two hundred and eighty-two feet of sea-going luxury, including a helicopter landing pad; and, in my opinion, one of the least attractive vessels ever launched. The German cruiser was smaller but in the same category. Her technical equipment was superb and I wanted experience of all the most modern devices. Also it polished my German.'

'Do you speak many languages?' Caroline asked.

'Only Gernan, French and some Spanish. There aren't many parts of the world where you can't get along with one of those three, plus English. How about you?'

'Fairly good French. Nothing else.'

Safely away from the disputatious subject of Todd, they continued an easy conversation until they arrived at the place where there were some small boats for rent.

It was, without question, the happiest morning of Caroline's life. From the moment when Hawk held out his hand to her and, steadied by the firm grasp of his lean brown fingers, she stepped into the well of the boat, she felt as much at ease there as the rest of her family felt when they swung into the saddle.

Later, thinking over her first sailing lesson, she realised it would have been normal to be nervous of doing the wrong thing, as she always had when on horseback. Especially as her instructor was a man who, when he chose, could fluster her more than anyone she had met.

But she wasn't nervous. She was confident. And Hawk proved an excellent teacher who, far from being bored by demonstrating and then letting her try the basic elements of seamanship, seemed to enjoy it as much as she did.

The breeze ruffled his thick dark hair, and his bronzed skin gleamed in the sunlight as he showed her how to handle the little dinghy. Inevitably there was a good deal of physical contact between them. At first she was too intent on what she was doing to be more than vaguely conscious of it.

But, towards the end of the morning, when she no longer had to concentrate quite as hard, she was often sharply aware of their bodies touching as they changed places, or moved their positions to improve the boat's trim.

If Hawk was equally aware of it, he gave no sign. At lunchtime, when they pulled the dinghy ashore, the conversation stayed on impersonal subjects such as weather signs and tide tables.

After lunch he surprised her by saying, 'If you don't mind, I'm going to catch up some sleep. I've had several short nights this week.'

Watching him set the alarm on his wrist watch, she wondered why he had gone short of sleep. Sailors were said to have a girl in every port. Perhaps there was one in Baltimore with whom he kept late hours when there.

She watched him lie down on the sand, his sweater folded into a makeshift pillow. Within minutes he was asleep, his deep chest rising and falling.

Caroline also lay down, but on her side, facing towards him, her head pillowed on her elbow. Her gaze ranged slowly over his supine form from his deck shoes and bare brown ankles up the long blue-jeaned legs and powerful thighs. She wished she could lie close beside him, her head on his shoulder, his arm round her.

Every hour in his company made her more deeply in love. But what he felt was still a mystery.

She must have fallen asleep. She was woken by something brushing her cheek. For an instant or two, disorientated, she thought she was lying under the beech trees at Thornbridge Manor and one of her mother's dogs had snuffed her cheek, or licked it. When she opened her eyes, she found Hawk on one knee beside her. 'Time to go back, sleepyhead.'

There was a note in his voice which she wanted to believe was tenderness. Had she been lying on her back, she might have remained there, looking up at him, mutely inviting him to kiss her. Because she was lying on her side, the arm she had used as a pillow felt cramped and uncomfortable. As she sat up and stretched it, he rose, still looking down at her but from a greater distance than before. Seen from the ground, his six feet three or four inches seemed a giant's height.

He offered a hand to help her up, and she took it, her fingers tingling with pins and needles as full circulation returned. Hawk drew her upright. For several seconds they stood close together, her face raised expectantly to his.

She felt certain he wanted to kiss her as much as she wanted it. But he didn't. He turned away and began to gather up their gear.

For some moments longer she stood there, watching him, baffled. Although he was busying himself with other things, now she could see that he wanted to make love to her. But, for a reason she couldn't fathom, he was controlling the urge. Why? If, as Todd alleged, he had been and possibly still was a notorious womaniser, why not with her?

He was taciturn on the way back; speaking only when it was necessary to give an instruction. Thinking of the evening ahead, she wondered if he planned to eat out. If not, they would be alone together for hours; a circumstance which might strain even his self-control.

However, when they returned to the house, they found Todd there. He was waiting for them on the back stoop, a box full of young plants beside him.

'I've been visiting with an old lady who gave me these for your garden. They should be planted right away, but I wasn't sure where you would want them, so I waited until you came back. I spent half an hour in a friend's jacuzzi this afternoon and it's cured my stiff back. I feel fine now.'

Caroline didn't know whether to be relieved by his presence or vexed. She wanted to be alone with Hawk, yet was half afraid of where it might lead. She knew she was his for the taking—but she didn't want to be taken without love and commitment on both sides.

'We do need new plants. Thank you, Todd. Where do you think these should go, Hawk?'

'That's your province. I know nothing about gardening,' he said indifferently. 'Excuse me, I'm going for a tub.' He left them together on the stoop.

By the time she and Todd had attended to all the plants, Hawk had bathed and changed, and reappeared with a glass of beer. When he offered one to Todd, the younger man said, 'Yes, thank you. By the way, I thought Caroline might be tired after a day on the water, and not feel like cooking—

especially with the kitchen the way it is—so I booked a table at the Ships Inn. For the three of us. I hope that's okay?'

When Caroline woke the next morning, she spent some time thinking about their strange evening *à trois*.

Obviously Todd saw himself in the role of a sheepdog protecting a lamb from a wolf, and the situation was not without its funny side. After dinner he had virtually invited himself back to their house for more coffee, and had remained rooted in the parlour until she had announced her intention of going up to bed.

Hawk could easily have got rid of him, had he wished, but had chosen to let him remain. She could only suppose that it suited him to have Todd there.

By the time she went down to breakfast the workmen had arrived. At no time that morning were she and Hawk alone together. When he left, soon after lunch, he didn't kiss her goodbye as he had the previous weekend.

Before the end of the following week the telephone had been installed. After she let him know her number, Hawk rang her every night for a short conversation. But he didn't come back for the weekend, being heavily engaged in matters to do with his ship.

The weekend that he was away, Todd brought her a copy of *Old Houses On Nantucket* which he had tracked down in New York. Knowing how much it must have cost him, her pleasure was mixed with embarrassment. She felt obliged to accept his invitation to dinner on Saturday night, but avoided spending time with him on Sunday with the legitimate excuse that she had too much to do preparing for the Wigans' arrival.

Hawk escorted them over from the Cape, having landed his plane at Hyannis instead of Nantucket.

The day before Caroline had spoken to Emerald on the telephone. She had thought it would be nice to celebrate the completion of the new kitchen by cooking a special dinner for them on their first night. In case there was anything which Mrs Wigan didn't like to eat, she had consulted her daughter before planning the menu.

When they arrived, it seemed doubtful that, without Hawk to pull and Emerald to push, Mrs Wigan would have succeeded in emerging from the taxi. She was an extremely stout woman wearing a pink and purple dress with a pink bag and matching shoes which looked uncomfortably tight on her plump little feet. The size of her feet and hands suggested that, basically, she was a petite woman. Neither her choice of clothing nor the blue rinse on her white hair was flattering to her high colour.

However, as she stood on the brick path, catching her breath after the effort of getting out of the taxi, Caroline noticed that the Yorkshirewoman had one of the most goodhumoured faces she had ever seen.

She went down the steps to greet her. 'Welcome to Captain Starbuck's house, Mrs Wigan. I'm Caroline Murray.'

'Pleased to meet you, Miss Murray.' Observant brown eyes looked her over and seemed to approve what they say.

Perhaps, long ago, Mrs Wigan's eyes had been as large and limpid as her daughter's. Now they were small and beady, reduced by the fullness of her cheeks. A slimmer woman of her age would have had wrinkles and crow's-feet. Her skin was unlined and of a delicate texture which owed nothing to make-up; she was not wearing any. But she did have on a great deal of jewellery; large gold ear-rings, three strands of pearls, a gold watch on one wrist, a jingling charm bracelet on the other, and a variety of rings including a very large solitaire diamond on the same finger as her old-fashioned plain gold wedding ring.

'As soon as I've shown you your rooms, I'll make some tea,' said Caroline, as she led the way upstairs. 'How do you like it? Strong or weak?'

'It can't be too strong for me, my dear,' said Mrs Wigan. 'I know they say strong tea is bad for you. What isn't bad for you nowadays? Three tea-bags to the pot is how I like it. I wouldn't use tea-bags at first, but they do save the mess of loose tea-leaves, so I've come round to using them now.'

By the time she reached the top of the staircase, she was short of breath and had to pause, her eyes taking everything in.

'My word! You've some lovely furniture. My husband liked everything modern. But to my mind there's nothing to touch the stuff they made years ago, all done by hand. When Albert and I was first married, we had furniture left to me by my old granny. Then he began to make money and out it all had to go. I would have kept it, myself, but there was no budging my hubby when he took an idea into his head. "From now, my lass, you're having nothing but the best," was what he said to me. And I did.'

There was pride in her voice, but also a faint hint of wistfulness which made Caroline suspect that Albert Wigan's idea of the best had not always been what his wife wanted.

Both Mrs Wigan and her daughter seemed delighted with their bedrooms, and appreciative of the fresh flowers and other welcoming touches.

They had so much luggage that it was necessary for Hawk to take the taxi back to the dock and pick up several more cases which had been left there. While he was gone, Caroline made the tea and carried the tray upstairs. Both bedroom doors were open and mother and daughter were busy unpacking. It was as well Caroline had put plenty of hangers in their closets. Between them they had enough clothes to stock a boutique.

'Miss Murray's brought the tea up, Emmy,' Mrs Wigan called out.

'Okay, Mum, I'll be there in two ticks.'

'Why don't you call me Caroline, Mrs Wigan?'

'All right, dear, if you've no objection.' The older woman unfolded an evening dress adorned with much sparkling embroidery and slipped a hanger inside the neckline.

Coming closer to Caroline and speaking in an undertone, she said, 'I knew there was romance in the air the day Hawk came over to see me. He didn't say anything, of course, and he's not one to show his feelings, but I had my suspicions immediately. Quick on the uptake, that's me. There'll be wedding bells before long if I'm not much mistaken, I said to myself. But I haven't said anything to Emmy. Let things take their course—that's my motto. She——'

At this point Emerald came in, and her mother said no more.

A few moments later Caroline left them to drink their tea in private. She went to her own room, closed the door and sank down on the side of her bed with her face in her hands.

Mrs Wigan was nobody's fool. If she felt sure that Hawk had encouraged them to come to Nantucket to facilitate his courtship of her daughter, she was probably right.

Dear God! What an idiot I am, Caroline thought, in despair. I could bear it if he really loved Emerald. But I'm sure, if he does ask her to marry him, it will only be for her money. Does Mrs Wigan know that? Perhaps she does. Perhaps she thinks it doesn't matter as long as her daughter loves him.

CHAPTER SIX

AT dinner that night, Hawk shocked Mrs Wigan by telling her how, in 1857, the crew of a coastal trading schooner sailing from Nantucket to New York had thrown overboard fifty cats which were part of the cargo.

'Whatever did they do a wicked, cruel thing like that for?' she exclaimed, her round face aghast.

'They'd had a run of rough weather and thought the cats were responsible. When they'd tossed them overboard the weather changed, confirming their opinion.'

'What a very odd cargo,' said Caroline, half suspecting him of inventing the story.

'They were Maltese cats. The merchant they were consigned to sued for two thousand five hundred dollars.'

'I see.' She met his gaze with composure, her feelings under control now.

For the main course she had roasted a chicken.

'Will you carve or shall I?' she asked him, when she brought it into the dining-room, golden brown and garnished with watercress.

'I'll carve.'

Although her stepfather was an expert carver of poultry and roast joints, she had found, at her small supper parties in London, that it was usually best to tackle the carving herself. Not without certain misgivings she returned to the kitchen to bring in the potatoes and the broccoli.

When she returned with the vegetable dishes, she could see at a glance that Hawk had not botched the carving. Two slices of breast, a wing with a strip of breast attached, a drumstick and the upper leg joint were neatly aligned on the platter, and he was beginning to carve the bird's other side.

Watching his shapely brown hands deftly repeating the process, she wondered where he had learned that accomplishment. Not that his past or his future were of any concern to her now that she understood the reason why he had changed tack in his attitude to her.

She looked across the table at Emerald, who tonight was wearing a see-through crinkle gauze shirt with a flounced linen skirt of the kind which started to crease the moment it left the ironing board. A dramatic necklace made of shells, pieces of coral and gold beads, which she said she had bought in Palm Beach, was displayed in the opening of her shirt—unbuttoned almost to the waist—with dangling ear-rings to match which were really too long for her short neck.

Caroline's mother would have said that everything about her, including her glittery eye make-up, was unsuitable for the occasion. But Caroline herself could see that, unsuitable or not, Emerald looked very pretty and sexy. Especially from a man's point of view.

Her manners were going to need some polishing. It never occurred to her to check that everyone else had helped themselves to both vegetables before she started to eat, and she showered pepper and salt on both the soup and the main course before she tasted them.

But minor lapses of that sort were of less importance than her friendly nature and basic intelligence, thought Caroline. Without those qualities she would never make a satisfactory wife for the master of a cruise ship. With them, if she put her mind to it and was given some tactful guidance, she could easily acquire more social graces.

What Caroline had not bargained for was that Hawk would see her in the role of Emerald's mentor.

The following morning, while she was preparing breakfast, before the Wigans had come downstairs, he came into the kitchen and, after some general conversation, said, 'It would be a good thing if you could encourage Emerald to get more out of staying on the island than she seems to have done in other places. She's not as dumb as she looks. If she could be persuaded to have a look round the museums, as well as the shops, she might find they're not as dull as she seems to imagine.'

'All right. Next time I go in, I'll take her with me,' she agreed.

As he knew, she now had a season pass to the town's two museums and other places of interest. When she had the house full of visitors, she wanted to be able to answer everything they asked her about Nantucket.

'I notice there's another letter to Miss Edith Pell on the hall table,' he went on. 'You appear to write to her more often than to your family. Is she your best friend?'

'She's part of my family. She was my stepfather's nannie when he was little and, later on, she was ours. She's very old now, a semi-invalid, and she loves getting letters and postcards.' Her face clouded. 'I might not see her again if I don't go back until next winter.'

He said, 'You're a nice girl, Caroline. There are not many who would bother to write to an old lady as regularly as you do.'

Against her will she felt herself warmed by his praise. But it left a bitter aftertaste. A nice girl. An attractive girl. But not the heiress to a fortune.

'I heard from my brother yesterday,' she said, in a matter-of-fact tone. 'You remember my telling you that Kiki had left him all the books at the Villa des Anges?'

'Yes.'

'Rob made enquiries through the lawyers about who has inherited the house, but apparently they can't tell him until later in the year—I can't imagine why not. However, in the meantime he can leave the books where they are, and make use of the house in the long vac. But I'm hoping he'll want to come here and see my house ... our house,' she corrected herself.

In the following fortnight she found herself spending much more time with the Wigans than she had originally envisaged. Before their arrival, if she had had nothing to do, she would have picked up the book she was reading or gone to the Atheneum to borrow another. Neither of the Wigans were readers. Their relaxation was talking and, although they could always enjoy talking to each other, it was even better to have someone new to talk to.

Within a few days of their arrival, Caroline had learned as much about Mrs Wigan's past life as if they had known each other for years. By the end of the week her guest was not only coming into the kitchen to talk to her while she was cooking, or sitting in the parlour while she dusted it; she was lending Caroline a hand.

'Let me peel those pears for you, love,' or 'I'll polish the table. I like to make myself useful,' she would say.

At first Caroline demurred. But soon she began to realise that Agnes Wigan was a woman who genuinely enjoyed all the tasks which kept a house looking immaculate.

Emerald's great interest was clothes. It was by mentioning that the exhibits in the Foulger Museum included a wedding dress that Caroline lured her inside the place.

Once there, Emerald found it more interesting than she had expected. Indeed, it was she who noticed the framed declaration of marriage made by a Nantucket Quaker, Barzillai Macy.

'Have you seen this, Caroline?' She read it aloud. *'Friends, I take this my friend Mary Hussy to be my wife, promising through divine assistance to be unto her a loving and faithful husband until it shall please the Lord by death to separate us.* That's nice, isn't it?'

'Yes,' said Caroline hollowly.

The girl's tone, and her dreamy expression, sent a sharp pang of misery through her. How long would it be before Hawk was making the same kind of promise to Emerald?

Although from what she had heard, Nantucket summers weren't always dry and sunny, that June the weather was perfect.

Emerald spent a lot of time sunbathing in the nude up on the walk where, lying on a towel-covered air-bed, she could toast every inch of herself without being seen.

Sometimes Caroline joined her up there. Less uninhibited than Emerald, she didn't shed her bikini, partly because, if the telephone rang, it would be she who dashed down to answer it, and partly because it didn't cover much of her anyway.

One afternoon, while Mrs Wigan was resting in her bedroom and the two girls were basking on the walk, Caroline asked a question which had been on her mind for some time.

'That day you came here by yourself, Emmy; did you notice Hawk or did he notice you?'

'He noticed me. I was looking in a shop window. He tapped me on the shoulder and said, "It's Emerald Wigan, isn't it? What are you doing here?"' She rolled from her front to her back and sat up to apply some more oil. 'It was clever of him to recognise me, because when we went on the cruise I had my hair down to my shoulders and I wasn't using henna then.'

Caroline had hoped for a different answer, and the rider which Emerald had added made her feel doubly depressed.

'If we're going to have dinner at the Chanticleer this weekend, I shall need a new dress,' Emerald went on. 'Will you help me choose one, Caroline? Hawk was talking about you one day, and he said you had very good taste.'

The reported compliment gave Caroline no pleasure, because it was not hard to guess the motive behind it.

'How kind of him,' she said dryly.

Emerald dribbled some oil on her thighs and began to spread it with her fingertips. Watching her, Caroline realised that the long, pointed, pearl-pink nails were now the same length as her own and painted with natural varnish.

'Have you got a serious boy-friend in England?' Emerald asked her.

She had already told Caroline all about her love life, as she called it. But this was the first time she had asked about Caroline's relationships with men.

'No.'

To avoid further questions, Caroline scrambled to her feet.

'It's time I made your mother's tea and toast.'

The Chanticleer at 'Sconsett was said to be Nantucket's best restaurant. Having heard that President Nixon and his entourage had dined there in 1980, Mrs Wigan had booked a table for a party to include Hawk and Todd.

In spite of her belief that Hawk had his eye on her daughter, she didn't discourage the younger man from helping Emerald with her sketching. No doubt she could tell he was more interested in Caroline.

Helping Emerald to find a dress in keeping with the new, more understated image she seemed to be striving to attain was a task which, had her own feelings not been involved, Caroline would have enjoyed.

They had been to half a dozen shops, and Emerald had tried on at least twenty styles—some of which pleased her but would not please Hawk—before Caroline spotted a very plain cotton dress, the colour of amontillado sherry.

'There's nothing much to that,' said Emerald, when Caroline took it off the rail.

'But the colour will be wonderful with your tan, and the most successful dresses hardly ever do look stunning on a hanger. You have to try them on.'

Somewhat reluctantly, Emerald retreated into the fitting-room while Caroline said to the assistant, 'I think it will need a gold belt. Perhaps you have one on another dress which we could try for effect?'

'It's not bad ... I think I like it,' said Emerald, a few minutes later when, with a gold kid belt produced by the saleswoman, she looked at the effect in the showroom mirror. 'What do you think?'

'You look lovely, Emmy,' said Caroline.

She meant it. The expensive simplicity of the shirt-style halter and swingy skirt, with slit pockets in the seams of the slightly gathered centre front panel, did far more for Emerald's figure than the show-everything styles of her existing wardrobe.

Hawk should have returned that evening, but telephoned to say he would be delayed. As Caroline was busy in the kitchen when he called, Emerald answered the telephone.

'He'll be back before lunch tomorrow,' she reported, after talking to him for six or seven minutes.

When Todd called, the following morning, Caroline was arranging flowers. The others were out, having their hair done. He didn't knock but, knowing the door would be unlocked if she were at home, opened it and called, 'Hi! It's me. Anyone around?'

Busy with her flowers, she called back, 'I'm in the parlour.'

When he appeared in the doorway, she saw he was carrying a parcel, attractively gift-wrapped.

'Oh, Todd—not another present!' she exclaimed, as he handed it to her.

'This one is an advance on Christmas,' he said, with a smile.

It looked as if it might be another book, but a smaller and slimmer volume than the one he had given her before. However, as she took off the wrapping, the present was revealed as a photograph in an expensive leather frame.

It was a photograph of the head and shoulders of a young man—not a studio portrait but an enlargement of an outdoor snapshot. A breeze had been ruffling his hair at the moment he grinned at the camera. Fair hair, bleached by the sun which had given him his tan. High cheekbones. White teeth. A cleft chin. A face she had never seen before but which she recognised instantly because it was so like her own.

Tears sprang to her eyes and her throat tightened. '*My father!*' she said, in a husky whisper.

As, in an instinctive gesture, she held the frame against her heart, embracing the likeness of the man who had given her life but had never seen her, Todd put his arms gently round her.

It seemed only a comforting gesture at a deeply emotional moment. She accepted it as such, unable to put into words how much it meant to her to have this longed-for memento of her other parent, the one she most closely resembled both in looks and in temperament.

For some moments, while she strove not to shed the tears which pricked her closed eyelids, Todd's hands moved over her back, tenderly patting and stroking, as if she were an upset child. Gradually the uprush of emotion subsided, and Caroline began to recover her command of herself. It was then, as her wet lashes lifted and she essayed a tremulous smile, that he bent to kiss her lightly on the cheek.

This gesture also she accepted submissively, her own feelings being far removed from any awareness of Todd as a man. He was, at that moment, a friend towards whom she felt a deep gratitude.

When, with startling suddenness, he pulled her against him and began to kiss her on the mouth, she was caught completely off guard.

Before she had a chance to break free, the door opened and someone walked in on them. As suddenly as he had pressed his mouth over hers, Todd raised his head and released her.

The photograph still clasped to her chest, Caroline turned her head and met Hawk's unreadable gaze.

'Excuse me.' He turned and walked out, closing the door behind him.

With a smothered cry of dismay she started to follow him, then checked. In a swift revulsion of feeling, the look which she turned upon Todd was now full of reproach for putting her in a false position.

'Caroline, I——' He broke off. Whatever he had been about to say remained unspoken as he turned away towards the window.

Longing to run after Hawk and explain that what he had seen had not been what it must have seemed, she knew that she couldn't. It would be too much of a give-away; and what did it matter to him whom she kissed or who kissed her?

Lowering the photograph to look again at her father's cheerful young face—he looked about nineteen or twenty, and bursting with health and *joie de vivre*—she asked, 'How in the world did you get hold of this?'

'The same guy who helped me to check out Hawk traced it for me. I've also got a whole lot of clippings about the accident, and the nice things people said about your father, which I thought you would like to have. They include various pictures of him, but it was a lucky chance that one of the papers which carried the story still had that photograph on file and my friend was able to borrow it and have it copied.'

'I don't know how to thank you, Todd. It's a wonderful present. I can't tell you how much I appreciate your going to so much trouble to get it for me.'

'I would go to a lot more trouble than that to please you,' he said, with emphasis.

But to her relief he didn't attempt another embrace, and a few minutes later Emerald and Mrs Wigan returned.

Her mother, the two men and Caroline were already having drinks in the parlour when Emerald made her entrance that evening. She was wearing a great deal less make-up, and her only jewellery was the tiny gold lightship basket pendant she had bought on her first day on the island. Even her new gold sandals had less stilt-like heels than her others, enabling her to move more gracefully. It was clear now she had the potential to become a strikingly lovely woman, and both men expressed their approval in terms which made her blush with pleasure.

Later, when Todd was assisting Mrs Wigan to insert her bulk into the taxi, and Hawk was locking the front door, Emerald had a chance to whisper to Caroline, 'I should never have chosen this dress if you hadn't come with me. Did you hear what he said?'

Caroline smiled and nodded. She had heard Hawk's complimentary remarks and read the approval in his eyes as they appraised Emerald's new look.

Neither Todd's little car nor the taxi being large enough to carry the whole party, Todd and Caroline followed behind.

'By the way, I shan't be going back to New York on Monday morning,' he told her, as they set off behind the cab. 'I'm on vacation for two weeks. I was going out to the west coast to stay with my sister in California, but I changed my mind.'

She felt him glance meaningly at her, but she pretended not to notice, saying, 'Wherebouts in California does your sister live?'

'In Carmel.'

By questioning him about California, she managed to keep the conversation off personal subjects until they arrived at 'Sconsett.

On fine summer nights the dining area at the Chanticleer was a courtyard surrounded by rose-covered trellises. A round table had been reserved for them. The maître d'hotel drew out a chair for Mrs Wigan, who then pointed out where she wanted the others to sit.

Caroline realised at once that she had made a mistake, putting Emerald next to Todd and Caroline next to Hawk. As the two men moved round the table to draw out chairs for the girls, she took the one next to Todd. It might give him the wrong impression, but at least Emerald would be where she wanted to be—and where her mother wanted her.

The cuisine was mainly French, classic and nouvelle, with some New England dishes. They all began with smoked fish, after which both the men had Nantucket rabbit cooked with mushrooms and a mustard sauce, and the women had duckling with apple.

During dinner the conversation turned to the race from Newport to Lisbon, now only a short time ahead.

Emerald said, 'Hawk was telling us on the way here that there's going to be a Captains' Ball the night before the race, Caroline. Would you like to go? I should.' Without waiting for Caroline's answer she turned away. 'You could get tickets for us, couldn't you, Hawk?'

'Tickets, yes—but what about partners?' he asked, with a teasing smile.

She laughed. 'What's wrong with you and Todd? You could come too, Mum. You'd like Newport. It's where all those famous millionaires like the Vanderbilts used to live. Don't you remember the lady in Palm Beach telling us? She used to go there for the summer. Super shops, so she said.'

After a couple of drinks, Mrs Wigan tended to revert to the Yorkshire dialect of her youth. Her round face lit up. 'Aye, and that's where Jackie Onassis were wed, the first time. Is it far from here, Hawk? How would we get there?'

'From the Cape it's no distance—maybe a couple of hours. You could hire a car at Hyannis.'

'We don't drive,' said Mrs Wigan.

'Caroline does,' put in Todd.

To her dismay, she found herself being involved in a plan to spend several days at Newport. When, in an effort to extricate herself from these arrangements, she suggested hiring a chauffeur as well as a car, Mrs Wigan dismissed the idea as a waste of money.

'And if there was one thing my Albie couldn't stand, it was waste,' she said firmly. 'No, love, you can shut up the house and come and enjoy yourself with us.'

'We'll *both* need new dresses for a ball,' said Emerald excitedly. 'Will you still be on holiday then, Todd?'

'No, but it makes no difference. It's easy to get there from New York,' he assured her.

A few days after the dinner party at the Chanticleer, Caroline was taking Mrs Wigan's early morning tea to her when she met Hawk coming downstairs.

He stood aside to let her come past. As she did so, he said, 'Are you avoiding me, Caroline?'

'Avoiding you? No! Why should I?' she replied, with a show of amazement at such a strange question.

'If you're not, how about coming sailing this morning?'

This time she was genuinely surprised. What devious game

was he playing? Keeping the Wigans on tenterhooks, perhaps? If so, he need not look to her to be the pawn in his gambit.

'Thank you, but I'm afraid I'm too busy this morning,' she said, continuing on her way.

Mrs Wigan was sitting up in bed, a pink net over the rollers which she put in her hair every night. Caroline wondered how she could bear to sleep in them, and if she had gone to bed in them when Mr Wigan was alive.

She remembered Nannie telling Rob that before he proposed to a girl he should take a close look at her mother whom she would be sure to resemble in thirty years' time. Perhaps that was not always true, although it seemed more than likely in Emerald's case. Had Hawk ever looked at Mrs Wigan in that light? she wondered.

His own looks were the kind which wore well. His crisp, thick hair might go grey but probably wouldn't recede; and, at an age when many men were already in physical decline, his body was still lean and hard.

'Do you know something, love?' said Mrs Wigan, as Caroline placed the tray on her bedside table. 'I've felt more myself since I've been here, and I reckon it's because you've let me help you in the house. I'm not cut out to be a lady of leisure, as they say. I need something to do. Being idle doesn't suit me. Now why don't you give me a treat and let me cook the meal this evening? I'm in the mood to make Albie's favourite steak and kidney pudding, and I know Hawk and Todd would enjoy it—men always do.'

'All right, if you really want to. Why not?' said Caroline, smiling.

Privately, she thought Albie's favourite rather stodgy for a warm summer evening, but she had suspected for some time that what had ailed Mrs Wigan had been not having a home of her own. Luxurious rented houses with staff to run them might be some people's idea of heaven, but Agnes Wigan was essentially a home-maker. Deprived of the tasks she enjoyed, she felt aimless and unhappy.

As it happened, during the day the sky clouded over. By mid-afternoon the town's trees and hedges were being refreshed by a downpour which brought a marked drop in the temperature. Rain was still streaming down the window-panes when Mrs Wigan served her steak and kidney pudding, followed by apple pie and cream.

'Main Street was like a stream when we came back from Todd's place,' said Emerald. She had spent the afternoon with him, having a lesson in the use of oil paints.

Although he was nice to Mrs Wigan about her cooking, Hawk's mood that evening was tinged with irritability. Perhaps he didn't approve of Emerald spending so much of her time with Todd, or perhaps the reason for his barely concealed ill humour was that he knew he ought to be in Baltimore, attending to the final arrangements for his ship's passage from there to Newport.

Caroline, who had spent the afternoon reading in her bedroom, knew that he had spent much of the afternoon on the telephone. Who he had been calling, and why, she had no idea. But it must have cost a good deal of money.

When Mrs Wigan had called her down to have tea and freshly-baked parkin—a Yorkshire cookie made from oatmeal, butter, syrup, ground ginger and allspice—Hawk had said he would give Caroline a cheque to cover the cost of his calls.

As soon as Todd had left the house, Caroline went to bed. Like all the other bedroom doors, hers had a lock on it now—not that she ever used it—and the walk-in closet in the corner of her room had been converted into a compact bathroom.

Before she was ready for bed, she heard Mrs Wigan slowly climbing the stairs, leaving Emerald alone with Hawk. Surprisingly, it was only a short time later that she heard their voices on the staircase.

She was trying to concentrate on the final chapters of *Moby Dick* when there was a light tap on her door. Assuming it was Emerald outside, she said, 'Come in.'

To her astonishment, it was Hawk who entered, closing the door quietly behind him. He was still dressed.

Caroline stiffened. 'What do you want?'

'To talk to you alone, which seems impossible during the day.'

He sat down on the edge of the bed and, removing the book from her hands, put it with others on the night table.

'What does Todd mean to you, Caroline?'

'He's a friend.'

'Nothing more? Are you sure of that?'

'Certainly I'm sure.'

'Would you count me as a friend?'

Uncertain where this was leading, she said cautiously, 'Yes . . . I suppose so.'

'You can't give an unqualified yes?'

Something in his manner made her nervous. 'Yes . . . all right . . . yes,' she amended.

'In that case I claim the same privileges you allow your other friends,' he said smoothly.

The next instant she was in his arms, her head bent back, her protesting lips crushed beneath his.

For a moment or two she tried to fight him. It wasn't possible. Not only because he was much stronger, but because her own body refused to resist what her senses had craved since his last kiss. With an incoherent sound, she surrendered to his arms and mouth.

A long time later he said, 'Now perhaps you would like to explain why I came back to find you in Todd's arms.'

'I wasn't . . . at least, it wasn't the way it may have looked when you walked in on us. He'd just given me a photograph of my father. It was such a shock—though a lovely one—that I almost burst into tears. Todd had been patting my back. Then, quite unexpectedly, he kissed me. That's all there was to it . . . truly.'

As she finished explaining about Todd, she remembered Emerald. Emerald whom—such was the sorcery of his kisses—her mind had conveniently blanked out during that wild blaze of passion which had flared up between them.

Hawk said, 'Okay, I'll take your word for it. But how come I've been getting the cold shoulder?'

At that moment, with his arms round her and her own arms round his strong neck, the answer seemed ridiculous. She knew, without having to be told, that he wouldn't have come to her bedroom and kissed her in that famished way if Emerald was part of his life-plan.

'Tell me something first,' she murmured. 'Why, after behaving so outrageously at the beginning, did you suddenly stop flirting with me? That day we went sailing I expected you to kiss me again, but you didn't.'

Hawk tilted her face up to his. 'For the first time in my life

I was serious. I wanted to make sure we could be friends as well as lovers. But from that point on you became less and less friendly. Why, Caroline?'

She moved his hand from her chin and hid her face against his shoulder.

'I was jealous of Emerald.'

'Of Emerald! For God's sake—why?' He made her look up at him again.

'She told me the first time I met her that she thought it was fate . . . meeting you again.'

'You took that seriously? I can't believe it! If you asked her now she'd say it was fate meeting Todd. She has a crush on him now. I thought you'd seen that for yourself, and it was the reason you sat between them at the Chanticleer.'

'Oh, no. I swopped seats because I thought you and she——' She let that statement trail, but added, 'Mrs Wigan thinks you want Emerald.'

'Then Mrs Wigan is a fool. Her daughter is not only years too young for me, we have less than nothing in common. If you were jealous of Emerald, you can't be as bright as I thought you were,' he said roundly.

'You were jealous of Todd,' she reminded him.

'With reason. He's a good-looking, interesting guy who's in love with you. What does Emerald have to appeal to me . . . apart from her mother's steak and kidney pudding'—with a hint of a smile.

'She's very pretty . . . and very rich,' said Caroline.

As she felt him tense, she knew she had said the wrong thing.

'You believed that her money—her father's money— would interest me?' Suddenly his mouth was as grimly compressed as Captain Starbuck's.

'Hawk, please don't be angry. I admit . . . for a while . . . I did think that. Especially when Emerald's mother——'

She broke off as he withdrew his arms and rose from the bed.

'If you thought that, Caroline,' he said coldly, 'you didn't begin to trust me. If you don't trust me now, you won't later.'

She searched for words to defend herself and found none.

After a pause, he said, 'One of the hazards for any officer on a cruise ship is a certain type of female passenger who leaves her inhibitions ashore. To cope with women of that type—and they have to be handled with tact—is difficult enough. To have to deal with jealousy in private would be too much.'

'But I shouldn't be jealous in those circumstances. You don't understand. I——'

He cut her short. 'With rare exceptions, my encounters with women haven't given me too high an opinion of them. I thought you were different. A mature, intelligent girl who could cope with life without tranquillisers or therapy. A beautiful girl who, somehow, hadn't slept around. A girl with the character and courage to insist on keeping this house when I wanted to sell it.' He paused and his vivid blue eyes held a curiously bleak look. 'You were someone I didn't think existed—or not for me. But it seems my feelings weren't mutual.' His mouth curled into a sneer of bitter self-mockery. 'While I was putting you on a pedestal, you were writing me off as a prize——' He bit off the word he had been going to say and substituted '—rat.'

He moved to the door and, with his hand on the latch, said, 'If our instincts about each other ran counter to that extent, I don't think there's much future for us. I would have staked my life on your integrity. Clearly you didn't think I even knew the word.'

He walked out of the room.

Caroline's first sight of *Damaris* was from the terrace of Hammersmith Farm, overlooking the passage from Rhode Island Sound into Narragansett Bay and Newport harbour.

She and Mrs Wigan and some other people were waiting for a guided tour of the interior of the house, when someone said, 'Oh . . . look at that!' and she roused from her unhappy thoughts, and turned to find out what had caused the admiring exclamation.

What she saw made her draw in her breath. Gliding gracefully over the expanse of shimmering blue water on the far side of the split-railed paddock below the terrace was a four-masted, white-hulled sailing ship of such heart-wrenching beauty that even the most garrulous tourists fell silent and stared at her in wonder.

Some time earlier the ferry to Block Island had steamed past, the noise of her engines making the flagstones vibrate.

But *Damaris*—and Caroline knew instinctively that this lovely vessel had to be Hawk's beloved barque, and that he was somewhere on board her—passed with no sound, propelled by the same fresh breeze which was pushing some cottonwool clouds across the hot July sky.

She had neither seen nor heard from him since the night he had walked out of her bedroom. But he had written to Mrs Wigan, enclosing tickets for the Ball, and telling her he had arranged accommodation for them at the Sheraton-Islander Inn on Goat Island in Newport harbour.

This had turned out to be a luxurious two-bedroom suite in a motor hotel where the facilities included a saltwater pool and sauna as well as a heated indoor pool. It was many times more expensive than the motels where Caroline had stayed on her trip from Boston to Hyannis. But as Newport was packed with yachting enthusiasts, she was surprised he had been able to get them in anywhere.

Mrs Wigan, who had been looking round the sunken garden, came back to where she was sitting.

'That's Hawk's boat going past, love.'

'I guessed it was.'

A woman came out of the house and introduced herself as their guide. Reluctantly, for she would have preferred to remain outside, watching the barque, Caroline followed Mrs Wigan into the spacious hallway of the rambling twenty-eight-room 'cottage' which had once been the home of a girl called Jacqueline Bouvier.

The day before they had visited four of the great stone mansions built around the turn of the century for men of unimaginable wealth, most of whom had lived in them only for a few weeks in summer. By the previous evening Caroline had had a surfeit of marble, enormous tapestries, old master paintings and ornate, gilded furniture.

But Hammersmith Farm was nothing like the millionaires' palaces. Although built in 1887, it had none of the oppressive grandeur of the Vanderbilts' houses. Here, although many of the furnishings were antique, the atmosphere was one of modern comfort. It might easily have been a country house in England.

As the tour group paused in the white-painted dining-room for their guide to point out the Regency chandelier and explain that the centre panel of the large bay window was electrically operated, Caroline was able to catch another glimpse of *Damaris*.

Since Hawk had returned to Baltimore, early the morning after his chastening indictment, she had not had a moment's peace of mind. At first she had thought him unjust. Now she knew he had been right to upbraid her. Trust was part of love—or it should be. But so was forgiveness. If he loved her—and he hadn't actually committed himself on that point, although he had seemed to imply it—surely, by now, he would have been in touch with her?

The tour group moved through a compact, up-to-date kitchen and climbed a narrow back staircase leading up to the bedrooms. The two rooms of greatest interest were those of the teenage girl who had subsequently become First Lady; and the bedroom of her mother and stepfather, Mr and Mrs Hugh Auchincloss, where, later, as wife of the President, she and her husband had slept when Hammersmith Farm had become a summer-time White House.

Here, two single beds were covered with quilted bedspreads of the same pretty flowery chintz applied to the wall behind them.

'Poor thing . . . if she'd known what would happen!' whispered Mrs Wigan lugubriously, as she waited her turn for a glimpse of the adjoining bathroom.

The last room they were shown was the Deck Room, a huge room with a high beamed ceiling, wide sea views—which no longer included *Damaris*—and a grand piano.

The guide pointed out the stuffed pelican suspended from the ceiling which, becoming entangled in Mr Auchincloss's fishing line, had drowned before it could be rescued. There was also a stuffed pheasant which, flying against one of the windows, had broken its neck. He had left instructions in his will that it was to remain in the room it had seemed so anxious to enter.

'You should have come with us, Emmy. You missed a treat,' said Mrs Wigan, when they returned to their suite. She began to describe the house, while Caroline went to the window and looked at *Damaris*, now lying at anchor with her sails furled.

She was wondering if they would see anything of Hawk

before the Ball the next night, when someone pressed the buzzer, and she opened the door to find a young man in a spruce white uniform standing outside. She knew instantly that he must be one of Hawk's junior officers and her heart leapt with hope.

But he brought no message for her. His errand was to see Mrs Wigan.

'Captain Lowell sends his compliments, ma'am, and he hopes you three ladies will join him for dinner on board. I'll come over and fetch you in the launch at seven-thirty, if that's convenient?'

Hawk was waiting at the head of the gangway ladder when the tender brought them alongside.

'Welcome aboard, ma'am.' He smiled down at Mrs Wigan as, draped in purple nylon chiffon, she reached the top of the ladder.

'You look very pretty tonight, Emmy.' Again a smile creased his lean cheeks.

Only when Caroline stepped aboard was his welcome markedly formal, as if he were greeting a stranger.

Seeing him in his Naval-style mess dress, it didn't surprise her that women threw themselves at him. Later, in a large saloon between decks, where drinks were being served before dinner, she saw more than one glamorous woman smiling alluringly at him as he circulated among the fifty or sixty people who had been invited to dine on board.

At dinner Caroline found herself next to the First Officer. He told her that the young people—girls as well as boys—who were going to help sail the ship to Europe were having a seafood buffet supper on deck before going to the local discos.

He was an interesting man who kept up an easy flow of conversation, as did her other neighbour. But from time to time she could not help letting her glance stray to the Captain's table and the darkly bronzed face of the man who never once glanced in her direction.

After dinner groups of people were shown the magnificent staterooms built for the opera singer and her friends. Then the party continued with some of the guests strolling about on deck and others sitting in the comfortably furnished library and smoking and writing rooms.

Had it not been for Caroline's secret heartache, it would have been a magical evening. Now that it was dark, the barque's masts, rigging and spars were lit up with strings of white lights. With the lights from the waterfront where several of the wharves had been extensively renovated into shopping and restaurant complexes, and also the lights from the many cruisers and yachts which had come to see the tall ships, Newport harbour presented a dazzling scene.

When, an hour after dinner, Hawk had made no attempt to seek her out, she knew there was going to be no chance of even a few words in private with him. Yet she knew that, if he had wished to, he could have contrived to neglect his duties as host for a short time. She was forced to conclude that he felt they had nothing more to say to each other.

Somehow, when the time came to say goodnight, she managed to hide her pain behind a social mask.

'Thank you for a pleasant evening, Captain.' Deliberately, she was even more formal than he had been when he greeted her.

'I'm glad you enjoyed it.' His handclasp was firm but brief.

As she descended the ladder, and the junior officer helped her into the tender, it was almost impossible to believe that the man she had just shaken hands with had ever held her in his arms.

It was almost one o'clock in the morning when the lights festooning the barque were switched off, except for her riding lights.

From where Caroline sat by her bedroom window, she could still see the towering masts—one hundred and ninety feet tall, the height of the tallest white pines, so the First Officer had told her—and the lighted portholes which indicated that, although the last batch of youngsters had returned aboard at half past twelve, it would be some time before everyone on *Damaris* was asleep.

It was past one, and she was still hunched in the chair, watching the ship which meant so much to him, when a movement on deck caught her eye. As she watched, a man in a white shirt came to the starboard rail and stood there, looking in the direction of the Inn.

It was difficult to be sure at such a distance, but she was almost certain it was Hawk. For a long time—more than a quarter of an hour—he stayed there, as still as a statue. Then he turned away and disappeared, leaving Caroline to climb into bed, feeling a little more hopeful that he might not be obdurate for ever.

Until she woke up the next morning, it had been her intention to go to the Ball in a long black skirt borrowed from Emerald and a white silk shirt of her own. However, while accompanying Emerald on her search for a suitable long dress on the afternoon of their arrival, she had seen one she would have liked for herself, had it not been an unjustifiable extravagance.

This morning nothing which might make Hawk soften towards her seemed unjustifiable. She was waiting outside the shop when it opened. To her relief the dress was still there; a drop-dead ankle-length chemise of olive green silk chiffon given impact by a belt of bright turquoise ribbons, stitched together round the waist and then fluttering loose to the hem.

'It's a copy of an Oscar de la Renta,' the saleswoman told her. 'It looks wonderful on you.'

Caroline smiled, knowing it did. After signing the several travellers' cheques needed to pay for it, she spent the rest of the morning searching for sandals and a purse. Might as well go the whole hog, she thought recklessly.

About an hour before the Ball was due to begin, Todd arrived at the Inn, wearing a white dinner jacket and accompanied to their suite by a waiter with a bottle of champagne on ice which Todd had ordered by telephone from the downtown hotel where he was staying.

From the way Emerald's face lit up when he entered their sitting-room, Caroline knew that Hawk had been right in thinking that it wasn't only Todd's help with her painting she wanted.

Although she looked very pretty in a strapless, boned-bodice dress of pale peach taffeta with a tiered skirt shading to deep apricot at the hem, it was Caroline to whom he said, 'You look fabulous.'

In 1982 the Captains' Ball had been held at Rosecliff, a mansion famous for its heart-shaped staircase, built eighty years earlier for Mrs Herman Oelrichs whose father had made his fortune in the California Gold Rush. This year it was being held at The Elms, a château-style house which had narrowly escaped demolition by a land development firm from whom it had been saved by the Preservation Society of Newport County.

Todd drove the car they had hired up to the palatial entrance and, after they had climbed out, drove away to find somewhere to park. As they entered the foyer and handed over their tickets, the young officer who had been in charge of the tender the night before came down the stairs from the inner hall, making a beeline for Emerald and, with her mother's permission, sweeping her off to be among the first on the dance floor.

'By the way, love,' said Mrs Wigan, as they strolled through the great house, admiring the superb flower arrangements, 'I've been meaning to say that, if you should want to go back to England unexpectedly, you needn't worry about leaving me and Emmy by ourselves. To tell you the truth, I feel better with some housework and cooking to occupy me. I'm not cut out to be idle, and that's a fact. So if you want to go home and see your mum, you go ahead.'

'Thank you, but I wasn't planning to go home until next winter,' said Caroline.

'No, maybe not, but you never know what might come up. Life is full of surprises,' the older woman said sagely. 'Ah, there's Hawk and one of his officers. Let's go and say good evening to them.'

Caroline would have preferred to have left it to the men to approach them, but she was obliged to follow Mrs Wigan to where they were standing. When he saw her, she thought she detected a flicker of warmth in Hawk's eyes. But it was his subordinate who asked her to dance.

From then on she was seldom off the floor. All his officers—except the two whose wives were present—wanted to dance with her. It was from one of them that she learned that Hawk never danced.

'Although I'm sure he regrets it tonight,' he added gallantly.

To be so much in demand would have been flattering if she had been heart-free. But when there was only one man whose arms she longed to feel round her, the attention of the others meant nothing.

After dancing almost non-stop for more than an hour, she was glad when Todd suggested a stroll round the garden.

At first he made casual small-talk. Then, suddenly, he said, 'Caroline, I've tried to convince myself that you and I had a future together. Now I know that isn't to be. You're in love with Hawk, aren't you? You have been since you first met him.'

She gave him a startled glance; her first thought being to deny it. Then, with a slight shrug, she nodded. 'Perhaps not quite from the first, but almost. Stupid of me, isn't it?'

'I thought so at the beginning. I was as jealous as hell,' he admitted. 'When I told you those things about him, I was hoping it would put you off him. What I didn't tell you was the big thing in his favour. Not that you would think it important—you're not that kind of girl.'

'The thing in his favour?' she queried.

'You'll find it out pretty soon—when whatever is wrong between the two of you is straightened out. He's crazy about you, Caroline. When you aren't looking at him, he looks as if he could eat you. And when he isn't looking at you, you look at him the same way. Emmy sees it; so does her mother. What none of us can understand is what's keeping you from getting together?'

'What do you mean . . . Emmy sees it?'

He said, 'I think when she first arrived here, she had a yen for him herself. At least that's the way she *had* felt when they took that cruise on his ship. It took her a while to realise she'd grown out of that earlier crush. She sees now that he's a lot too old for her, and she's not all that keen on his life-style. But her mother knew that right away. There are no flies on old Mrs Wigan. She's been giving me hints for some time that I should forget about you. In fact the other day she came right out with it and said she'd known that Hawk was in love with you from the day he went over to the Cape and fixed up their visit to Nantucket.'

Stunned by the realisation of her total misunderstanding of Mrs Wigan's remark on the day of her arrival, Caroline gazed at him in silence.

'What *is* the problem between you and Hawk?' he asked

gently. 'I don't feel it can be me. I don't think he rates me a rival.'

Caroline pulled herself together. 'I think he may have, at one time. But what has gone wrong—and I don't think it can be put right—is that I ... I accused him of being after Emerald's money.'

'I put that idea in your head. At the time, you didn't agree. The irony is——' Todd stopped short.

'The irony is?' she prompted him.

'Never mind that now. Look, why don't you go and find him right now and try to straighten things out? I'm sure he'll meet you half way. If he really cares for you, he will. All you have to do is give him a lead. That's not too much to ask in these days of women's liberation, is it?'

'No ... I guess not,' she answered doubtfully, turning her head towards the lights of the house.

He gave her a gentle push. 'There's no time like the present.'

For a moment longer she lingered. But only to say, 'Todd, you're such a nice man. I hope it won't be too long before you find ... the right person.'

'I hope not, too,' he said wryly. 'Off you go ... and good luck!'

With an uncertain smile, she left him, walking slowly at first, then more quickly. Half way across the lawn she picked up her skirt and began to run, suddenly feverishly impatient to put Todd's conviction to the test.

At first Hawk seemed to have disappeared. She could not see him anywhere. Yet, if not the tallest man present, he was tall enough to be easily distinguished in a crowd.

When it seemed that he must be outside, she caught sight of his broad-shouldered back and hurried towards him, only to be stricken with nervousness when she was a few steps away.

He was conversing in German with two other uniformed men; one a grey-haired man in his sixties with four gold rings on his sleeves and a row of medal ribbons on his chest, and a younger man whose uniform indicated that he was from a different ship.

Reluctant to disturb what seemed a serious conversation rather than social platitudes, Caroline hovered behind him, her eye on his well-brushed dark head.

Let Todd and the others be right . . . please let them be right, she prayed silently.

The younger officer noticed her. He said something to Hawk which made him swing round to face her.

'Did you wish to speak to me, Caroline?'

His blue eyes were cool, his tone crisp. She felt he must be annoyed by the interruption.

As she stood there, tongue-tied, paralysed by nervous embarrassment, the younger man said something else. The two officers moved away, leaving Hawk and her alone—to the extent that none of the people nearby was paying any attention to them.

He lifted a questioning eyebrow. 'What is it? Is anything wrong?'

She shook her head. 'There's something I'd like to discuss with you. Could we walk in the garden?'

'By all means.'

Perhaps because he had been with two Europeans whose manners were sometimes more formal than those of the English and the Americans, he gave a slight bow of assent and offered her his raised forearm.

Slipping her arm inside his, she laid her hand on his sleeve, but so lightly she could scarcely feel the muscular strength beneath the white barathea.

As they made their way through the throng of well-dressed men and women, she still had no idea how to give him the lead recommended by Todd. Liberated she might be, but not liberated enough to say boldly, I love you: do you love me? That must remain his prerogative. Yet there must be something which would be tantamount to I love you. But what?

As they stepped into the garden, Hawk asked, 'What is it you want to talk about, Caroline?'

Although his tone was a shade less forbidding than before, it was still anything but encouraging. For a moment her mind went blank. She couldn't think what to reply. And then, as if it were someone else speaking, she heard herself saying, 'I should like to sail with you tomorrow. I feel it would be an experience I should remember all my life, and this may be my only chance to cross the Atlantic on a windjammer. Is that possible? Could you find room for me?'

There was a very long pause during which she withdrew her arm and braced herself to accept a crushing rejection.

At last he said coolly, 'Yes, I imagine we might. But what about Mrs Wigan and Emerald? How are they to manage in your absence?'

'I know Mrs Wigan wouldn't mind taking over the running of the house, and I'm sure Emerald wouldn't object. She has her painting to keep her happy, and her social life is beginning to snowball. I don't think they would be inconvenienced if I were away for the rest of the summer.' She drew a deep breath. 'To be honest with you, I'm beginning to wonder if I *am* cut out to run a guesthouse. Or to settle down in Nantucket. It's a place I shall always love, but maybe it isn't *my* place.'

They were crossing the lawn in the direction of the sunken garden, their shadows stretching ahead of them; his longer and sharper in outline than her smaller, slighter silhouette, its edges blurred by the softness of her hair and the filmy material of her skirt.

He said nothing for such a long time that she felt obliged to go on, 'I suppose for a girl who isn't committed to a career—and I realise that I'm not—there is no fixed, special place. She . . . she has to wait until she marries and then go wherever her husband's work takes him.'

'You'd better not let any feminists hear you talking like that,' he said dryly. 'Every woman should be her own person, doing her own thing, not tagging along in a man's footsteps.'

Although he hadn't turned down her impromptu suggestion of sailing on *Damaris* tomorrow, the conversation was not going in the direction she had hoped for. She decided to take a leaf out of his book and let his remark pass in silence.

After a moment or two, he said, 'You realise we might run into some heavy seas before we reach Lisbon? Even at this time of year the Atlantic can be rough.'

She nodded. 'I'll chance that.'

'How would you feel about sharing accommodation?'

'I don't mind that either.'

His hand fell on her bare shoulder, bringing her to a standstill and turning her towards him.

They were out of range of the golden lights of the mansion.

Here, where they stood face to face, there was only moonlight and starlight, and Hawk had his back to the moon so that his face was in shadow, his expression unclear.

'Even if the quarters you had to share were mine?' he asked, in a harsh tone.

Without hesitation, she answered, 'That would make the voyage an even more wonderful experience.'

His fingers tightened. 'Are you sure about that? Think carefully.'

She smiled, her eyes clear and trusting. 'I'm sure.'

An instant later, regardless of who might be watching, she was locked in a crushing embrace, being kissed with a fiercely possessive ardour to which her whole being responded with joyful relief.

When, at last, Hawk raised his head, she was breathless and trembling—and happier than she had ever been in her life.

'Unfortunately, you can't,' he said huskily. 'Can't share my quarters, I mean.'

'Why not?'

'Because there's no way we can be married before the race starts.'

'Does it matter? We can get married after the race.'

'That's what I have in mind. Meantime I'll stick to my cabin and you can have one of the staterooms. I don't want your honeymoon spoilt by not having your husband's undivided attention, which is going to be next to impossible during the race. So we'll do things the old-fashioned way. I'll present myself to your family, and we'll have a traditional wedding from their house, and then we'll go off somewhere quiet and have a month by ourselves. How does that sound?'

'Wonderful! But will you be able to take a month off? What about the Mediterranean cruises?'

Although he still had both arms round her, his embrace had slackened. Now he tucked her right arm through his left one, and began to stroll back to the house.

'My side-kick can take care of those.'

Caroline remembered something Todd had said earlier. She said, 'Todd says there's something about you which I don't know. Something very much in your favour, although I might not think so. What does he mean?'

'I think he must have found out that I'm not only Master of

Damaris but also chairman and major shareholder of the company which owns her,' Hawk answered.

Twenty-four hours later, *Damaris* was at sea with all sails set.

After dining in the ward-room with Hawk and the other officers who were not on watch, Caroline had spent the rest of the evening on deck. At this early stage of the race all the Class A vessels competing—square-riggers of more than a hundred and fifty tons and other ships of five hundred tons and over—were still within sight of each other.

To port she could see the topsail schooner *Juan Sebastian de Elcano* which was Spain's contender, and the Norwegian training ship *Christian Radich* with the figurehead of a woman under her bowsprit. To starboard lay the German naval barque *Gorch Fock* with her eagle figurehead, and the distinctive dark and light hull of the Italian Navy's *Amerigo Vespucci*.

They were such an extraordinary sight—like a glimpse into another century—that she watched them entranced, with no idea how long she stood with her elbows on the varnished rail and the light breeze whipping her hair.

'Isn't it time you turned in?'

She glanced round to find Hawk standing close behind her, no longer in the uniform he had worn earlier but wearing a plain navy sweater over an open-necked shirt.

'I'm not tired ... and they're so beautiful,' she said dreamily.

'But not as beautiful as *Damaris*,' he answered, with a smile in his voice. 'Come: I'll show you something special.'

Earlier, watching the crew and the trainees going aloft, she had hoped he would never expect her to climb the rigging. She hadn't a good head for heights.

Now, when she realised he was going to take her out on the bowsprit, she felt a twinge of panic. It was only her desire to please him in every possible way which prevented her from drawing back; and her confidence that as long as he was beside her no harm would come to her. Also there was a safety net rigged under the bowsprit so that if anyone did miss their footing, they wouldn't plunge into the sea directly in front of the bows.

Lying out on the flying jib boom was a fantastic experience.

As well as the triangular staysails, the six great sails on the foremast soared skywards towards the stars. First the vast silent motionless foresail; above it, almost as large, the two topsails; above them the upper and lower topgallants and, finally, the royal, with behind it a glimpse of the skysail at the summit of the mainmast.

What surprised her was that none of these huge stretches of moonlit canvas showed even a ripple of movement. They appeared to be carved out of alabaster, and yet she could feel their power almost lifting the ship from the water in a series of rhythmic upsurges.

'I understand now why you love her so much,' she said quietly.

'But not as much as I love you,' was his instant reply.

Several weeks later, on the evening of her wedding day, Caroline sat on the terrace outside one of the bedrooms at the Villa des Anges, re-reading a letter written by Kiki Lawrence. It had been held by her New York lawyers until Caroline had written to tell them of her impending marriage and to ask them to send her the jewelled love-knot which they still had in their safe, and which she wanted to wear on her wedding dress.

They had responded with a cable asking the name of her husband-to-be. When told, they had written to Hawk informing him that Kiki had left him the villa in France as a wedding present.

To Caroline they had sent the jewel, and an envelope marked *For Caroline Murray, if and when she becomes Mrs Hawkesworth Lowell*. Had this circumstance not come about, the lawyers had been instructed to destroy the letter unopened.

> *My darling Caroline*, Kiki had written,
> *If the day comes when you read this letter, my dearest wish will have been realised. You—the most beloved of all my 'adopted' grandchildren—will have found the love of your life and the happiness which, alas, I missed.*
>
> *You were still in your teens when I first began to wonder if in you, when you were older, Hawk might find the girl who meant more to him than his adored Damaris.*
>
> *Many times in the past few years I have been tempted to*

arrange for you to meet each other. But I knew that, at twenty, even at twenty-two, you were still too young for him. I feel now that, to be on the safe side, I must wait until you are twenty-five, by which time he will also be at the right age to marry.

However, as I may not be here to supervise that meeting in person, I have devised a scheme to bring you together in my absence.

As you will, by now, have discovered, you are not the first woman in Hawk's life. Don't be jealous of your predecessors, Caroline. None of them touched his heart. I am certain that, after your marriage, your only rival will be the beautiful sailing ship which, being very much your father's daughter, you will soon come to love as much as Hawk does.

Looking back on my life, I realise that my love for Ben, like that of most very young girls, was based on illusion. I endowed him with qualities he did not possess—but which his grandson does. Hawk, in Ben's place, would have followed me to New York, or waited for me to return to Nantucket and to him.

The letter ended, *It pleases me to think of the two of you sailing all over the world together, with my house in France and Ben's place in Nantucket as bases on land when you need them.*

Caroline folded the paper and put it on the table beside her. Since their arrival at the villa, she had had a shower and hung up her going away clothes and a couple of evening outfits. Her trousseau consisted mainly of bikinis, some pretty wisps of lingerie and the long loose robe of white voile trimmed with old, hand-made lace which was all she was wearing at the moment.

She was waiting for Hawk to reappear, not having seen him since he had gone off to shower in another of the villa's many bathrooms.

It was cooler now than when they had landed at Nice airport. A light breeze was wafting the heavenly scent of white jasmine to her. All the flowers in the garden were white; white pelargoniums growing in ancient stone urns, white hydrangeas, white lilies, and the waxy white *stephanotis floribunda* which had been among the flowers in her bouquet and which, here in the south of France, grew as a climber, its fragrance rivalling that of the jasmine.

Footsteps crossing the bedroom made her turn to smile at her husband as he came to join her, bringing with him champagne and glasses.

'The kitchen is full of good things to eat later on, but I think for the moment all we need is a glass or two of this to complete the unwinding process,' he said.

Caroline murmured agreement, her eyes on his powerful brown torso. He was wearing a dark brown bath towel wrapped round his hips. Like hers, his feet were bare.

'Come and sit on the wall with me. You can't see the sea from that chair,' he said.

As she rose and the breeze blew the transparent voile against her, moulding her body, she saw desire in his eyes and felt an answering longing to feel his strong arms tighten round her.

From the wide parapet surrounding the terrace, they could see the whole garden with its flights of stone steps descending to the private cove where the water shaded from aquamarine to dark green.

They sat on the sun-warmed stone, drinking the chilled golden wine and looking down at the tall, tapering spires of the cypresses which punctuated this and all the hillsides of the Côte d'Azur.

'Come closer.' Hawk reached out an arm and drew her to him.

As she leaned against him, she was conscious of the primitive fear that life had given her too much—more than she deserved—and to be so intensely happy might make the gods jealous.

Then he turned her face up to his and their champagne-cooled lips met and warmed in the first private kiss of their marriage.

ROMANCE

ROMANCE

Next month's romances from Mills & Boon

Each month, you can choose from a world of variety in romance with Mills & Boon. These are the new titles to look out for next month.

BAY OF ANGELS Margaret Rome
YOURS...FAITHFULLY Claudia Jameson
DARK HERITAGE Yvonne Whittal
LIFELONG AFFAIR Carole Mortimer
A PRECIOUS THORN Kate O'Hara
HARD TO HANDLE Jessica Ayre
EDEN'S LAW Pamela Pope
FLORIDA FEVER Elizabeth Oldfield
THE DAUGHTER OF NIGHT Jeneth Murrey
PASSIONATE PROTECTION Penny Jordan
BUT KNOW NOT WHY Jessica Steele
TEREBORI'S GOLD Lynsey Stevens

Buy them from your usual paperback stockist, or write to: Mills & Boon Reader Service, P.O. Box 236, Thornton Rd, Croydon, Surrey CR9 3RU, England. Readers in South Africa-write to: Mills & Boon Reader Service of Southern Africa, Private Bag X3010, Randburg, 2125.

Mills & Boon

the rose of romance

Best Seller Romances

These best loved romances are back

Mills & Boon Best Seller Romances are the love stories that have proved particularly popular with our readers. These are the titles to look out for this month.

BOUND FOR MARANDOO Kerry Allyne
REILLY'S WOMAN Janet Dailey
NOT A MARRYING MAN Roberta Leigh
CHARADE IN WINTER Anne Mather
ACROSS A CROWDED ROOM Lilian Peake
CARIBBEAN ENCOUNTER Kay Thorpe

Buy them from your usual paperback stockist, or write to: Mills & Boon Reader Service, P.O. Box 236, Thornton Rd, Croydon, Surrey CR9 3RU, England. Readers in South Africa write to: Mills & Boon Reader Service of Southern Africa, Private Bag X3010, Randburg, 2125.

Mills & Boon
the rose of romance

An orchestra for you

In the Rose of Romance Orchestra, conducted by Jack Dorsey of '101 Strings' fame, top musicians have been brought together especially to reproduce in music the moods and sounds of Romance.

The Rose of Romance Orchestra brings you classic romantic songs like Yours, Just the Way You Are, September Song and many others.

We promise you a new dimension of pleasure and enjoyment as you read your favourite romances from Mills & Boon.

Volumes 1 & 2 now available on the Rose Records label wherever good records are bought.

Usual price £3.99 (Record or Cassette)

VOLUME TWO

VOLUME ONE

THE ROSE OF ROMANCE ORCHESTRA

Yours·Theme from Dr.Zhivago·Romeo & Juliet·You Don't Bring Me Flowers
Just The Way You Are·Cavatina·Can't Smile Without You·September Song
Days Of Wine&Roses·Send In The Clowns·Shadow Of Your Smile·All By Myself

Mills & Boon

The rose of romance.